Her Maine Reaction

A Pine Cove Novel
Book 2

Rebecca Gannon

Copyright © 2019 Rebecca Gannon

All rights reserved.

ISBN: 9781712274033

No part of this book may be reproduced or transmitted in any means, electronic or mechanical, including photocopying, recording, or by any information storage and retrieval system without the written permission of the author, except for the use of brief quotations in a review.

This book is a work of fiction. Names, characters, places, and incidents are either products of the author's imagination or are used fictitiously. Any resemblance to actual persons, living or dead, events, or locales is entirely coincidental.

More by Rebecca Gannon

Pine Cove Series
Her Maine Attraction
Her Maine Reaction
Her Maine Risk
Her Maine Distraction

To Ashley, thank you for being the fabulous you.

CHAPTER 1

"Ashley! Get back out here!"

Rolling my eyes, I grab the two bottles of whiskey I came to the storage room for, and head back down the hall.

I fucking hate this place. It was supposed to only be temporary, but temporary has turned into long-term. I've lost count now of how many men have 'accidentally' brushed my ass as I've walked by, or how many have looked down my top as I've placed their drinks in front of them. And while I used to enjoy the attention, I don't anymore.

Not since that damn barbecue last summer. Over seven months ago.

I've tried to forget, and I've tried to move on, but I can't. And I hate him for that.

"Ashley! Hurry up!" my manager, Rick, yells again.

I also fucking hate him. I've worked here for six months, and there hasn't been a single night that's went by where he hasn't tried to get me to go home with him. It's not that Rick is bad looking, I guess, he just has this creepy way about him that screams 'stay away!' I can't pinpoint it exactly, but I still don't like being alone with him at the end of the night when we're cleaning up. I don't know how many more times I can politely say no before I straight up tell him to fuck off.

"Ashley!" Rick pops his head out from behind the bar and into the hallway where I'm literally standing only a few feet away.

"Rick, I've been gone 30 seconds, calm down."

"We're just busy. Hurry up," he snaps back. He's been doing that more and more with me lately, probably getting fed up with me turning him down every night.

"I know that. I did hurry. I was gone 30 seconds," I repeat in a calm voice, holding back what I wish I could say.

I seriously fucking hate him. But I need this job, so I keep my mouth shut and slip back behind the bar. I've appropriately nicknamed him Rick the Dick, and he's definitely living up to it tonight.

No matter the time of year, or the weather, we're always packed from wall to wall with people looking to get hammered and find a one-night stand.

I'm jealous. I haven't had a one-night stand in seven months and I'm going batshit crazy. Forget a one-night stand, I haven't had any sex in seven months and I'm going batshit crazy.

It's not for lack of trying, though, I just can't do it anymore.

I got a taste of something raw and intense, and I can't forget it. It's always on my mind. *He's* always on my mind. I've tried going out, and going on dates, but it's useless.

Damn it! Now I'm thinking about that night again—and him.

The bottle in my hand almost slips out as I pour two shots of vodka for the Barbie dolls in front of me. I know they'll have men fighting each other by the end of the night to get them to go home with them.

I miss that. The feeling I'd have knowing I could get any man in the room I wanted. I mean, I know I still can, but I don't want to. And that's the problem.

Taking a deep breath, I slide the glasses towards the girls and take their money as they knock the shots back like pros.

All these months later, and I still lay awake thinking about his hands and lips burning my skin – marking me, claiming me. I didn't know I wouldn't be able to go back to my life like he was any other man, and I can't shake the feeling of how it felt to have his eyes on me, or the way he knew exactly what I needed without having to say a word.

This time the bottle of vodka really does slip from my hand and crashes to the floor, shattering on impact.

"Ashley!" Rick the Dick yells, his eyes angry.

"Sorry, I'll clean it up." Grabbing the broom from the side of the bar, I quickly sweep the glass up and throw it in the trash before washing my hands and getting back to work. I seriously need to stop thinking about that night. It's never going to happen again, and I need to accept that.

For the rest of the night, I feel Rick watching me, his eyes running up and down my body every time I laugh or smile. I know, because the hairs on the back of my neck would stand, and a weird prickling sensation would spread across my skin.

While we're cleaning up after closing, his leering starts to feel different. I'm trying to focus on wiping down the bottles on the rack, but I can't shake the feeling that something is off.

As I'm placing the bottle of Jack Daniel's back in its place, Rick's arm snakes around my waist from behind and he whispers in my ear, "Hey, I'm sorry about getting mad at you before." His arm feels like a slimy snake trying to coil around its prey, and his breath on my neck sends thousands of little bugs crawling all over my skin.

"It's fine, Rick," I say through gritted teeth, trying to take his arm away. But he just tightens his grip.

"I hate that every night, all the men get to look at you, talk to you, and make you smile and laugh. But I don't. You keep turning me away like you're not interested, but I see it in your eyes that you want me."

"Rick, please let go of me. Right now," I demand, my voice cold and hard.

"I know you feel it between us, Ashley. You just deny it because I'm your boss."

"No. Let go." I try and pry his arm away again, but he pulls me back against him, and I can feel his bulge against my back. Cringing, I try and get loose, but can't.

"You like that don't you? You can feel what you do to me, can't you?"

"No!"

His arm loosens, but he doesn't let go. Instead, he spins me around and pushes me back against the bar, making the bottles behind me rattle against each other as he steps forward, caging me in.

"I know you want me, Ashley." Rick's disgustingly warm breath blows in my face and I turn my head away so I don't inhale it. "I can feel it. You're always swaying your hips and flipping your hair. I know you want me to look. And I love looking at you."

This is the last straw. He's gone fucking crazy! "Rick, get away from me!" I yell in his face. "I don't want you!"

He pushes his hips into me. "Stop refusing me. Just give in, Ashley." Grabbing me behind my neck, he slams his mouth down on mine, and I seal my lips closed. His grip is rough, and I can't move my head away. When his tongue tries to break through, I snap out of it and fight back.

I use every ounce of strength I have to yank my head to the side and buck my hips forward. With the few inches I'm granted, I lift my leg and knee him in the crotch.

"ARRGGHH!" Rick yells as he moves back and stumbles to the ground, holding his—what I'm hoping is broken—penis.

Stalking forward, I bring my fist back and punch him in the face as hard as I can. "You're fucking crazy! I quit, you disgusting bastard!" I yell, my voice coming out broken and raw.

I grab my purse from beneath the bar and empty the entire tips jar into it. With one last look over my shoulder at Rick writhing on the ground, I start running down the hall and out the back door. The second I'm in my car, I lock the doors and start the engine, peeling out of the parking lot as fast as I can.

Seriously?! What the fuck just happened?!

Stretching my neck from side to side, I can still feel his rough hand around my neck, and I know I'll be bruised from his tight grip. I knew there was something off about him, I just never thought he'd do anything as stupid as force himself on me.

Thinking about his cold, clammy, wet lips on mine, my stomach recoils, and I gag. I rub my lips on my sleeve and try to rid myself of the taste, but it's still there.

I focus my attention on driving, but the adrenaline that was pumping through my veins is starting to wear off, and my body starts to shake.

I suck in as much air as I can, refusing to shed a single tear over what just happened. My dad taught me how to handle myself, and I know he would be proud of me if I could tell him.

Thinking about my dad will make me cry, though, so I focus back on the lines on the road.

At least I know my mom will be asleep and I won't have to be subjected to her incessant questions. She could always just look at me and see that there was something wrong.

Six months ago, I never would have had to worry about that. But after what happened with my last job, and I started working at the bar, I had to move back home with her to save money. But I don't like to dwell on that. I have to move forward.

Pulling into the driveway, I turn the car off and just sit for a minute, taking a few deep breaths. Just when I thought my life couldn't get any more of a hot mess, it just did.

Sighing, I drag myself out of the car and shuffle inside, making my way upstairs. I just want a hot shower and my soft bed. I need to wash away the grimy feeling that Rick left on my skin. Convulsing at the thought, I strip my clothes off and step under the hot stream of water, my muscles starting to relax for the first time all night.

I don't know how long I stand there, but my fingers are pruney, and my skin is red from the heat. Stepping out, I wrap myself in a fluffy towel and look in the mirror. Sweeping my hair over my shoulder, I turn my head, and see the finger print bruises already starting to form on the sides of my neck.

Fucking Rick the Dick. I hope I did some damage. He doesn't deserve to use his dick anymore.

Good thing it's winter and I can hide behind sweaters and scarves, because I really don't feel like explaining this to people.

Walking back down the hall to my room, I throw the towel off of me and drop it on the floor, not caring about where it lands, as I put on a long t-shirt.

I slide into bed, and the cool sheets greet me as I curl into my thick comforter, my eyes closing the second my head sinks into my soft pillows.

****

Waking up to the sun streaming through my window, I groan and roll over, burying my head into my pillow, trying to give myself just a few more minutes of peace. But the events of last night come rushing back to me, and I groan again, feeling the dull throb in the back of my neck from where that asshole gripped me.

Throwing my arm out, I reach for my phone on the nightstand and scroll for the number I need. I know she's awake. She talks about watching the sunrise with her man all the damn time.

"Hey, Ash," Ally greets cheerily on the third ring.

"You really need to stop being so cheerful so early in the morning."

"Sorry." She laughs. "Jake and I–"

"Yes, I know. You two woke up early to have sex and watch the sunrise."

She laughs again. "Okay, what did you call for then, if not to hate me for having sex with my man?"

Ugh, lucky bitch.

I've known Ally since freshman year of high school, when the four of us–me, her, Elizabeth, and Melanie–were put together in a group for orientation. And we've all been best friends since.

Last year, Ally moved to a cute small town in Maine called Pine Cove, and she fell in love. That bitch. Her and Jake found the rare kind of love that we all only dream of finding, and get sick of seeing and hearing about pretty quickly if we ourselves don't have it.

Rolling onto my back, I groan at the pain that travels across my shoulders from my neck.

"I called because Rick tried to force me to have sex with him last night."

"WHAT?!" she yells, and I have to hold the phone away from my ear for a second.

"Yeah, when we were cleaning up last night. He obviously couldn't take another night of rejection, so he pinned me to the bar, pushed his dick against me, and kissed me. It was disgusting. And my neck is fucking killing me from where he grabbed me."

"He grabbed your neck?" she practically growls.

"Yes. And then I kneed him in the balls and punched him in the face before taking all of the tips and running out of there. I never thought he'd do something so stupid."

"I'm assuming you quit then?"

"Yes. And now I really have no idea what I'm supposed to do. You know I can't get a job at any law offices around here, and that bar was the only high paying one in the area. I just don't know what to do."

"Why don't you come up and stay with me for a week?" Ally suggests. "You need a break, and I don't want that creep coming around looking for you after what happened."

"I don't know. I don't want to intrude on you and Jake." They moved in together after he proposed at the end of last summer, and I really have no desire to hear them having hot sex at all times of the day. I also have no desire to watch them being all cute and in love while I'm lonely and single.

"I can ask Dottie if the cottage is free. I doubt anyone is clamoring to rent in the dead of winter, so she may let you stay there for really cheap, or even for free." Dottie is the cute old lady that Ally rented from last summer when she moved to Maine. And apparently, she played a major role in getting her and Jake together. She's a crafty old broad.

"Really? Because I don't have any money to spare. Especially now that I'm jobless again."

"Let me call her right now, and I'll call you back, okay?"

"Thanks, Ally."

"Of course, Ash. I'm sorry that this happened. I'm glad you fought back and taught that fucker a lesson, though. Just sit tight, and I'll call you right back."

"'Kay. Love you."

"Love you, too."

After hanging up with Ally, I feel a little better knowing that a plan is in motion.

Rubbing my eyes, I throw the blankets off of me and shuffle down the hall to the bathroom. I wash my face and brush my teeth, and then sweep my hair back and turn to see the marks on my neck. They've gotten darker and more pronounced, with four finger marks on the left, and one on the right.

My anger flares inside of me again.

I don't understand what that asshole was thinking. I've said no every night for six months, and so he decides that means I want him? He's fucking delusional! I don't know why men always think that I'm flirting with them, and then get all put out when they finally realize that I'm really not interested in them. I was already driven out of one job because it, and now a second.

Is it me? Am I doing something that makes them think this?

My phone vibrates on the sink counter, interrupting my thoughts, and I see Ally's name flash across the screen.

"Hey, what did she say?" I ask right away.

"Dottie said she'd love to have you stay for as long as you'd like. She hasn't had anyone interested in renting for the winter."

"Did you ask about payment?"

"Yeah, don't worry about money. She needed someone to check up on the place and make sure that it's staying clean and that everything is working through the winter, anyhow."

"I can do that."

"And if something isn't working, Jake can come and fix it."

"Ah, yes, the handyman trick. Should I do what you did?"

"No, because he's mine, bitch." She laughs. "But we can arrange for another hottie to show up if it'll make you feel better."

"Thanks for the offer, but I'm kind of put off of men right now after last night."

"Oh, right, sorry."

"It's fine. I'm more pissed off than anything else."

"Good, you should be."

"Thanks for asking Dottie for me. I really love that cottage." When I visited her last summer, Ellie, Mel, and I stayed there with Ally. There was something special about it.

"Me too. I miss it sometimes."

"But now you live with your hunky Thor, and that's better than a cottage by yourself."

"True," she says, a wistful tone in her voice. Lucky bitch. "Oh, and you'll want to come as soon as possible. There's supposed to be a big snow storm coming in a couple of days and I don't want you driving in it, or having to wait until after it passes to come up."

"Shit, okay. I'll come tomorrow then."

"Good. I'll meet you at the cottage to give you a set of keys and remind you where everything is that you'll need."

"Sounds good. I'll text you when I leave, and then when I'm an hour or so out."

"Perfect. Oh, and pack warm clothes. It's freaking freezing here. The other night, it was -4. It definitely never got that cold in Jersey."

"Oh lord, -4?"

"Yup. So pack heavy."

"Thanks, Ally-cat, I really appreciate this. I just need to get out of this place and regroup. Maybe think about a different career."

"One without a sleazy asshole as your boss?"

"Exactly."

"Okay, see you tomorrow."

"See ya," I say, and hang up.

But when I put my phone back down, it hits me.

Shit.

Going up there will mean that I'll more than likely run into him. I'll have to look into his handsome, sexy face, and those eyes that haunt my dreams every night.

Shit.

Sighing, I take one last look at my neck in the mirror, and then go back to my room. I pull out my suitcases from the closet and lay them out on the floor, throwing in almost every warm piece of clothing I own.

Maybe seeing him will make me stop thinking about him.

Well, that's a load of bullshit. I can only hope that maybe he's gotten ugly and less manly and muscly over these past few months. That would solve everything.

CHAPTER 2

"Ashley, honey, are you sure you should be traveling to Maine now?" my mom asks for the fiftieth time this morning.

"Yes. I have to beat the storm that's supposed to hit in a few days."

"But why are you going now? It's January. What if you get stranded in the snow?"

"I'm not going to get stranded. Ally and Jake are there." It's the truth, I just didn't tell her that I'm not staying with them. She'd freak if she knew I was staying out in a cottage by myself where anything could happen to me. Including getting stranded.

"Well, that makes me feel a little better. But why now? Did something happen? Don't you have work?"

"Mom, you have to stop with the twenty questions. I asked for a little time off at the bar because we're slow, and I just need to get away for a few days." The lies just keep coming. If she knew I was forced to quit another job because of sexual harassment, I don't know what she'd start thinking about me.

"Alright, honey. I'm sorry." I can hear the twinge of sadness in her voice, and I immediately feel guilty. I know she's only worried because I'm all she has left now.

"I know why you're worried, but I'll be fine. I promise."

She pulls me in tight for a hug. "I know you'll be fine. You're strong." I don't know if she can sense I've been lying to her about why I'm going on this trip, but her words bring tears to my eyes that I have to quickly blink away.

"I'll call you when I get there."

"You better."

Smiling, I kiss her cheek and take my last bag out to my car.

"Love you, Ashley," my mom calls from the door.

"Love you, too," I say back as I get in behind the wheel.

****

Six hours, and three coffee stops later, I've finally made it to the Pine Cove exit off of the highway. The sun is shining bright above, and the ground and pine trees are covered in a blanket of snow. It looks like they just had a snow storm, and the sky hardly looks like another one is coming, but I guess in Maine, snow is always just around the corner.

The closer I get to Pine Cove, the more nervous I feel. My hands are sweating on the steering wheel, my left leg is bouncing, and I can't stop chewing on my lip.

What was I thinking coming back here? I mean, I knew I'd eventually have to come back for Ally's wedding, and I'd have to face him again, but I thought I'd have more time to prepare myself. This trip was too impulsive.

Turning right onto Main Street, my heart starts to pound in my chest, and my skin breaks out in a cold sweat. I slow down when I see The Blueberry Café, and pull into a spot right out front. I need a cup of Courtney's strong coffee to calm my nerves. And maybe one of her pastries. Sugary treats and coffee go hand in hand for me.

Courtney is only four years older than me, and at 32, she owns the café. She's married to hot fireman in town, too. Just like Ally, Courtney came to Pine Cove for a fresh start in life, and she found her forever here with the café and her hunky husband. She had her life together when she was my age, and yet I'm bumbling around like an aimless drifter.

Maybe this place possesses some kind of small-town magic that draws in the lost souls of the world and finds them a home. Or, maybe this town just has an obscene amount of hot men that know how to make women fall in love with them so they'll stay.

Either way, I do know that Courtney's coffee and pastries are magic, and I could use some of both right now. Opening my car door, a blast of frigid air blows in my face and I immediately close it again. Holy hell, it's freezing!

Reaching into the back seat, I grab my scarf and wrap myself up before attempting to step out of the car again. It's only a few steps to the café's door, so I tuck my face down and hurry inside. The familiar bells jingle above my head, and the warmth welcomes me like an old friend.

I love this café. The floors are blue and white tiles that are laid down in an old checkered style like those authentic black and white ones in diners. Bistro tables are set up all on the right side, and the left is made up of cases filled with pastries and desserts, including pies, cakes, cookies, cupcakes, and donuts. It's a haven for those in need of a sugar pick-me-up.

Unwrapping my scarf, I start to walk towards the counter, but when I look up, I freeze on the spot.

He's here.

What the fuck?

Shouldn't he be working?

I haven't mentally prepared to see him yet.

No. I'm not ready.

He's not facing me, though, so if I back out slowly, he doesn't have to know that I was ever here.

But of course, my plan is ruined the second Courtney spots me over his shoulder.

"Ashley?" she asks, smiling, surprised to see me.

The man who's occupied my every thought and dirty dream for the past seven months stiffens, and slowly turns to face me.

The breath I've been holding suddenly rushes out of me as our eyes lock. I definitely wasn't ready to see him yet.

My chest tightens as his eyes run up and down my body, feeling them on me as if I were naked, and he's remembering everything we did in explicit detail.

When his eyes meet mine again, they're darker. Fuck, he's even more handsome than I remember. My fantasies haven't been doing him justice.

"Ashley." His voice flows over me like a warm breeze on a summer afternoon, and a shiver runs down my spine. Just my name from his lips is enough to make my blood rush—pounding in my ears. No man has ever made me feel like this, and I hate it. He makes me feel weak and vulnerable, and those are two things that I most definitely am not.

He's watching me, waiting for me to say something.

"Ryan," I manage to say, despite the fact that it feels like my throat is closing.

He takes a step towards me, and I resist the urge to take one backwards, staying planted where I am.

"You're back." He smirks, and my eyes dart down to his delicious lips that I've been dying to taste again.

Clearing my throat, I look back up, and see that his eyes are even darker. He knows exactly where my mind went. "I'm just here to visit Ally."

"How long are you here?"

"I don't know."

"Where are you staying?"

"Dottie's cottage." Why am I answering all of his questions? It's none of his business.

"Alone?" His voice drops an octave, and I suddenly snap out of the spell I'm under.

"That's none of your concern," I tell him, finally finding my voice. Steeling my spine, I walk past him and towards Courtney, but his spicy scent fills my nose, and I all but stumble the rest of the way to the counter.

"Hey, Ash." She smiles, her eyes holding a knowing look.

"Hey, Courtney. How have you been?"

"I'm good. How are you? What brought you back?"

"Uh"–I shift my eyes to the side–"I just needed to get away for a little while."

"Is everything okay?" she asks, her brows pulling together.

I know Ryan's still behind me, so I need to choose my words carefully. "Oh, yes, I'm fine."

"Doesn't sound like it."

"Maybe we can talk later?" I whisper, hoping she catches my hint. Her eyes dart over my shoulder and then back to me, and I know she gets it.

"So, what can I get for you? It's on the house."

"Oh, thanks." I smile, grateful. "I'll have a coffee and one of your amazing bear claws. I've been dreaming of them for months now."

Smiling, she pours me a coffee, and grabs a bear claw from the case. "To-go?"

"Yes, thanks. I'm meeting Ally at the cottage soon."

"She didn't tell me you were coming."

"I only decided yesterday. Ally said a big storm was coming in a few days, so I just packed up and came today."

"You two have the impulse gene, don't you?" She laughs. "She came here last year only a few days after being fired from her job." My eyes dart to the side, and I shift on my feet.

"Yeah." I smile weakly, taking the brown bag and cup from her.

Adding a little cream and sugar to my coffee, I steel myself to face Ryan again. I've felt his eyes on me the entire time.

Turning, I find him sitting at a table near the door, his gaze on me, never wavering. My god, he's sexy as hell. He exudes power and authority in his sheriff's uniform as he sits with his legs apart and his arm resting on his thigh as he sips his coffee. My eyes take in all of him – from his boots, to his gun, to his badge. Everything makes me want him more. When I finally take in his face, I see that sexy little smirk playing on his lips again, and I want to kiss it away.

His short blonde hair is begging for me to touch it, and his clean-shaven face shows off his square jaw and high cheek bones. The longer I stare at his perfect face, the wider his smirk gets, until he's full blown smiling at me, and I feel like I'm going to pass out. His straight white teeth graze his bottom lip and he rubs his jaw, making me wish those same teeth were grazing my neck as he pinned me against the wall.

Snapping my eyes up to his, I know he can see where my thoughts have gone again, and I grip the paper bag in my hand a little tighter. I hate how he has this power over me. I never let a man make me feel like I'm not in control of my body or my mind. But with Ryan, that's not even an option.

Turning back to Courtney, I hold up my coffee and force a smile. "Thanks, Courtney. Me, you, and Ally should have a night at The Rusty Anchor while I'm here." A low rumble from Ryan makes my forced smile morph into a real one. Does the idea of me going out upset the sheriff? Well, that's just too damn bad.

"Yes! I haven't had a good night out in such a long time."

"Good. See you."

"Bye, Ash."

Avoiding looking at Ryan again, I walk out of the café with my head held high. I refuse to let that man affect me any more than he already has. I refuse to go back home again with more memories that I can't get out of my head.

Thinking about it now sends flashes of him pushing me against a tree, his hot breath against my neck, kissing his way up to whisper sweet, dirty things, in my ear.

Shaking my head, I push the memory back down and get in my car. I need to get a grip on where my thoughts keep going.

The drive to Dottie's is just as I remember, with pine tree lined roads, except this time, everything is covered in snow. It's beautiful. I've always loved the winter and snow. It's a fresh, white, sparkled blanket that provides a clean slate on the world around you.

Glancing in my rearview mirror, I see an SUV not too far behind me. And as if the driver can sense that I'm looking at them, blue lights start flashing at me.

Are you fucking kidding me right now?

Sighing, I roll my eyes and pull over. Is he serious? Did he really follow me so he could pull me over? Is he on some sort of power trip?

Parking, I turn my car off, and watch in my mirror as Ryan gets out of the SUV cruiser and places his sheriff's hat on his head. Damn it, even that stupid hat looks hot on him.

Slowly walking towards my driver's side window, I eat up every inch of his 6'3" frame with every step he takes.

When he reaches my window, he taps gently, and I roll it down, waiting for him to say something first. I refuse to give in to his authority that he thinks he can just throw around. I'm just a game to him–something he thinks he can win or play around with.

"Do you know how fast you were going Ms. Ames?" Ryan's silky voice floats into my car, and my pulse starts racing from that alone.

"I was going below the limit," I answer, keeping my eyes straight ahead. "There was no reason to pull me over."

"I know."

"Then why did you? That's harassment." His low chuckle vibrates through me, and when I see his hand coming towards me, I jerk out of the way. "What are you doing?" I ask sharply, looking him straight in the eyes.

"Trying to get you to look at me."

"Why?"

"You know why," he says, his voice dropping a few octaves.

"No. I don't. And I need to meet Ally, so…"

"So…what? Are you asking me if you can go?" The hint of humor in his voice makes my blood boil. He's such an ass.

"No. And you pulled me over for no reason other than to make me see you as someone who can control me. And you can't. So I'm leaving. Don't pull this shit on me again, Ryan. Just leave me alone while I'm here."

Bending down, Ryan rests his arms on my window frame. His sexy face is less than six inches from me, and his eyes are on mine, challenging me. "Why are you so mad at me, Ashley?" Jesus, my name just rolls off his tongue like it was always meant to say it. "Is it because you went back home and realized you'd never find a man there that could give you what you need?"

Curling my fingers into my palms, I resist the urge to slap him. "Fuck you."

"I know you want to, sweetheart." I know I want to, too. "I bet you've thought about me often."

Try every fucking day.

Turning my car back on, I throw it in drive, and barely give him a chance to step away from my window before I step on the gas. My tires sputter in the snow, but then level out as I hightail it to Dottie's. I don't care if I just sped away from a sheriff. I know he's not coming after me.

I can't fucking do this. Why did I come here? I knew I'd see him, and I knew I'd want him all over again. The second I followed him into those woods last year, there was no going back. And the thing is, that I hate to admit to myself, is that I don't want to go back.

Even before I visited Ally last summer, I was sick of dating around. No man ever had the ability to hold my attention, or spark my interest for longer than a week or two. I was always bored. I thought the problem was with the men I chose, until I began thinking that maybe it was me.

But then Ryan showed me what it was like to be with a real man, not the boys back in Jersey that try to pass as men, and I know it exists–passion.

Gripping the steering wheel tight, I check the rearview mirror to make sure he's not following me, and I make the last turn onto Peach Place. When I reach the driveway with the mailbox marked 25, I turn into it, and make the long drive through the snowy pine trees. A minute later, it opens into a clearing, and a cute little blue cottage welcomes me.

The last time I saw it, it was bursting with flowers all around, and color was everywhere I looked. And while that was beautiful, there's something about the simplicity of a snow-covered cottage amongst the trees. It makes me feel like I'm in a Hallmark Christmas movie, and the owner is going to be a handsome stranger who I run into all over town while I'm here.

Okay, I need to stop watching those movies every chance I get.

Parking next to Ally's car, I wrap my scarf around my neck a little tighter and climb out, the freezing cold air whipping at my face immediately. Hurrying up the porch steps, I knock on the front door, and bounce from foot to foot to keep my blood circulating.

Ally opens it a few seconds later with a huge smile on her face. "Ashley!" she yells, pulling me inside and hugging me tight.

"Hey, Al." I laugh, squeezing her back. "I've missed you."

"Me, too." She had come home for Thanksgiving with Jake a couple of months ago, but then decided to stay up here and celebrate Christmas with him and the Taylor's. I definitely had a twinge of jealousy knowing she was spending time with Ryan, but I wasn't going to tell her that. No one even knows about what happened between Ryan and I last summer. I couldn't tell my best friend that I hooked up with her man's older brother...

"So, I now know what you meant by it being cold. I'm freezing."

"I just turned the heat up for you. It was on low so the pipes wouldn't freeze, but it should warm up soon. And you can turn the electric fireplace on too."

Closing the door behind me, I unwrap my scarf and smile, looking around the living room. "It's the same. I love it."

Ally smiles too. "I know. I loved this place. I never changed it while I was living here, even though Dottie said I could."

"There's nothing to change." The muted pastels of the décor make it feel homey and lived in. The beige couch has a light pink, lilac, and cream crochet blanket draped over the back, and the chair in the corner has a similar one thrown over the side, along with a fur throw pillow. The walls are lined with bookshelves and pictures of flowers that tie in with the rose patterned side table lamps and area rug. Dottie loves flowers.

"Exactly. Now, let me show you where the heat switches are and everything else." Following her down the hall, she stops at the end, right before the kitchen, and points at the dial on the wall. "This is for the heat. But I also took out all of the extra blankets from the closets and piled them on the bed in the purple room. I knew you'd like the pink room like I did, so I changed the sheets and added an extra blanket. Uh, what else? Oh, the keys," she says, pulling them out from her pocket. "This is the front door, and the other is the back. With the snow covering everything, I don't know if you'll be walking around the property, but if you do, be careful. Don't slip and fall into the ocean."

"Yes, mom," I say, rolling my eyes. The cottage sits on the coast, and last summer we all sat out in Adirondack chairs and drank cocktails while talking and watching the boats pass. It was so nice. But, right now it's all snow and ice, and I don't plan on falling down the rocky edge into the freezing Atlantic.

"Sorry, I just don't want you stranded out there and then freeze to death."

"Wow, thanks for that image. It's safe to say I won't be wandering around. Trust me."

"Okay." She smiles. "Now, a huge storm is coming in a day or two."

"That's okay. I'll just raid the bookshelves, drink wine by the fireplace, and relax. I could use that."

Ally's face drops. "I'm sorry this happened to you. What the hell is with that guy?"

"I don't know." I shrug. "I knew he was interested in me, considering he asked me out every damn night I was there, but…" I shake my head. "Whatever. I handled it, and I need to move on. Again."

"You'll find something."

"Not in the field I want. You know that."

"Sorry."

"It's fine," I say quickly. "I don't want to talk about it. Thank you so much for asking Dottie for me."

"Of course." She smiles. "I'm so happy you're here."

"I already stopped at the café on my way here and told Courtney we needed to have a girl's night at the bar. So, when are you free? Can you pull yourself away from Jake?"

"Yes." She laughs. "How about tonight? Or are you too tired?"

"No, I'm not. I could really use a night out after everything."

"Perfect. I'll pick you up at seven? We'll have dinner and drinks."

"A lot of drinks," I correct.

"Yes, a lot. Sorry." She laughs. "Okay, I'll text Courtney and tell her the plan. Now, let me help you bring your stuff in so you don't have to take more than one trip out into the cold."

"Thank God. I don't think I'll be leaving this house much unless it's necessary."

Taking just one trip, Ally and I manage to haul in my two big suitcases to the pink room. She's right, I did want that one.

Dottie's cottage has two bedrooms, each virtually the same, with light brown wooden dressers, paintings of flowers on the walls, a floral patterned rug, and wrought iron beds with big, fluffy floral comforters on top. The only difference being that one is pink, and the other is purple.

"Did you bring enough shit, Ashley?" She jokes.

"Shut up. Yes, I did bring enough. I brought all of my winter stuff. I didn't know what to expect. You made it sound like the arctic tundra, which to be fair, it kind of is. So I'm glad I brought everything."

"Don't be dramatic," she says, rolling her eyes.

"Dramatic? My face is frozen and my nipples have been as hard as rocks since I got here."

"Ashley!" she exclaims, laughing. "Okay, I'm going to go. But I'll be back soon."

"Alright. Go make out with your man and I'll just be here freezing and figuring out what people wear to go out in when you can't show any skin for fear of exposure."

"You'll figure something out. I believe in you." She jokes, closing the door behind her.

CHAPTER 3

Looking in the mirror, I do a little twirl and smile, fluffing my hair. Just because it's winter, doesn't mean I can't be cute. I went with a short black and white plaid woven wool skirt, sheer tights, black suede over the knee boots, and a tucked in, tight burgundy turtleneck sweater. My boobs look good, my waist looks slim, and the boots make my legs look longer. And luckily, the tights make what would be an inappropriately short skirt sexy, not slutty.

My naturally curly brown hair is long and wild, and I only put on a little extra makeup than usual to make my hazel eyes pop. I've been known to draw men in with the mysterious gold, brown, and green colors of my eyes, and over the years, I've learned to use them to their full advantage.

But they've also gotten me into some trouble this past year. Jackass men tend to think that just because I smile and make eye contact with them, it means I want to fuck them every which to

Sunday. They always say they knew I wanted them, that it was in my eyes. The most notable examples being my last two bosses. Fucking dicks.

Hearing my phone buzz on the bed, I pick it up to see a text from Ally saying she's here. I throw my lipstick and phone in my purse and walk around the house to make sure the back door and all of the windows are locked before slipping on my coat and scarf.

Stepping out onto the porch, I lock the door behind me.

Holy balls it's cold! Maybe sheer tights wasn't the best idea.

Hurrying to her car, I climb in, rubbing my hands together. "I need food and alcohol. ASAP."

"Me, too. Courtney is meeting us there. She had to run home to change, and then I think Jack is driving her."

"Good. Because we're going to get fucked up, and we'll need a ride home later."

Shaking her head, Ally smiles. "At least we'll be responsible about our inebriation."

"Exactly."

****

Walking into The Rusty Anchor, I smile, loving that it's just as I remember it. The floors are a dark wood that matches that of the ceiling and the horseshoe shaped bar at the far end of the room. Two pool tables separate the bar area from the twenty or so tables that are scattered on the side closest to the door, and the walls are a deep navy blue, and are lined with neon signs, posters, and all sorts of nautical memorabilia.

Choosing a table closest to the bar, we take our jackets off and sit. Looking around, I take in the people, not sure if I'm hoping, or dreading, to see the familiar face of a certain Pine Cove resident.

"Looking for someone?" Ally asks.

"Oh, no. Just looking around," I quickly say, standing. "I'll get the first round."

Walking up to the bar, I see that the sexy bartender, Alex, is still working here.

"You're back." He smiles, his emerald green eyes gleaming mischievously. "And just as beautiful as I remember." And he's just as good looking as I remember. His dark hair, green eyes, and tattoos scream 'a good time with a bad boy.' But sadly, he doesn't even compare to Ryan. Not even close.

"I am." I smile back.

"Just you this time? Not the whole entourage?"

"Yeah, just me. I needed a break, and Ally invited me up," I tell him. "I'll have a Jack and coke, and Ally will have—"

"A gin and tonic. Her usual."

"Yeah." Watching him make our drinks, I smooth my hands down the sides of my skirt and look around again. I don't know why I want to torture myself this way. I want to see him, and I don't want to see him. I want to kiss him, and I want to slap him.

Oh, for fucks sake, what I want is for him to pin me up against the wall and take me the way he did all those months ago.

"Here you go, gorgeous. The first round is on me." Alex winks, sliding the two glasses towards me.

"Thanks, Alex." I smile, turning back to Ally, seeing that Courtney has arrived.

"Hey, Ash," she greets, taking her coat off and hanging it on the back of the chair.

I place the two drinks down on the table. "Hey. Let me get you a drink. Alex said the first round is on him."

"Of course he did," she says, rolling her eyes.

"A free drink is a free drink." I laugh, walking back up to the bar and flagging Alex down. "I need a drink for Courtney now, too."

"So, I should expect it to be a wild night then?"

"Yup. Just keep 'em coming."

Shaking his head, he smiles, and makes a drink for Courtney without even having to ask what she wants.

"Thanks." I smile. "I promise we'll be good."

"But you won't be."

"I know." Shrugging, I smile and flip my hair over my shoulder and walk back to the table.

"Thanks," Courtney says when I hand her her drink. "So, what's new with you? What sparked this impromptu trip?"

I shrug, taking a sip of my rum and coke, letting the liquor warm my insides a little. "I just needed to get away."

"There's more to it. Spill."

"Wow, did you wear Ally down too when she first came here?"

"Yes. So spill."

My eyes dart to Ally, and she just shrugs, letting me decide my fate. "Fine," I sigh. "I quit my job. My manager had been hitting on me every night after my shifts for the past six months, and then the other night, he took matters into his own hands."

"What does that mean?"

"He tried to force himself on me, and so I kneed him in the balls and punched him in the face. Then I stole all the tips from that night and ran out of there like I was on fire."

"Are you serious? What a fucking dick!"

"I know. And that wasn't the first time this happened to me. This year, actually."

Her eyes widen. "What?"

"Long story. But I'll just say that my previous boss thought it was okay to force himself on me too."

"What the hell is with these guys?"

"I don't know. But the bartending job was the best one I could find. They're always packed, so the tips were really good. But now I don't know what I'm going to do. I already had to move in with my mom to save money when I started that job. And now I'm unemployed and live at home. At 28." Taking a long drag from my drink, I lean back in my chair and close my eyes.

"There's no shame in that, Ashley," Ally says. "That was me last year, and look at me now."

"Yeah, but you had a choice in everything that happened."

"I was fired, Ash."

"Yeah, but you were able to choose what you did next. I don't have that luxury."

"But you'll figure it out."

"That's easy for you to say. You're not banned from your profession because of a handsy dick, or was forced to quit the only other well-paying job in the area because of another handsy dick." Sucking down the rest of my drink, I get up to go get another one. Thinking about my situation makes me want to down an entire bottle of wine, and then wash that down with five shots of tequila.

"Alex, I need another one. And a shot of tequila."

He raises his eyebrows. "That bad, huh?"

"What?"

"Why you're here."

"Maybe." I shrug. "I don't know."

"Well, tequila is always a good start for solving your problems." He slides a shot glass, lime wedge, and salt shaker towards me. But I down the shot plain, not needing the lime or salt. I like the burn of the tequila as it slides down my throat and pools warmly in my stomach.

"I'll be back in a little while for another," I tell him, grabbing my rum and coke and taking a sip.

"I like a woman who can handle her tequila." His voice dropped a few octaves, and it vibrates through me in a way I wish turned me on like it would have before Ryan.

"I bet you do. But you can't handle me."

"You could let me try. I'm sure you'd see otherwise."

"Thanks, but no. I'm not really getting involved with any men right now."

"Ah, so your drinking has to do with a man, then."

"Maybe. But not because I got my heart broken or some shit like that. They're just fucking assholes."

He smiles wide, showing off his perfect, white, straight teeth. "Assholes are the most fun, baby."

"Oh my god." I roll my eyes. "You're hot, Alex, I'll give you that. But I'm not in the market for a man, or a fling. Just alcohol and my friends."

"Alright, let me know if that changes, though." He winks. "I can help you forget your problems for an hour or two."

Laughing, I grab my drink and step away. "You're relentless. I'll let you know if I need your services, slick." I know I won't, though.

Nodding, he winks and moves down the bar to help someone else.

Courtney wags her eyebrows at me when I sit back down. "So, Alex?"

I wave her off dismissively. "Oh, he's a harmless flirt who wants to show me how assholes can rock my world or some shit like that."

"What?" she sputters. The sip she was taking dribbles down her chin, and she quickly reaches for a napkin to blot it away.

"Yeah, but I turned him down."

"You did?" Ally asks, sounding incredulous. "Why?"

"What? You think I have sex with anyone who gives me attention?"

"Don't get defensive. I just thought you may want a distraction while you're here."

"Oh, she has one already. Right, Ashley?" Courtney's eyes dance with mirth. Shit. I forgot she saw what happened earlier in the café with Ryan.

Ally's confused eyes dart back and forth between Courtney and I. "What do you mean?"

"I mean," Courtney continues, "that Ashley has her eyes on another Pine Cove hottie."

"I do?" I ask innocently.

"Who?" Ally asks.

"No one."

"Who?"

Sighing, I lean back in my chair and sip my drink. I didn't plan on spilling this secret tonight – or ever.

"Ashley?" Ally asks again.

"Ryan," I mumble.

"What?!" she shrieks, slapping her hands on the table. "How? Why? When? What?"

"Shut up, Ally! Geeze."

"Well, what the fuck, Ash?"

"She was all flustered and nervous this afternoon when she ran into him at the café. It was cute."

"It wasn't," I shoot back, narrowing my eyes.

Ally pins me with a stare. "Why were you flustered?"

"Because last year at the barbecue, we sort of… Uh… Hooked up." When I came with Ellie and Mel to visit Ally last summer over Memorial Day Weekend, we all went to the Taylor family barbecue at Jake and Ryan's parent's house. "I may have let my drunken confidence take charge over me."

"What?!" she shrieks again. "Ashley! Why did you never tell me? Wait, you had sex with him that same night you first met? At his parent's house?"

"Make me sound a little sluttier, why don't you? I couldn't help it," I sigh. "I'd never seen a sexier man in my life. And I thought it'd just be a quick thing, and I'd get it out of my system."

"But?"

"But… I'm going to need another shot. Be right back." Walking up to the bar, I order two more shots of tequila and knock them back before returning to the table. "I've never experienced anything like him before. And I haven't stopped thinking about him since."

"Really?"

"Yeah." My voice comes out small and resigned. It feels good to actually admit this out loud. "I finally found a man who captures my attention–fully–but he lives here, and I don't. He was amazing, too. He was like a fucking animal in those woods. I had scrapes on my back for weeks."

"Wait. That was you in the woods?" Ally smiles, covering her mouth with her hand.

"Yeah?"

"Jake and I were out there too." She giggles. "And when we were walking back to the party, we heard two people going at it."

"I guess brothers think alike." I laugh, but then sigh. "And then we parted ways and never spoke again. Not that I expected us to or anything. Trust me, I'm not delusional. I'm just pissed. I went on dates, tried kissing other guys, but all I could think about was Ryan." Rubbing my forehead, I start to feel the effects of the tequila and rum.

"Well, you're here, and he's here. You could always just do it again and see if it was a one-time thing, or if you actually feel something for him."

"Seriously?" I ask, not sure if I heard her correctly.

"You should do it," Courtney agrees. "You two were practically eye fucking each other this afternoon."

"No, we weren't."

"I've never seen him look at someone like that before. I've known him for years, and he's always been single. Or if he wasn't, he's good at hiding his women. And he's never looked at one like he wanted to eat her alive right then and there."

"Holy shit! He was?" Ally asks.

"No, he wasn't."

"Yes, he was," Courtney confirms.

"Well, even if he was, the fact that he pulled me over five minutes later on the way to the cottage just to shove his authority in my face, makes that a moot point."

"Wait, he did?"

"Yes. And then I sped away from him while he was still standing at my window. I hope he jumped back in time so I didn't run him over."

"You did what?"

Shrugging, I sip my drink again. "He was pissing me off with his sexiness, so I drove off."

"Isn't that illegal?" Ally asks.

"I don't know, and I don't care. And we need more drinks."

"I'll get them this time," Courtney offers, leaving me alone with Ally's hard stare on me.

"Yes?" I ask her.

"Ashley. Why didn't you tell me?"

"I didn't tell *anyone*."

"Why? Do you regret it?"

"No," I say quickly, making her smile.

"You know, we could devise a manipulative plan like Courtney did for me when I first got here. We can get you Ryan."

"Who said I want him? I'm only here for a week."

"And you think you'll get attached?"

I don't answer. Instead, I suck down the rest of my drink and look around the room as it starts to fill up with Saturday night patrons looking for a good time. I already am attached. Hell if I know why, considering we barely spoke. But he pinned against a tree and took me like a man who just got out of prison and hasn't seen, or had, a woman in years.

Was it hot and sexy? Yes. Was it the best I've ever had? Yes. Am I getting hot just thinking about it? Yes.

"You're already attached, aren't you?"

"I barely know anything about him."

"Well then, let's change that."

"No," I say flatly.

"Come on, let us," Courtney says, placing a fresh round of drinks down on the table. "We both did it, and now we're in love."

"Who said anything about love?"

"No one. I'm just saying it could happen."

"I don't need love. I have other shit to worry about."

"Ashley, I know you. All you've ever wanted is love. That's why you've tried every dating app in the world, and have given so many men a chance when they don't deserve one. You were searching for what we all want."

"Okay, Dr. Phil. Yes, I want love, and happiness, and all that shit."

"And I know you've never been caught up on a man before."

"I know," I sigh, downing my drink in a few gulps. I don't think there's enough alcohol in this bar that could make me forget the way my skin tingled when Ryan's eyes met mine today, and then trailed down my body. It was like he could see under my clothes, and read every thought in my head.

"Let's just enjoy the night, because we're probably going to be too far gone to come up with anything good," Ally says.

"True." I laugh. "I'll get us some shots and another round."

"We still have full drinks. You're the only one who downed hers in thirty seconds."

"Well, yours better be gone by the time I get back." Standing, I push my hair behind my shoulders and saunter up to the bar. I tend to get a little sassy when I drink.

"Another round please, Alex. And three shots."

"Already? Courtney just got you a round."

"Judgy much? We can handle our liquor."

"Never said you couldn't, beautiful," he says, holding his hands up in defense. "You have a ride home, right?"

"How sweet. You're concerned for our safety. And yes, I'm sure either of their men will have no issue coming to pick us up."

"Okay." He nods, pouring our shots.

Taking two trips back to the table with our drinks, I hold my shot in the air and propose a toast. "To reunions, a good night, and fun."

"Here-here!" Ally and Courtney say together as we clink glasses and shoot our shots back.

The song changes in the bar, and I gasp. "Oh my god, I love this song! Come on!" I yell, standing, trying to pull them to their feet. "Let's dance!"

"Oh, no. No, no, no," Courtney chants. "I don't dance."

"Yes, you do, and you will." Dragging them to their feet, I pull them towards the small makeshift dancefloor that's really just a few tables pushed out of the way, and I start to spin around. Raising my hands above my head, I move my hips, and sway to the rhythm of the song. Grabbing Ally's hand, I twirl her around, and we move to the beat.

Smiling at Courtney, I grab her next, and pull her towards me so I can show her how to move. Laughing, she goes with it, and we start to move together, until a hand snakes around my waist, and I freeze.

Spinning around, I come face to face with some drunk asshole who thinks he can just put his hands on me without asking.

Pushing him away, I level him with a death stare. "What the fuck are you doing? Don't touch me."

"Baby," he slurs. "I think you could use a man like me with the way you're moving. I'll take care of you *real* good."

"You're disgusting," I sneer.

"Come on, baby," he slurs again, reaching for me.

"Get the fuck away from me." Stepping back, I bump into Ally, and she finally realizes what's happening.

"What's wrong?"

"This fucker thinks he can just touch me."

"The way you're dancing"–he licks his lips–"makes a man want a taste of that fine body."

"Gross," Courtney says, grimacing. "Get out of here."

Another drunk asshole walks up to our little party, and sways next to me. "Is he bothering you, beautiful?"

"If you're talking to me," I start, "then no. I can handle this on my own."

"I can help you, sweets." He winks, turning to the dick who touched me. "Leave her alone."

"Is she yours? You should keep a better handle on her."

"I'm not property, and I'm standing right here. I can speak for myself, you chauvinistic fuckers." I'm raging on the inside right now. I feel like I'm some sort of douchebag magnet. I'm just trying to have fun with my friends.

"Let's just go back to our table," Ally whispers in my ear. "I'll call Jake to come and get us."

"Fine," I huff, wanting to get away as quickly as possible.

But after turning away, one of them grips my arm. "Where do you think you're going?"

Freezing, I look down at the hand on my arm, my blood turning to ice in my veins. He's seriously touching me again? Turning slowly, I meet his bloodshot eyes of the first dick with my steely gaze. "Get your hand off of me." My voice is low and menacing.

"Or what, baby? You're going to stop me?"

"She won't, but I will," the second asshole says as he breaks the grip on my arm and swings his fist, connecting squarely on the first guy's jaw.

His head snaps back. "The fuck?!" he yells, his nostrils flaring, and his chest heaving.

Charging forward, he knocks the guy to the floor, and starts punching him in the face. The sound of knuckles meeting bone and flesh sends chills down my spine, and I start to back away, my eyes wide.

"Hey! Hey!" Alex yells as he comes out from behind the bar. Pulling them apart, he pushes the first asshole back, and two guys come out of nowhere to hold him back from charging forward again.

Backing up, I sit back down at our table, my legs no longer able to support me.

What's happening? I don't even know these people, and they started fighting because of me. Over me?

I stare blankly at the table in front of me.

I don't know how much time passes, or how many swirls of the wood I've circled with my eyes, but my drunken haze is broken through by Ally's voice.

"Hey! Ashley!" Looking up, I blink a few times, and focus in on her concerned eyes. "Are you okay?"

"Sure." I nod, but I don't really know.

"I called Jake and told him what happened. He'll be here soon to pick us up."

"Great," I say, my voice sounding dead to my ears.

I think she says something back to me, but my eyes are on the door of the bar that just opened, and Ryan walks in with a deputy in tow, his presence bringing me a comfort I'm not ready to analyze.

Scanning the room, his eyes land on the scene to my right, but then dart around until they meet mine. Even from this distance, I can see him searching my face to see if I'm okay. I'm clearly not.

His jaw tightens, and he tears his eyes away, making his way over to Alex and the two assholes.

"Can we go?" I ask, my eyes following every step Ryan takes, admiring his powerful presence.

"I don't know. Maybe he needs a statement from you or something," Ally says.

"I don't care. I just need to leave."

"Okay, yeah, sure. Let's go."

Standing, we all put our jackets back on, and I keep my head down as we weave our way through the crowd and outside into the cold night. But I don't feel it. I don't feel anything, really.

"He'll be here in a few minutes."

Remaining quiet, I lean against the wall and close my eyes. Taking a deep breath, the cold air makes it feel like a thousand tiny needles are pricking my lungs, but it does nothing to break my trance.

How did my life become such a shit show?

When the door next to me swings open, I open my eyes and see the deputy that came here with Ryan walking one of the guys out. He pushes him towards his cruiser, and shoves him in the back – handcuffed.

Next, Ryan emerges with the other, and walks him over to his SUV, putting him in the back too. Spotting Ally and Courtney huddled together, his eyes scan the shadows of the building until he finds me. Slamming the door to his SUV shut, he walks towards me, his long legs eating up the distance in a matter of seconds.

I try and look away from him, but his eyes hold mine captive until he's standing right in front of me.

"Ashley, are you okay?" he asks, and I nod. "Tell me what happened." His eyes are hard and angry, but full of something else, too.

Swallowing, I try and get my dry throat to work, but I can't. No words will form.

I'm saved by the rumble of a truck pulling into the parking lot that makes Ryan stiffen, turning towards the source. But when he sees it's Jake, he relaxes and turns back to me. "Go with Jake. I'll talk to you later."

Nodding again, I push off the wall and slowly make my way over to the white pickup truck. Ryan opens the back door for me and I grip the inner handle hard, using all the strength I have left to lift myself up inside.

He rounds the truck and talks to his brother for a minute, and then steps away, letting Jake drive off.

Closing my eyes, I lean my head against the window, the cool glass relieving my heated skin as I drift off to sleep.

CHAPTER 4

Something warm touches my face and my eyes jolt open, searching the dark.

"It's just me," a low voice says that I immediately recognize.

"Where am I?"

"At Jake's. But I'm going to take you home now."

I pull the blanket that's around me a little tighter. "Uh…"

"I promise I'll be good." He chuckles softly. "I just need to get your statement about tonight. And I doubt you want to still be here when Jake and Ally start going at it."

"Oh my god," I groan, throwing the blanket off of me. "No, I don't. That's why I'm at Dottie's."

Standing too quickly, my head pounds, and I start to sway. Reaching out into the dark to grab onto something before I fall, an arm wraps around my waist before I get the chance to.

"I got you," Ryan whispers in my ear. His warm body against

mine sends a shiver down my spine, and he tightens his grip before letting go and taking my hand.

I look around, but I can't see or hear anything. The moon is hidden behind the clouds tonight, so there's no light coming from anywhere. The only thing keeping me steady is the strong, warm hand engulfing mine. But then he releases it, and I panic for a second, until I feel him behind me again.

"I have your coat," Ryan whispers, helping me put it on.

Opening the front door, he takes my hand, and we step out into more darkness. Shuffling closer to him, my head turns in every direction, ready for something to jump out at us. "I've got you," he says again, and my heartrate kicks up. "There's nothing out here, I promise."

"Okay," I whisper, somehow knowing that he'd protect me even if there was.

Ryan opens the passenger door of his black pickup truck for me, and I hop up inside. When he rounds the front and climbs in, the second he closes the door, it feels like the cab shrinks to the size of a thimble–allowing me only short, shallow breaths.

Starting down the driveway, I focus on breathing evenly so he doesn't see how he affects me. Shoving my hands in my pockets, I keep them hidden so I don't give in to my urge to reach out and touch him.

The ride seems to go on forever as he winds through the pitch-black streets of Pine Cove. When he finally pulls into the driveway of the cottage, I practically jump out of the truck the second he puts it in park.

I need air. His scent is everywhere, and I can't take a breath without the spicy, woodsy smell filling my lungs.

Hurrying to the front door, I pull out my keys, but it's dark, and my fingers are numb. I can't find the right key.

"Let me," he says, covering my hand with his. Slipping the keys out from between my fingers, he unlocks the door and pushes it open, motioning for me to step inside.

When I hear the door close, I turn and find him behind me. "What are you doing?"

"I said I have to ask you a few questions."

"Now?"

"Would you rather come by the station in the morning? Or maybe I should stay the night and you can tell me over coffee?" He smirks.

The audacity of this man.

"No. You're not staying the night. Let's just get this over with. But I'm tired and still a little tipsy, so I'm making coffee first."

Unwrapping my scarf, I toss it on the couch along with my jacket, and walk down the hall to the kitchen. Placing a fresh filter in the coffee maker, I scoop out the grounds, and press brew. I need water first, though. My throat feels like the Sahara. Grabbing a bottle from the fridge, I down half of it in a matter of seconds, reviving myself slightly.

It's time to get out of these clothes and into sweatpants.

Bending down, I start to unzip my boots, but I hear a low groan behind me. Spinning around, I find Ryan standing in the doorway, his heated eyes on me.

"Why are you watching me?"

"Because I can," he says simply.

Rolling my eyes, I walk past him and into the pink bedroom, making sure the door is closed behind me before I start undressing. He definitely doesn't get the privilege of seeing all of this.

Taking my boots off, I peel down my tights, and shimmy off my skirt, before stepping into a pair of comfy sweatpants. I replace my sweater with a long-sleeved t-shirt, and then shove my feet into my fuzzy slippers.

When I reemerge in the kitchen, I find Ryan leaning against the counter, a steaming mug of coffee in hand. His eyes take in my new outfit and his lips turn up, fighting a smile.

"What? Is there something wrong with this?" I ask, waving a hand down my body.

"Not at all, sweetheart. It only makes me want to look at you more so I can try and catch a glimpse of that sexy body you're hiding under there."

I don't even know how to respond to that.

"Let me make you a mug. How do you take your coffee?"

"Cream and a little sugar," I tell him, taking a seat at the small, round kitchen table. "Why aren't you in uniform?" I ask, trying to distract myself from him being here, alone with me.

"Would you prefer if I was?" He smiles, his perfect smile. "I didn't think you'd respond well to me if I showed up in it, though. I thought we could talk as friends."

"We're friends?"

"Are we not?"

"I don't know. I wouldn't say we are."

Ryan just smiles, and I watch him as he makes my coffee. He adds the perfect amount of both cream and sugar that I like, and then saunters over and places it in front of me before taking the seat across from me.

"Don't you need a notebook or something?" I ask.

"Yes. But if you're more comfortable just talking to me, that's fine."

My brows furrow. "How is that fine? It doesn't seem very official. Aren't you the sheriff?"

"I have a good memory." He smirks.

"Fine," I sigh, taking a sip of coffee. The hot liquid flows down my throat, and gives my brain the jolt it needs to focus on telling Ryan what happened. "We were having a good time catching up – Ally, Courtney, and I. And after a few drinks, and a couple of shots, a song I like came on, and I dragged them up to dance. Then some dick thought it was okay to snake his sleazy arm around my waist, call me 'baby,' and tell me it looked like I needed a man like him to take care of me by the way I was dancing." Ryan's jaw clenches, and he grips the mug in front of him a little tighter, the blue in his eyes turning to ice.

"I told him to fuck off, but he kept saying shit to me. Then some other asshole comes up to us, thinking he's helping in defending me, but he only made it worse. The first guy thought that he was my boyfriend coming to my defense, and he told him he should keep a tighter leash on me, or something like that. I tried to walk away at this point, but then he grabbed my arm."

"He touched you again?" Ryan asks through clenched teeth.

"Yeah. And that's when the other guy pushed him away and punched him in the face. But that only seemed to anger the guy more, and he charged at him, knocking him to the ground. Then he started punching him in the face over and over again." A shiver racks my body and I hold the hot mug close to my face. "That sound."

"It's okay. Everything's fine now," he says, trying to soothe me.

"I know," I say defensively, eyeing him over the rim of my mug. "I can handle myself. I've been doing it a lot lately."

"What do you mean?"

"Nothing." Looking away, I pick a spot on the wall behind him, and study it.

"Hey," he says, trying to get me to look at him. "Ashley." His smooth voice floats over me like I'm submerging into a warm bath, and my eyes have no choice but to drift back to his.

Even from here, I can see the light blue centers of his eyes are rimmed by a darker navy – almost as if the light is trying to push away the dark, but it still creeps in no matter what.

I see that in him. He's good and he's light, but he's also something else. And it's that something else that drew me to him in the first place.

The longer I look, the more the dark overtakes the light.

"What's on your mind, Ashley?" he croons, pulling me in.

I shake my head weakly. "Nothing."

"You sure?"

"Yes, and I'm done with my statement. So, you can go."

"What if I said I didn't want to leave?" His voice is low and seductive – hypnotic.

"I'd say that's too bad, because you have no choice in the matter."

"I know you want to remember again, Ashley." His voice drops even lower, his eyes melting into mine.

"Remember what?" I ask as he stands, closing the distance between us.

Leaning down, he braces his arms on the table, his face just a few inches from mine. My breaths are coming shallow, and my hands shake around my mug.

"You felt it. And I can tell you it was just the beginning. I can give you so much more, sweetheart. You can deny it, and you can pretend all you want, but I know."

My eyes dart down to his lips. They're right there.

He exhales. That simple act parts his lips, and I want to taste him. I want to see if he's as sweet as I remember.

Tilting my chin up, he lowers a fraction of an inch. Our breaths mix, and I'm dizzy.

I'm riding on the thin edge of sanity, and just the slightest touch would push me over into a frenzy I know I wouldn't be able to control.

That's how he made me feel last time. Unhinged. I was out of control, and he was in charge. He gave me the freedom to relinquish the power I desperately try and hold on to at all times.

I could give in right now. I could feel that freedom again so easily.

Ryan can give me that one thing I didn't know I needed.

"You feel it right now," he whispers, and my eyes lift to his, seeing the need in them.

In slow motion, he moves his head lower, closing the distance. His eyes morph, and my vision blurs. I need this kiss.

But the second I feel the warmth of his lips a millimeter from mine, I pull back.

I know he's just playing some sick game with me, and he wants to see if he can unravel me. I know he didn't spend seven months thinking about me night and day, reliving every touch, kiss, and electric current that flowed between us. I'm sure he's had sex countless times since then, and I'm just a blip on the radar of his conquests.

I'm the one who can't get past a one-night stand.

I'm such a fucking cliché for all women everywhere.

Closing my eyes, I turn my head away and take a deep breath. I refuse to let him play me. Sure, we'd have a wild time that I know would blow my mind, but I also know that I'd want more. I can't be hung up on him for another seven months when I go back home. I've already been miserable wanting something I can't have.

"You need to go," I tell him, my voice soft.

This time Ryan doesn't say anything, he just straightens and walks out of the kitchen.

A minute later, I hear the front door close, and I take a shaky breath in.

I wanted him to go, but I didn't want him to leave.

Sighing, I cover my face with my hands and rub my temples.

The man I've been dreaming of was right in front of me, and I turned away from him.

Groaning, I push my hair away from my face and look around the small kitchen. His tall frame took up so much room, it felt like he dominated the space. But now that it's just me, it feels small and empty – a little like my heart.

Okay, snap out of it, Ashley. Even I'm depressing myself.

Steeling my spine, I finish my mug of cold coffee and bring mine and Ryan's to the sink. Leaning on the edge, I remind myself that I'm a strong, independent woman who can get through anything, and can handle whatever's thrown at me.

I can handle Ryan. I have to.

I came here to get away from the shit storm that is my life, and yet instead, I've crash landed in the path of the only man who has the power to ruin me.

Closing my eyes, I take a couple of deep breaths.

An hour ago, I was woken up from a drunken stupor, only to be brought back to Dottie's cottage and made to give a police statement because two assholes decided that they knew what I needed – them. What the hell? Can I not just get away from the stupidity and general dumbass-ness of men for a few days?

Blowing out a lungful of air, I straighten. Walking through the house, I shut off all the lights and make sure the front door is securely locked before climbing into bed.

With thoughts of what it would have been like to actually kiss Ryan again on my mind, I drift off into a deep sleep.

CHAPTER 5

I wake to the dull, grey light of the morning, and curl a little tighter into the comforter, wishing for just a few more minutes of sleep.

I can already feel a massive headache coming on because of last night. I should just go home now and start looking for a job. Staying here longer will only guarantee more headaches and run-ins with a man that can't be mine. Well, he could be for a few days, but then what? I'd leave in an even worse condition than I came here in.

Stretching out, I swing my legs over the side of the bed and my feet meet the cold wooden floors, sending chills through me. I look around for my fuzzy slippers and slide my feet inside, the fur hugging my already frozen toes like a warm blanket.

Shuffling down the hall, I start a fresh pot of coffee, and make it a little stronger than usual. I'm going to need the caffeine if I plan on functioning like a human today.

Yawning, I lean on the counter and look out the little window above the sink. It definitely looks like a snow storm is coming. The sky is grey today. A vast change from yesterday's blue. We hadn't had any snow in Jersey yet, so I'm actually really excited.

I've always loved sitting by the window and watching it fall. Anything that was once imperfect is covered by a fresh white slate, and then it's suddenly beautiful again.

If only that could be true for life. I don't regret anything I've done – my dad taught me that. But it would be nice to just cover my past up with a blanket of white, and call it beautiful.

But I can't.

The ugly is what drives me forward to seek more, and want better. I refuse to settle in any part of my life. I know what I deserve, and I will never feel bad about that. It doesn't make me selfish, or picky, or full of myself. It just means I hold myself to a higher standard that won't be lowered. And there's absolutely no shame in that.

Sighing, I pour myself a mug of coffee and add a little cream and sugar before shuffling out to the living room.

I haven't had a day to do absolutely nothing in I don't know how long. Turning on the TV, I search around until I find a crime show that I haven't watched in forever. Murder and coffee on a Sunday morning sounds perfect to me.

And that's how I spend the rest of my day – curled up on the couch under a blanket, binge watching CSI: Miami. I love that damn Horatio Caine.

It would be nice to have a man that reliable in my life again. His team members come to him with any problem, and they know Horatio will do everything he can to help them.

Besides my dad, I've never had that.

He was my rock in life. He was there for me, always. And since he's been gone, I've had to figure out how to be that person for myself.

There were times when I wished I had someone to share my

burdens with, and help me carry the weight of the world when it got too heavy on my shoulders. But it was in those moments that I became stronger, and more resilient.

Despite that, though, I'm at a place in my life where I don't want to carry every burden on my own anymore. I'm tired of searching for something I'm not sure even exists, and yet I continue to believe it does.

As the sun sets, and the sky grows darker, I realize that most of the day has passed me by, and I'm starving.

Grabbing my phone, I text Ally and ask her if she wants to grab dinner. I told her not to think that she has to be available for me every day just because I'm here, but I'm not really looking forward to going out to eat by myself.

Standing, I stretch my stiff limbs, and head down the hall to the bathroom. A hot shower revives me, and snaps me out of the contemplative state I was in. I just need to push forward until everything works out how it's supposed to.

I put on black skinny jeans, a black tank top, and a long beige cardigan sweater. Adding a long necklace and my leather booties, I put on a little makeup and dry my hair so it's wild and curly.

Checking my phone, I see Ally still hasn't answered me, but I can't wait any longer, I need food. Grabbing my purse, I put on my coat and scarf before stepping out onto the porch and locking the door.

Damn, I think it's gotten even colder.

Pulling my coat together, I run to my car and blast the heat as soon as I get in.

People in Maine must have to wear bras at all times or else their nips would be hard as rocks and protruding through every layer of clothing. I've been known to let the girls go free when I'm just running errands and have on a sweatshirt or something. But I definitely couldn't do that shit here. Nope. It would be VNs–visible nipples–even through the thick material of a sweatshirt.

After letting my car warm up for a few minutes, I start the trek through the darkness into town.

I guess I'll go back to The Rusty Anchor. I sure as hell am not sitting at a full-blown restaurant by myself. I can blend into a bar way easier.

I'm just going to have to sit somewhere I won't be bothered by any assholes thinking that I'm some whore up for grabs. I still don't get that. Do I give off some slutty vibes or something? All I do is act normal. It's not my fault if men read into what's not there.

Pulling up to the bar, I wrap my scarf another time around my neck, and shove my hands into my coat pockets as I walk quickly inside.

Trying not to look around, I head straight to the bar, and sit at the far end against the wall. Unwrapping myself, I lay my coat and scarf on the stool next to me so no one gets the idea that it's available, and push my curls away from my face. I give Alex a small smile when he sees me.

"You're back already? Last night didn't scare you off?" he asks.

"Nope. And I'm just here for food. I'll be good, I promise."

"We'll see." He smiles, handing me a menu.

"I don't need it. I'll have a cheeseburger, medium well, with fries and barbecue sauce, please. And a Bud, thanks."

"No problem, gorgeous."

Shaking my head, I lean against the wall and scan the room, curious to see if those guys are here again. Luckily, I don't see anyone familiar.

I honestly don't know when the last time I went out to eat on my own was, let alone braved a bar alone. Pulling out my phone, I busy myself scrolling through social media, not really caring what the people I knew fifteen years ago are doing, but at the same time, do. Seeing how happy and in love most of them are, and how they have these big important jobs in the city, makes me feel a little inadequate, and if I'm being honest, like a loser.

Sighing, I throw my phone back in my purse and look around again. A young couple sits at a table nearby, their heads together, smiling at each other with hearts in their eyes. Oh, young love. How naïve and pure. You think everything is perfect, and that it'll stay that way, but then you learn the truth a short while later. The real world will test you, and throw you curve balls that will either make or break you as a couple.

Most don't make it.

The times I thought I was madly in love all fizzled out the moment the first storm came.

But those two look really into each other, so I hope they make it. We need more love in this world.

"Here you go," Alex says, placing my food and beer in front of me.

Oh my god, it looks and smells amazing. "Thank you."

"Sure. Let me know if you need anything else."

"I will."

Dipping a fry into the barbecue sauce, I pop it in my mouth, and hold back a moan. It's so good. Crispy and hot. Perfect.

The bar starts to fill up as I devour my burger, and I'm not ashamed to be shoving food in my mouth like I haven't seen any in days.

"Need another beer to wash that down with?" Alex laughs, leaning his arms on the bar – his muscles flexing.

"Shut up. I was hungry. And yes, I would like another one."

Sliding a full glass in front of me, he asks, "Anything else? I'm slammed, so you'll have to get me while you can." He winks. "My other bartender just called saying she can't come in, even though she was supposed to be here an hour ago." Sighing, he wipes the few drops of beer that spilled over onto the wood.

I don't know what comes over me, but I find myself asking him, "Do you need help?"

"Are you asking to work?"

"If you need help." I shrug. "I bartended back home, and I honestly have nothing to do now that I ate. Ally never texted me back."

Laughing, he motions for me to come on back. "Alright, I'll give you a chance. But if you become trouble or can't handle it…"

"Then I'll go. But trust me, I can keep up."

Hopping down from the stool, I grab my stuff and walk around through a side door that leads to a small room next to the bar. Hanging my coat and scarf on a hook, I hide my purse in the cabinet below, and take my sweater off, leaving me in just my black tank top and jeans. I make sure my hair is covering my neck so my bruises aren't showing, and I step out behind the bar.

Alex looks over at me and smiles. "I thought you said you'd be good tonight."

"What?" I ask, looking down at my outfit. "I'm not bartending in a freaking sweater."

"Okay, but you better not start any more fights."

"Come on, that wasn't my fault. Those guys were assholes."

"Alright, just get your ass to work." He jokes, walking over to a pretty woman to take her order. Rolling my eyes, I go in the opposite direction, and head straight for the two girls laughing and flipping their hair–obviously trying to get the attention of the guys a few seats down.

"Hi." I smile. "What can I get for you?"

"Two vodka sodas," the blonde one answers.

Nodding, I fill two glasses with ice and pull out a lower shelf vodka from the holder, pouring perfect portions. Filling the rest of the glass with seltzer, I garnish with lime wedges, and slide them forward.

"Do you have a tab open? Or do you want to start one?"

"Start one," she says, handing me a card.

"Okay." Walking over to the register, it takes me a second to figure out the system, but when I do, I'm golden.

Moving around the bar for the next hour is easy. I never minded bartending, I actually really liked it. I love the hustle and bustle, and mixing the drinks perfectly so that people can't tell how drunk they're getting. It's an art.

"You're doing good," Alex says as he brushes past me.

"I know," I reply, throwing him a smile over my shoulder.

Pushing my hair back, I smile at the guy in front of me. "What can I get for you?"

"A beer. And your number."

"Sorry, that's not on the menu tonight. But I can get you a beer. What kind?"

"Heineken."

"Coming right up." I nod, bending down to the fridge below to pull out a bottle. Popping the cap, I slide it towards him. "There you go. Do you have a tab?"

"Don't need one," he says, standing and placing a ten on the bar. "Keep the change."

"Thanks."

Another guy takes his spot, and I look up, seeing someone who looks a lot like Ryan, but not, at the same time. He's wearing a Pine Cove Fire Department sweatshirt and his blue eyes study me for a second before recognition hits. "You're Ally's friend, right?"

"Uh, yes?"

"I'm Tyler, Jake's brother." He smiles, holding his hand out for me to shake.

"Oh, right. I thought you looked familiar. What can I get for you?"

"Just a Bud. I'm waiting for my brother."

"Jake?"

"No, Ry. He's supposed to meet me after his shift, but he usually stays later. That guy seriously needs to get a life."

Oh no. No, no, no.

Ryan is coming here? Now?

I force a smile. "Yeah, I'm sure he does." My voice comes out weird to my ears, but Tyler doesn't seem to notice.

Grabbing a glass from the cooler, I pour his beer and place it on a coaster in front of him. "Do you want a menu before the kitchen closes?" Why am I asking that? I don't want them sitting and eating in front of me where I'll be forced to look at them, and Ryan will just stare at me.

"Yeah, thanks."

Shit.

Handing him two menus, I smooth my suddenly sweaty palms on the sides of my jeans, and move down to the next customer. I need to focus.

After fifteen minutes, I start to relax again, smiling and laughing with the people of Pine Cove who come up for drink after drink. The people here are so nice. The cold weather definitely brings them flocking here as something to do.

As I'm smiling at a man who's a little older, but still handsome, I feel a tingling sensation run down my spine.

He's here.

I'd know the feeling of his eyes on me no matter where I was.

Turning slowly, I meet Ryan's hard gaze, and my blood starts to rush a little faster in my veins. His clenched fists rest on the bar as his eyes take me in from head to toe.

He looks good. His t-shirt hugs his biceps, showing off his well-defined arms that look like God sculpted himself. I remember how strong they are, and I'd love to feel them wrapped around me again.

Tearing my eyes away, I take in a shaky breath, and walk over to him.

"What can I get for you?" My voice is barely above a whisper, but I know he can hear me.

"What are you doing?" His harsh tone snaps me out of whatever haze seems to cloud my brain when he's around.

I blink. "What do you mean?"

"Why are you back there?" His hard eyes dart to Alex, and then back to mine.

"Why do you care?" I snap back, not liking his questions.

"I don't," he says through clenched teeth.

Glancing down, I raise my eyes again and look at Tyler, who's smiling. "So, Ashley. Do you know my brother?"

"Not really."

"Huh. It seems like you do."

"Do you know what you want to eat?" I ask him, trying to get him to drop it.

"Yeah. I'll have a dozen wings and another beer. Ry?" He turns and smiles at his brother, who's still looking at me like I'm offending him by being here.

"Same," he says, his voice deep and rough.

I remember how that gruff voice felt against my neck as he pushed into me over and over. Biting back a moan, I pour him a beer, and slam it down a little too hard in front of him, not looking him in the eye.

Hot and bothered, I spin around and march over to the computer to put their food order in.

This man will be the fucking death of me.

I try and ignore him, but I feel his gaze on me the entire time I'm moving around the bar. And like a moth to a flame, my eyes search his out on their own, and every time, I feel like prey being captured by the beast.

He's too much.

He's too everything.

It's like he can see past all of my shit and down to the scared girl I still protect on the inside.

"Hey, Ash," Alex calls from behind me. "Food's up."

"Oh, okay." Heading back to the kitchen, I grab the two plates of wings and carry them back out to Ryan and Tyler. Placing them down, I get a smile from Ty, but not Ryan.

What is his problem with me being here?

I can't keep playing this battle of wills. I know I won't win. Sighing, I push a few stray curls away from my face and continue on down to another customer.

"Hey, gorgeous, I haven't seen you here before."

"Because I'm not from here. What can I get for you?"

"Whiskey. Neat. And you."

Internally rolling my eyes, I force a smile as I pour his drink. "Sorry, I can only provide the drink. Nothing else."

"Come on, darling. I can show you around if you're new. Where're you from?"

"I don't need showing around. I've been here before. Do you have a tab?"

"You've been here before? I would have remembered seeing a beautiful woman like you if you had."

"It was last summer. Do you have a tab?"

"I'll start one," he says, smiling. He's cute I guess, but my mind is on the man a few seats down. When the guy hands me a credit card, I make sure not to touch his hand as I slip it from his pinched fingers. "I'm Jeff."

"Let me know if you need anything else," I tell him, finally making my escape to the computer.

Eventually, Ryan relaxes, and I see him out of the corner of my eye smiling as he talks to Tyler. My god, that smile could make me do anything, no matter what it was, or where I was.

"Ash?" I hear a distant voice call.

"Ash?" Louder now, I snap my eyes back to the drink I was pouring and see that I basically filled the whole thing with vodka.

Shit.

Alex nudges me, and gives me a knowing look. "So, Ryan?"

"What?"

"What's the story there? He's been watching you all night."

"He has?" I ask innocently. "I haven't noticed."

"Bullshit."

"Okay, I have. What's your point?"

"Nothing." He shrugs, smiling. "It just seems odd, that's all. Ry is a private guy. And he's acting like a jealous boyfriend because you're working back here where all the guys can easily watch you, and flirt with you."

"Oh my god, Alex," I groan, rolling my eyes. "What're you, a girl? There's nothing happening."

Chuckling, he starts to pour a drink for the pretty woman in front of us. "Whatever you say."

"Yes. It is whatever I say," I huff, pouring the excess vodka into another glass and putting it aside for later. I'll definitely be making myself a drink after tonight. First, for helping out, and second, because I need it.

When it comes time for last call, the people remaining sway up to the bar to close their tabs.

"Hello again, beautiful." Great. It's the guy from before. Jeff?

"Hi. I'll close you out." Printing out his receipt, I hand it to him along with his card, and he grabs my whole hand, pulling me forward.

"Why don't you tell me your name, beautiful?"

"Because it doesn't matter." I force myself to not jerk my hand away and call him a bunch of names. I need to stay calm.

"It does to me." He winks, rubbing his thumb across my skin.

Ugh. No.

"I'm not really looking for anything right now," I say, trying to gently pull my hand away, but he won't budge. He just tightens his grip.

"What a coincidence. Me either." He flashes me a smile I'm sure usually works ninety nine percent of the time. Too bad I'm in that one percent that's not falling for it.

"I mean, *at all*. So I'm going to need my hand back." I again try and pull it away, but he doesn't budge.

"We could just grab drinks."

"She said no," a deep, angry voice says next to the guy. I didn't even see him walk up.

"Oh, Ryan, dude. Hey, how are you?"

"Let go of her and I'll be fine." He gives Jeff a hard look that would make any man wither.

Releasing me, I rub my hand to get the blood flowing again. I hadn't realized how hard he was gripping me.

"You okay, Ash?" Ryan asks, his eyes still on Jeff.

"Yeah."

"Get out of here, Jeff. And listen when a woman says no."

Nodding, he grabs his card, and leaves a twenty on the bar for me. "Sorry," he mumbles, walking away with his head down.

"Get your shit, Ashley. You're done for the night."

"No, I'm not."

"Yes, you are." His voice is barely concealing his anger as he moves his hard gaze from the back of Jeff's retreating figure to me. "Grab your stuff."

"It's fine, Ash," Alex says, coming up next to me and nodding at Ryan. "I can handle the rest. Thanks for the help tonight." He hands me a wad of cash and I shove it in my back pocket.

"Sure. It was no problem. See you soon, I guess?"

"Yeah."

A low growl sounds next to me and I know Ryan is losing his patience.

Good, so am I. With him.

Heading back into that small room off of the bar, I put my sweater back on and shove my arms inside my coat. Looping my scarf around my neck loosely, I grab my purse from the cabinet below, and sling it over my shoulder.

The second I open the door that leads back out to the main part of The Rusty Anchor, he's right there, waiting for me. "Let's go," he says, placing his hand on the small of my back, pushing me towards the front entrance.

"What's your problem?"

"Just walk," he says, growling in my ear.

I can feel the searing heat of his touch through all the layers separating us, and my steps hurry, even though all I want to do is defy him.

It's a reflex to want to do the opposite of what he says.

The few people left milling around pay us no attention as I'm all but pushed out the door. But he doesn't stop there. Leading me over to his big black pickup, Ryan opens the passenger door, and

"Ryan, please. Just drive," I sigh, and then it hits me. "Wait. What am I saying? Take me back to my car. I'm not leaving it at the bar. How am I supposed to get it back?"

"I'll take you tomorrow."

"What? No. Turn around."

"Nope," he says, shaking his head.

"Why are you being so weird?"

Silence. He doesn't answer me. He just keeps that sly smile on his lips as he drives down the dark roads towards the cottage. Crossing my arms over my chest, I watch the wall of black whirl by.

Turning into the driveway, the air in the truck starts to change. The static charge makes the hair on my arms stand, and I keep darting my eyes over to Ryan to see if he can feel it too.

He shifts in his seat, and tightens his grip on the steering wheel.

The crunching of the gravel beneath the tires is the only sound filling my ears, and the driveway starts to feel like it's miles long. When we finally get to the end and he parks, I look around in the dark to see if anything is out there. But all I get is black.

"I'm tired from tonight. So, I'll see you around. And don't worry about my car, I'll just ask Ally to take me."

"I don't mind. I'm the one who made you come with me."

"Yes, you did. I don't know why, but it doesn't matter. Goodnight."

Reaching out, Ryan grabs my arm before I can open the door. "It matters," he says, his voice low. Meeting his eyes, I can see that he's waging some sort of battle on the inside. "And you know why."

My mind is blank. I can't think straight when he's looking at me like this. "Why what?"

"You know exactly why I'm driving you home. You know exactly why I'm mad that you had men all over you last night, and tonight. And you know exactly why I want to carry you inside right now and push you up against the wall."

"I really don't," I whisper, my heart racing, my skin hot.

"You're pretending it didn't affect you, but I know you've

practically lifts, and throws, me inside.

"Ry–" I start, but I'm cut off by the slamming of the door.

What the hell?

When he gets in behind the wheel, he doesn't even look at me as he starts the truck and throws it in drive.

Staring at him wide-eyed, I can't hold back any longer. "Ryan, what the fuck is your problem? I drove here, and I can drive home. Turn around."

"No," he says harshly. "Why were you working there tonight?"

"That's what this is about?"

"All the men in there wanted you, Ashley. And you started a fight last night. Why did you go back?"

"I was hungry, if you must know. Which, by the way, you have no right to know."

"And how did food turn into bartending?"

"Alex had a call-out, so I offered to help. I didn't want to just go back to an empty house."

"Isn't that why you're here?"

"I don't know why I'm here," I mumble.

"What?"

"Nothing."

"Why did you come back?"

"Am I not allowed to visit my friend? Did you think you'd never have to see me again? You're a little full of yourself if you think me coming here has anything to do with you."

A small, sarcastic smile plays on his full, sexy lips, and I want nothing more than to slap him, and then kiss him. "I didn't think you came back for me. I'm not that self-centered. I just meant, why did you run away to Pine Cove in the dead of winter?"

"I didn't run away." Looking out the window, I swipe my fing through the foggy condensation.

"That look on your face says otherwise."

"There's no look."

"There is."

thought about me. I know you've *been* thinking about me."

"You're not the first man to think that I'm just pretending not to like them," I tell him, then mumble under my breath, "At least you didn't force yourself on me."

"What was that?"

"Nothing."

"Who forced you?" His one hand tightens on the steering wheel, and his jaw ticks.

"Don't worry about it," I say, pulling my arm free. "Bye, Ryan."

"Ashley, wait!" he calls as I slam the door shut on him, quickly walking up the porch steps.

Fumbling around with my keys, my hands shake, and they fall, clattering against the wood.

"Ashley." Ryan's voice floods my ears, and I jump when I feel him grab my arm and spin me towards him.

When he takes a step forward, I take one back, trying to maintain a safe distance. But he follows me, the look in his eyes like that of a cheetah stalking its prey.

"Ashley," he says again, and my eyes lift to his. Big mistake. His blue eyes are glowing, the battle he's waging on the inside starting to show. "Don't be afraid."

I flinch at his words. "I'm not."

"You are. But you're safe with me."

"I'm not, and you know that. Just let me go."

"I can't."

"Why not?"

"You know why. You just keep denying it."

"I can't deny something that I have no idea what–"

His lips crash down on mine, silencing the rest of my words. The excuses I had at the ready all fly out of my head as the heat of Ryan's lips sear mine.

The tiny electric currents I felt being near him turn into full blown synapse malfunction. My body feels like it could power the whole town.

Ryan pushes me up against the door, and I melt into the kiss. His hands cradle my face like I'm precious, but his lips mold to mine like he wants to break me.

My hands grip his coat, pulling him towards me further, the below freezing air doesn't even faze me anymore with the heat being given off by our bodies.

It's even better than I remember.

His lips. His kiss.

I feel like I'm both floating on air, and drowning in the deepest of waters.

Ryan Taylor knows how to kiss a woman.

When his tongue slides against the seam of my lips, I moan, and tighten my grip on his coat to the point of numbness. Groaning, he slips his tongue past my lips and sweeps into my mouth.

If I wasn't already pushed against the door, I would be melting into the porch where we stand.

Kissing Ryan feels like the first time all over again. I feel like I've never been kissed before this moment.

Tilting my head, Ryan moves me how he wants me. He takes this kiss from me–he takes everything–and I don't mind. I want him to. I need him to.

Every fantasy I've had over the past seven months don't even come close to the real thing.

But Ryan pulls away just as quick as he took me. Panting, the white clouds of our mixed breaths in the cold air fills my vision, and I catch glimpses of his blazing blue eyes in the hazy mist.

"You felt it then, and you feel it now. I'm not letting you pretend anymore."

"I'm not," I pant, still heaving my breaths in and out.

Chuckling, he shakes his head lightly and smiles. "I can read you better than you think, sweetheart." Releasing me, he bends down and picks up my keys. Reaching for my hand, he turns it over and places them in my open palm, brushing his fingers against my sensitive skin, sending shivers up my arm. "I'll see you soon."

Nodding, I close my hand around the keys and watch as he takes a step back, and then another, before he turns and walks back to his truck.

What just happened?

Did I dream that?

Pressing my fingertips to my swollen lips, I can still feel Ryan's heat, and his taste.

It was real.

Fuck. I'm screwed.

CHAPTER 6

Waking the next morning, I stretch out in the bed and yawn, loving the feeling of soft sheets against my skin. Curling back into the covers, it takes my foggy brain a few seconds to remember what happened last night.

Groaning, I flop onto my back and stare at the ceiling. Why did he have to kiss me like that? Why did I even come here? I have to leave soon to go back to my real life, and I don't need the feeling of Ryan's lips on mine flooding my brain every second of the day for the rest of my life.

Throwing the sheets off, I slip my feet into my slippers, and shuffle down the hall to the kitchen. I need coffee. I can't process this without caffeine.

While it's brewing, I take a nice hot shower to warm my body, and wake me up further. I hate to admit that I hate the idea of washing off any trace of Ryan, but my chilly bones demand warmth.

Dressing in sweats again, I throw my wet hair up into a bun and I pour myself a mug of coffee, adding a little cream and sugar. Shuffling back down the hall to the living room, I settle into the couch. I don't feel like going anywhere today.

Oh, shit. My car! Damn it!

Groaning, I go in search of my phone, but something catches my eye outside the window. What the hell?

Opening the front door, I find my little Toyota parked right where it was last night before I went out.

Did I really dream all of that then?

No, I couldn't have.

Did Ryan bring it back?

Shaking my head, I close the door before I freeze to death, and go and find my phone. Messages from Ally are blowing it up, and I laugh, swiping her name to call her.

"Ashley!" she yells, answering right away. "I'm so sorry I missed your texts last night! I, uh, got a little distracted with Jake."

"Gross. And yeah, I figured. It's fine. I just went to grab dinner at The Rusty Anchor, and then ended up helping Alex out."

"What do you mean?"

"I bartended. It was fun, actually. Until Ryan walked in and sat with his brother at the bar the rest of the night."

"Seriously?"

"Yes! And then he got all mad when some fuck-tard wouldn't take no as an answer when he was hitting on me, and got all chivalrous and shit. Was it hot and sexy? Yes. But super unnecessary. I can handle myself."

"Of course you can, Ash. You know guys get possessive, though, and feel like they have to pee a circle around what's theirs so all other guys know to stay away."

"But I'm not his to pee around."

"Don't you want to be?"

"Ally, I live six hours away in New Jersey! I may want to jump his bones, and we have this intense chemistry I can't explain, but I don't know anything about him."

"Wow, you're as good at lying to yourself as I was."

"What's that supposed to mean?"

"Nothing. Do you want me to come over today?"

"No, it's okay. I think I'll just read or watch TV again."

"Okay, well you're meeting me for dinner then. Seven o'clock at Anthony's, okay?"

"Fine, bitch, whatever."

Chuckling, she says, "See you then."

"See you." Hanging up, I sit on the couch and grab the remote, but my phone buzzes with a new message.

Morning, sweetheart. I brought your car back for you, so you don't have to worry.

Something flares in my chest when I read his words. I don't know if it's the 'sweetheart,' or the fact that he's being nice.

I didn't ask you to do that. I was going to figure it out.

Now you don't have to.

I don't need your help, Ryan.

Why can't you just say 'thank you?'

I don't know! Tossing my phone over to the other end of the couch, I throw my head back against the cushions. What's wrong with me? I'm acting so unlike myself and I hate it. Why does it feel like defeat if I thank him for doing something nice for me?

I never let men get to me. It's usually the other way around. I'm the one in control. I'm the one to say when and where it happens, or doesn't. But Ryan has blown all of that out of the water.

He's in control. He's slowly stripping me of everything I've known for the past eight years, and I both love it, and don't.

I just want to feel. I haven't felt anything real in a very long time. I've jumped from man to man, trying to find something in them that I know isn't there. But I always hope. And I always wish.

No, Ash. Just let it all go. You live your life for you, no one else. No regrets.

Sighing, I turn on the TV and find a sitcom that I can get lost in for a while. Snuggled under the crochet blanket, I sip my coffee and watch episode after episode of Modern Family, and my mind starts to relax from all things Ryan.

After a few hours, I stand up and stretch, the growling of my stomach outweighing my drooping eyelids. Searching the cabinets high and low, the only food I find is a package of Oreos. Eh, I'm not complaining.

Pouring a fresh mug of coffee, I carry it, and the cookies, back to the couch, and settle in for another marathon of episodes.

It's some hours later that I open my eyes to the dim light of the room. Rubbing my eyes, I look around. The clock below the TV says it's already four in the afternoon.

Picking up my mug, I make my way back to the kitchen. I need some real food. But looking out the window above the sink, I realize I may have an issue.

Shit.

It's snowing. Hard.

I guess it started while I was napping, and it's seriously coming down. Oh my god, I'm freaking starving!

Rushing back to the living room, I open the front door and step out onto the porch. Damn it. Wrapping my arms around myself, I look out at the sea of white.

I don't think I can leave. It looks like a few inches have fallen in the past couple of hours, and I sure as hell am not shoveling a quarter of a mile driveway to get out.

It sure is beautiful, though. The pine trees surrounding the property are covered in fresh powder–like something off of a Christmas card. All that's missing is Santa in his sleigh flying in the sky above.

Watching my breath cloud in the cold air, I take a few steps forward and stick my hand out to feel the soft fluffy clumps of snow falling from the sky. It's like I'm in a snow globe.

Smiling, I tuck my arm back into me and head inside, making

sure to open the front curtains wide. If I have to be snowed in, at least I can watch it fall gently down.

Grabbing my phone, I send Ally a quick text.

Hey, I'm not going to make it to dinner. I'm snowed in already. I'll have to search the cabinets for food.

We're stuck too, no worries! And I left you a few bottles of wine in the cabinet by the sink, and then I think there's crackers in another cabinet. I left you a block of cheese in the fridge, too. That wasn't left behind by people. LOL.

AHH I LOVE YOU! I thought I was going to starve!

Well, you might if it keeps snowing... Lol.

As long as I have wine and cheese, I'm good.

I figured.

Don't judge, bitch!

Ash, please... We're like the same. That's all I need to survive, too.

Lol, okay. So I'll see you when this is all cleared out I guess?

Hopefully soon! I don't want you stranded.

Just send the search party tomorrow if it's still like this. I'll need more supplies! LOL

Will do!

I honestly have no doubt that Ally would make Jake find a way to rescue me if I was still stranded tomorrow. I mean, wine and cheese can only last me so long. I think. I've never actually tried to survive on only that.

I guess there's no time like the present.

I find the wine Ally said she left me, and I pour myself a big glass before settling back on the couch for an evening of binge-watching movies.

It's definitely a Hallmark Channel movie kind of night. As a hopeless romantic at heart, I can't deny the secret love I have for these movies. I'm guaranteed a happily ever after, and that's something I could use a little of right now.

Two movies, and many glasses of wine later, a few tears fall from my eyes as the couple finally kisses in the end. The snow is falling all around them, and he holds her tight as they profess their love for one another – after only knowing each other for a short time, of course. It never matters, though. They always know they're in love, and that's why I love these movies.

I wish real life could be that simple. And maybe it is for some people. But never me.

A few more tears fall from my eyes, and I look down at my empty glass. Wow, how many of these have I had that I'm crying over my lack of love life?

I either need to stop drinking, or I need more.

I'm going with more.

Pouring a fresh glass, I carry it with me to go in search of food. Scanning the fridge, I find the block of Irish white cheddar Ally left for me, and I grab a plate and knife, returning just in time for the start of the next movie.

CHAPTER 7

I'm fucking freezing. That's the only thought I have as I wake up shaking on the couch in the middle of the night – passing out somewhere after the third or fourth happily ever after movie and a bottle of wine.

Wrapping the crochet blanket as tightly as I can around me, I shuffle down the hall to the thermostat to check that it's on, but I can't freaking see. Fumbling around for the closest light switch, I flip it, and nothing happens.

Shit. No.

I flip it again and again, and nothing happens.

Hurrying into my bedroom, I try that switch, and nothing.

"Noooo," I groan. "Are you kidding me?" I ask into the darkness.

The power's out. Great.

Luckily, the snow makes it seem brighter outside, so I can still sort of see around the house.

Grabbing the extra blankets Ally left out for me in the other bedroom, I bring them back to the pink room, and layer them all on top of the comforter.

Burying myself below all the layers, my body continues to shake for a few minutes before it slowly mellows out, and I begin to relax.

Rolling onto my side, my eyes flutter closed, and I drift off back to sleep.

Sadly, though, I wake up a short while later–my nose frozen. Throwing the blankets over my head, I shimmy down the bed so my whole body is cocooned in the warmth.

It has to be like ten freaking degrees in here.

When my face finally heats again, I stick it back out so I don't suffocate, and pull the blanket half up my face.

Forcing my eyes closed, the only thing that relaxes me back to sleep is thinking about Ryan holding me and kissing me. He would wrap his strong arms around me, shrouding me in his warmth, and I'd drift off to sleep – content and happy.

****

As the dull light of the morning streams into the room, I shove my face into the blankets and warm my once again cold nose. This is ridiculous. How can I possibly still be cold?

Maybe tea would help? The stove is gas, so it should still work even without the power. But I don't want to leave the safety of this bed.

Groaning, I slip out of the bed and instantly regret it. Holy shit, it's freezing! Grabbing the top blanket, I wrap it tightly around me, and shove my feet into my slippers–which are also freezing–and all but run to the kitchen.

With a shaky hand, I fill the tea kettle and place it on the stove. Thank, God Dottie never changed over to an electric one.

Shifting from foot to foot, I keep my blood flowing while I wait for the water to be ready.

And of course, it feels like forever before the loud whistle of the kettle sounds, and I pour the boiling water into a cup, where I already have an earl grey tea bag waiting.

Looking out the kitchen window, I feel like I could cry. It's still snowing. Why is it still snowing?

It's been going strong for like eighteen hours or something. And the power has already gone out, so what am I supposed to do?

Oh my god, I'm going to be stranded here. And I'm going to starve. And I'm never going to have sex with Ryan again. Damn it! I think that's the worst part. And that definitely means I'm losing it.

Grabbing my tea, I take a sip and close my eyes. I need to relax.

Practically downing it in a matter of seconds, I refill it, and let the heat of the cup warm my frozen hands. Breathing in the steam, my lungs fill with the earthy scent, and I try and calm my nerves. If I let myself freak out, then I'll just spiral.

Everything will be fine. I'll be fine. Ally knows I'm here alone, and I know she wouldn't let me die here.

Yup. Sure. I'm just going to keep telling myself that.

Heading back to bed, I sit up against the headboard and tuck my legs under the blankets. I'll have to see if I can find a flashlight, candles, matches, and any spare food that's still good to eat. At least I know I have cookies and wine. I'm just hoping that's enough for me survive on until I can leave, or be rescued.

I should text Ally. Patting the bed down, I search for my phone, but come up empty. Shit. I think I left it in the living room last night. Banging my head back against the metal bars of the headboard, I close my eyes.

I really don't feel like leaving this bed again.

Holding the tea close to my face, I breathe in the steam as my fingers thaw out.

Finishing it, I place the cup on the bedside table and brace myself for the mission. I'm going to run really quickly into the living room, grab my phone, and race back. Maybe the running will keep me from feeling the cold.

1, 2, 3… I fling the covers off and sprint into the next room, but my phone isn't in sight. Oh my god. I start tossing the pillows and couch cushions until I find it wedged in the side of the couch, and I quickly run back to my room and the safety of the blankets.

With my jaw clattering together, I press my finger to my phone screen, but nothing happens. "Noooo, not this too!"

It's dead.

I have no heat, no hot water, no food, and no way of communicating to the outside world.

Great.

Okay, let me think.

I have winter clothes – hats, scarves, gloves. I just need to layer up.

Slipping from the covers, I make it a quick change, and throw my clothes off before redressing even warmer. I add leggings beneath my sweatpants, and put on a pair of thick boot socks before shoving my feet into my slippers again. Then I put on a fleece jacket beneath my sweatshirt, and zip it all the way up my neck. Lastly, I pull my hair from its bun and put on my knit hat with a big pompom on top.

Looking in the mirror, I smile. I love this freaking hat.

Digging out my gloves from my suitcase, I put them on, and blow hot air into my fists, trying to warm them up.

I guess I'm going to have to entertain myself today.

Grabbing a few blankets from the bed, I drag them out into the living room and throw them on the couch. Walking over to the bookshelves along the wall, I run my gloved fingers across the spines of the books. There are both older and newer romance novels, mysteries, fiction, and some good old classic literature.

Gold script against a black spine catches my eye over all the other books, and I pull it from the shelf.

Oooh, damn. It's a matte finished cover with glossy gold handcuffs, and nothing else. *Under Him*. The title gleams back at me and I flip the book over, reading the blurb, a small smile playing on my lips.

Settling into the couch, I wrap myself in blankets, and open to the first page. The gloves make it a little harder, but it's still manageable.

Page after page, I read, and I can't get enough. This book is freaking hot. I can't believe Dottie has this on her shelf–that saucy little minx. I'm getting hot just reading this. Who needs heat when you have this book?

I need wine with this. Throwing the blankets off, I head to the kitchen and open a bottle. Carrying it, a glass, and the package of Oreos back with me, I tuck my feet under me and pour myself a hefty glass of pinot.

Taking a few big sips, I open the book back up and bite my lip. This guy is sexy as hell. He's tall, dark, mysterious, and knows how to rock a woman's world. I wish I had a man who cared about me as much as this guy. The only difference being I don't need constant protection. I'm not a damsel in distress, and I never have been.

My dad raised me to be strong, fierce, and independent. I always knew I could count on him, but he also made me stand on my own two feet and tackle every mountain I faced. He was there only if I really, truly needed him.

I only need myself now. I know that.

But it would be nice to have someone there to catch me in case I failed. And I've been failing this year. More than I ever have in my entire life, combined.

But still I rise. I don't give up, and I won't give up.

Shaking my head, I take a few more gulps of wine and shove a cookie in my mouth. I just want to forget for a while that it's just me. Opening the book again, I decide it's safer to be lost in the life of this rich millionaire playboy who finally found the right woman for him.

Fiction is always better than reality.

As the minutes turn to hours, I lose myself in the words before me as I finish off the bottle of wine and the package of cookies.

I'm not complaining that I'm literally forced to eat cookies to survive, but I want real food. I want a big, juicy cheeseburger with bacon and avocado, and a huge side of fries – curly fries. Mmm.

Standing, I walk over to the window, and see that the snow is still steadily falling. What the fuck?! I'm never going to get food!

Walking around the house, I search for supplies. I find candles in the spare bedroom closet, and matches in a kitchen drawer. Setting them up on the living room table, I look around for a flashlight, but can't find one.

Ugh! Doesn't everyone who lives in the middle of the freaking woods have a flashlight?

Okay, relax. I'll be fine. I have candles and wine. Going back to the cabinet where Ally stashed me a few bottles, I'm happy to see she still believes me to be a wino. Which, if I'm being honest, I am. But so is she.

Grabbing the last two bottles, I bring them into the living room, and set them on the table with the candles. Being drunk will at least help me to sleep through the cold.

CHAPTER 8

Twirling around the living room, I watch as the flames flicker and cast shadows around the room. Humming my favorite song, I sway to the imaginary beat, feeling the warmth of the wine running through my veins.

It's dark out now, and it's still snowing, but I don't even care anymore. Let it fall, I say! Let it snow, let it snow, let it snow!

But then a loud thumping sound outside makes me scream, and I freeze where I stand.

What the hell was that?!

Oh my god.

What's outside?

I don't plan on dying today!

Running to the window, I look around, and am shocked by what I see. What the fuck?

Flinging the front door open, I take in what I'm assuming is a drunken fantasy, because Ryan is shoveling his way up the porch steps. It's like a rescue mission from heaven. My god, he looks sexy as hell.

His truck is behind him with a massive plow on the front.

He plowed his way to me?

"Ryan?" I question, not sure if I'm just seeing what I wish was real. "What're you doing?"

"Rescuing you." He smirks, that devilish little smile making my insides melt.

"Why?"

Pinning me with his blue eyes, he takes a step towards me. "I couldn't leave you stranded. You have no power, no phone, and no food."

"But why would you care? I'm sure there are other things the sheriff should be concerned with."

"Nothing more important, no."

Oh.

"Did you bring me food?" I smile, not willing to read into the fact that he thinks saving me was the most important thing to him.

Flashing me a sexy grin, he nods. "I did. I just have to go and grab it out of my truck." Leaning the shovel against the railing, he turns to leave, but I quickly step out onto the porch and reach for him.

"Wait," I say, my fingers clinging to his sleeve.

"Yes?" he asks, turning back.

I don't know what comes over me–maybe it's the wine, or the fact that I've been going a little crazy by myself–but I step into him, wrapping my arms around him. "Thank you," I whisper.

Circling me with his big, strong arms, I let myself relax in his embrace, and I get a taste of what it would be like to have this man as mine. He'd come to my rescue if I needed him. He'd care.

Lifting my chin from his chest, Ryan searches my eyes before lowering his head to place a soft kiss to my lips.

"I'll be right back."

"Okay," I say softly, stepping out of his embrace.

I watch him walk back down the steps, and jog over to his truck. He comes back with a huge bag, and we go inside together.

Walking over to the couch, Ryan puts the bag on the table—taking out a bottle of wine and two Styrofoam take-out containers.

"What did you bring?" I ask, sitting on the floor in front of the table, leaning back against the couch. I wrap a blanket around my shoulders and open one of the containers, smiling wide. "How did you know?"

"What?"

"This is exactly what I wanted. Did you hear my thoughts all the way across town?" He brought me a cheeseburger and fries, and I could cry with how excited I am to eat right now.

"No." He smiles. "I just guessed."

"Well, come on. Sit and eat with me."

Taking his coat off, I see he's still in his uniform, and I hold back a groan. He looks so good. I drink him in like I want nothing more than to rip his uniform off of him and lick him from head to toe. But then he clears his throat. Shit.

"See something you like, sweetheart?"

"Nope." Clearing my throat, I look back down at my food.

Chuckling, he walks over to the coat rack by the door, and hangs his up before heading down the hall to the kitchen. He comes back with a wine glass for himself and folds his large body down onto the floor next to me, opening the other to-go container.

Grabbing my burger, I lift it to my mouth and inhale the scent of salvation. And the second I bite into it, I moan, closing my eyes. "Oh my god," I say around a full mouth, not even caring. "So good."

"I know I am, sweetheart." He chuckles. "And I intend on reminding you of that."

Opening my eyes, I shift them over to Ryan's heated gaze. Swallowing, I pour out the rest of the wine from the bottle, and down it in a few gulps.

"I don't need reminding, Ryan," I tell him, popping a few fries in my mouth.

Tilting his head slightly, the corners of his lips rise. He knows I've been downplaying everything. And I'm done pretending he doesn't affect me the way he does.

Eating in silence, I practically inhale my food with how hungry I was. Out of the corner of my eye, I watch Ryan while he chews. His jaw flexes, his lips move, and his throat bobs when he swallows. He even eats sexy.

"Did Ally make you come?" I ask, needing to break the silence.

"No," he says, his eyes shooting to mine. "I called Jake to see if you were with them for the storm. I can't believe they let you stay here when it started snowing." Shaking his head, he rubs his hand across his jaw. "After my shift, I just got in my truck and came straight over."

"You called about me?"

"Why do you sound so surprised?"

"Because I am."

"Why?" he asks, studying me.

"I'm nothing to you. Why would you care if I was stranded out here?"

"It's my job," he says simply, and my heart drops.

Oh, right, his job. Being the sheriff must mean saving women when they're stranded. Why would I be different?

"So, do you often save woman in snow storms and bring them dinner?"

"Yes." He nods. "But never dessert," he adds with a small smile. Reaching into the bag he brought, he pulls out another container.

Smiling, I relax, knowing he's just joking. I seriously need to calm down. I don't know why I'm so wound up. Or, well, I do. It's just Ryan being here that's making me act so weird.

"Good. I'd be offended otherwise." Opening the box, I smile wider than before, turning to him. "You really do read minds, don't you?" A big, chocolate frosted brownie is staring back at me with whipped cream and sprinkles.

"Let's just say I can read you better than you may have thought."

"Can you, now? I thought I was more of a closed book."

"To others, maybe. But I can see the foods you desire."

Laughing, I grab a fork and dig in. "That's an interesting talent. Has it been useful to you for women in the past?"

"No. You're the first that it's worked on."

"Huh. Well, lucky me, I guess." Smiling, I put the forkful of brownie in my mouth and close my eyes, moaning. I can't help it. This is the most delicious thing I've ever eaten.

Opening my eyes, I see Ryan's are blazing.

"Sweetheart, you're going to have to stop making those sounds if you want me to be good."

"Who said I want that?" I ask, my voice low as I lick the fork clean – my tongue putting on a little show for him. He narrows his eyes, and I give him a sly smile as I stick the fork back in the brownie. I'm about to put it in my mouth when his hand reaches out and stops me.

"Let me," he says, his voice husky.

Turning my face towards him, Ryan pulls the fork from between my fingers and then puts it in his mouth – licking it clean the way I did.

"You just stole my brownie," I tell him, a little breathless as I watch his tongue lick his top lip.

"It is good." His voice floats over me like a hypnotic mist, pulling me under. "Do you want more?"

I nod, and he cuts off another piece, holding it up to my mouth. Opening for him, I keep my eyes on his as he feeds me. Moaning the second the chocolate melts against my tongue, Ryan's eyes turn molten – the light blue is being strangled out by the dark.

Pinching my chin between his thumb and forefinger, he holds me in place as he puts the fork back in the container and swipes his finger through the frosting, rubbing it across my lips.

When my tongue darts out, he grips my chin harder and shakes his head. My pulse quickens, and my breath comes a little shorter as he leans forward.

The second his tongue meets my bottom lip, a strangled moan escapes my throat. Gliding it across the expanse of my mouth, he sucks my lip between his, and I lean into him.

It feels like a thousand little sparks are igniting down my spine as he nibbles on my bottom lip.

"Mmm," he hums, pulling away, licking his lips. "It's even better tasting when eaten off of you."

With my lips parted, and my eyes hooded, I wait for him to make the next move. I need him to do something – more.

But he doesn't.

Releasing my chin, he reaches for the bottle of wine he brought and uncorks it, pouring himself a glass.

"Would you like more?"

Breathless, I whisper, "Yes." I need him to kiss me.

"Wine?" He smirks, but I gently shake my head no.

The smooth expanse of his square jaw is begging for me to touch it. I want to memorize the hard plains of his face with my fingertips.

Placing the glass to his lips, he takes a sip, and I watch his throat work. I want to feel that motion beneath my lips as I kiss my way up the column of his neck.

"Ashley." At the sound of his husky voice, my eyes snap up to his.

I feel like I'm in some hazy dream state. "Yes?"

"Why are you really here?"

"What?"

"Why did you come here?"

He's seriously asking me this now? I'm desperately wanting to kiss him, and he wants to talk?

Turning away, I grab the wine he just opened, and pour myself a full glass. Taking a sip, I lean back against the couch and stare into the flames of the candle.

"I quit my job. Not by choice." Apparently, the wine has caught up with me, and I'm feeling chatty.

"Why?"

"Because my manager was a handsy asshole who thought I wanted him. Just like the others."

"What others?" he asks, his voice hard.

"My other boss, those assholes the other night – take your pick." Sighing, I take another sip of wine. "I was a paralegal for a really prestigious firm back home. I had worked there since I graduated college, and I loved it. But late one night–about six months ago–the partner that I worked closely with, cornered me. He thought that I had been flirting with him, and teasing him, all that time I was working there. But I wasn't, and he didn't take the rejection well. And because of him, I can't get a job in my profession anywhere near where I live. He blackballed me.

"I went to school with a girl who works at another firm nearby, and she told me that my boss had told anyone who called for a reference that I was some homewrecker hoe looking to bed any and all of the wealthy men in the office."

"Fucking asshole. I'm sorry, Ash."

"It's fine." I shrug. "I'm used to men thinking I'm just some piece of ass that's teasing them because I smile at them."

"It's not fine," Ryan practically growls. "He wasn't man enough to take the rejection, so he ruined your career. That's not okay, Ash."

"I know," I whisper, taking a bigger gulp of wine than before. "But there's nothing I can do about it. So why dwell on it?"

Rubbing his jaw, Ryan lets out a frustrated sigh. "Did he put his hands on you?"

"No, not him."

"Then who?" he asks harshly, his eyes boring into mine.

"After my career was ruined, I moved back home with my mom and got a job bartending. It was fun, actually. I loved how busy it always was, and watching people get drunk and try and pick people up – it was fun." I smile. "But Thursday was different. My manager asked me every night after work since I started if I wanted to go out with him. I always said no. Then Thursday, he was weird. Mad at me or something. And while we were cleaning up, he came up behind me and pinned me to the bar."

Swallowing the lump in my throat, I look away from Ryan. I can't look at him while I tell him what happened. But for some reason, I want to tell him. I want him to know.

"He wrapped his arm around my waist and pushed himself against my back. He kept saying I wanted him, and that he knew it, and I was just denying it because he was my boss. Then he spun me around and grabbed me behind the neck." Pausing, I reach up and rub the side of my neck that I know still bares the evidence. "And he kissed me. It was disgusting." Shuddering, I continue. "When I finally got loose, I kneed him in the dick, and then punched him in the face as hard as I could."

Ryan pulls my hand away from my neck and takes my hat off, moving my hair off of my shoulder. He pauses, immediately going rigid, and I can feel the anger rolling off of him in waves.

Turning me so he can get a better look, he brushes his fingers across my neck – replacing the harsh touch of another man with his gentler one. When I feel the warm press of his lips against my neck, I lean into his touch and sigh. Each finger print left behind by Rick, Ryan kisses. And for the first time in a very long time, I feel cared for.

Kneading his thumbs into the knots between my shoulders, I relax into his touch. I've felt like the world has been weighing me down over the past few months, but now it feels like a distant memory.

Kissing his way up my neck, a soft moan escapes my lips when he reaches the spot behind my ear. My pulse quickens under his touch, and he digs a little harder into my muscles. Pulling me back towards him, Ryan turns my face so he can look into my eyes. And it's what I see there that makes my heartrate kick up to a speed I'm sure will make it give out.

Turning around to face him fully, the intensity of his gaze draws me in – hypnotic and controlling. I sit up on my knees, and he reaches for me, pulling me on top of him so I'm straddling his hips.

Lost in the swirling blues of his eyes, I lift my hands to his handsome face and trace his cheekbones with feather light fingertips. I make a sweep down the sides of his jaw, and slide my hands around his neck, leaning in, watching his eyes the entire time battle with restraint.

Just a whisper away, my bottom lip brushes his, and he tightens his grip on my hips.

It's in this pause that I feel everything. The magnetic force pulling us together, the tightening of my chest, the rushing of my blood through my veins, and his pulse beneath my hands.

My body hums alive with a need I've never had before.

I give in to the pull, pressing my lips fully to his, melting on impact. Ryan wraps his arms around my waist, pulling me flush against his rock-solid torso.

The little control I had flies out the window and gets lost in the snow storm as Ryan's tongue slides across the seam of my lips. Opening for him, he slips inside my mouth, and we both moan on contact, the taste of wine on his tongue forming an addiction I didn't even know possible.

Sliding his hands down my back, he skims the sliver of skin exposed between my sweatshirt and pants. His touch sears me, leaving goosebumps in their wake.

Ryan pulls back, and I gasp for air as he kisses his way across my jaw. Stretching my head to the side to give him better access, he swirls his tongue around the shell of my ear and sucks it into his mouth, biting down. Moaning, I give him the invitation he needs to lift my sweatshirt up and over my head.

Slowly, he unzips my fleece – his hot mouth leaving a trail of fire as he kisses, licks, and sucks his way down my neck.

The room is spinning, and my head is spinning. Dizzy, I close my eyes, and just let myself feel it all. My mind imprints this moment, knowing I'll have to take it back out when I'm home again.

Home again.

That thought snaps me out of the hazy spell I'm under.

I can't be with this man no matter how much I want to.

I pull away from him and run my hands up his head, feeling his soft hair tickle my palms until I'm cradling his face. Seeing the confusion in his eyes, I lean forward and kiss him softly before untangling myself from him and crawling back to where I was sitting before – a relatively safe distance away.

I hope.

"What's wrong?" he asks, his voice husky and sexy.

"Nothing. I uh… I just don't think we should get carried away. I know you think I'm some girl who sleeps with a man a second after she meets him, but I'm really not." I zip my fleece back up, and put my sweatshirt back on.

"Ashley," he murmurs, turning my face back towards his. "I don't think that. At all." His eyes are glowing – still turned on. He's just saying this so I'll climb back onto his lap. I knew my impulsive nature would catch up to me one day.

"You don't have to lie to save my feelings, Ryan."

"I'm not lying. And I wouldn't lie to you. I don't think you're anything but a beautiful woman I can't have, and a strong woman who deserves better."

I deserve better than him, or better in life?

Because I agree with the second, but I don't really think the first is possible.

"And now I'm just another man assuming you want him. I'm sorry."

He's apologizing?

"You're not assuming," I whisper. "I just have to go back in a few days, and I…" I look away. "I just can't."

What I really want to say is that I can't go back to dreaming of you every night, and reliving the same moments over and over in my head every day. He haunts me day and night, but he's the most beautiful nightmare I've ever had.

"Tell me about your family."

"What?" I ask, confused.

"Tell me about your life back home."

"Oh... Um. Well, it's just my mom and I." Hugging my arms around my waist, I lift my knees to my chest. "My dad died when I was 20. Eight years ago. He was the best person in my life."

Reaching out, Ryan strokes the side of my arm. "I'm sorry," he says, his voice full of regret.

"It was cancer. I knew it was coming, but I still wasn't ready. He was always there for me, no matter what. He taught me to be a strong woman and to stand on my own two feet, but I could always count on him to be there if I needed him. He was the only one in my life like that. Then, and now."

"What about your mom?"

"She shut down after he died. We have more of a superficial relationship. Everything is okay as long as we don't dive into the deeper stuff. Before, though, she was always happy – smiling, laughing, living life to the fullest. My parents were the epitome of true love. They lived, and loved, fiercely – with everything they had. But it was taken from them. Without choice." Shaking my head, I look into the flame of one of the candles, a ghost of a smile on my lips. "I can still hear my dad telling me to 'live big, and love hard', though. It was one of the last things he said to me during one his life lesson lectures he started giving me towards the end."

"And have you?"

"I think so. He told me he never regretted anything, even dying from cancer. He said that it just made him appreciate the time he *did* get to have, that much more."

"That must have been a hard realization to come to. I don't think many people would share that wisdom if they were in the same situation."

"I know. He was the best." A few tears escape my eyes, and fall against my knees. I wipe them away quickly, though. I don't want

Ryan to see me cry.

"Hey," he whispers, wrapping his arm around my shoulders, pulling me closer. I rest my head against his chest, and take a deep breath to calm my nerves. "He sounds like he was a great man. You're lucky."

"Is your dad not great?"

"Yeah, he is. As the oldest, though, I have a slightly different relationship with him than my brothers."

"How?"

"I had a lot of pressure put on me to be the best. The best student, athlete, role model, son, and brother. Anything you can think of, I was meant to be the best at it."

"Were you?"

"Yes," he sighs. "I couldn't disappoint my parents, and I couldn't let my brothers down. It sounds insignificant, and inconsequential, but it wore me down."

"It's not insignificant, Ryan. You should've been able to just be you, and have that been more than enough." I look up at him, and his eyes are clearer than I've seen them yet.

"Thank you," he whispers.

"For what?"

Shaking his head, he lifts my chin slightly, and plants a soft kiss to my lips – one that I can feel tug at my chest.

How did we go from hot and heavy, to talking about our dads, to kissing sweetly? Ryan's throwing me off balance and making me rethink everything I thought I knew about him, and me.

Resting my head back on his chest, I close my eyes. "Thank you for coming to save me. I thought my body was going to eat itself if I didn't get food soon. I also thought that I'd die a frozen popsicle."

His body starts to shake with laughter beneath me, and I playfully slap his chest. "Stop laughing."

"I'd never let you die a frozen popsicle. I have ways of keeping you hot for days."

"I know you do, sheriff." I smile. "And it's those ways that have been keeping me up at night." Oh my god. Shit. I just said that out loud?!

Tensing up, I try and pull away, but Ryan tightens his arm around my shoulders.

"Don't," he says, his voice hoarse. "Don't pull away."

I try and relax back into him, but it's hard. I just told him I've thought about him – often, and at night. I'm fucking pathetic.

He doesn't say anything, and I don't either. We just sit and breathe together. My head lifts with every inhale he takes, and lowers with each exhale.

The comforting motions lull me into closing my eyes, and I start to drift off.

****

Stirring, I feel myself being moved, but I don't want to wake up yet. I was dreaming of Ryan, and he was here with me. He was being sweet, and kind, and handsome, and sexy.

"Shh, I'm here," he says to me, and I snuggle closer, loving the warmth he's giving me.

It feels so real. His hard muscles against my softer frame surround me in a strength only a man like him could possess. I'm glad I can still dream of him. I thought maybe seeing him again would make the dreams stop, and I'd have to go back to the black bleakness I'm used to waking up to.

Sighing, I tuck my face into the crook of his neck and run my hands up his chest, feeling his starchy uniform beneath my fingers. That uniform does things to me that I can't explain. Well, I can, I guess. It makes my lady parts clench every time I see him in it. But it might just be Ryan that makes me crazy with need and think sexy thoughts.

"Ashley," he whispers, making the hairs around my ear tickle my skin.

"Mmm," I hum, loving the feeling of his warm breath spreading across my face.

I'm being laid out on something soft and cool, and the warmth of Ryan leaves me. A cold bed without him.

"No," I groan, searching for him again.

"I'm here," he says nearby, but he's moving farther away.

The soft pillow and cool sheets have me curling my body around the cold comforter for a warmth that isn't coming. I'm cold again.

Shivering, my jaw clatters and my body shakes.

He left me.

Even in my dreams, he leaves me.

I can't even dream of a perfect ending.

I just want to be warm.

"Hey, shh, Ashley." Ryan's soft, pleading voice is back, and I relax again, thanking my brain for bringing him back. He slips his arm under me and pulls me against him, his body heat giving me everything I've been missing. "Just sleep. I'm not leaving you."

****

Opening my eyes to a dark room, I feel disoriented. But the solid wall of muscle nestled tightly against me tells me that I didn't dream of Ryan carrying me to bed and holding me.

He stayed.

Smiling, I try and go back to sleep, but when my bladder starts to protest, I realize why I was woken up in the first place. Slipping soundlessly out from under Ryan's grip, I tiptoe out of the room, and down the hall to the bathroom.

When I slip back into bed, Ryan stirs as I lift his arm to place it around me again.

"Ashley?"

"Yeah?"

"Are you okay?"

"Yeah," I answer, pausing. "You stayed?" I ask, the words pushed from my lips.

"Is that okay?"

"Yes," I sigh, scooting a little closer to him. "I thought I was dreaming that you were here."

"No. But that explains why you were saying my name, though."

My eyes pop open. "What?"

"Don't worry." He chuckles, tightening his arm around me. "You didn't say anything too embarrassing. Well, except that you need me badly, and you want me to remind you why you followed me into those woods all those months ago."

"What?" I gasp. "I did not!"

"I know." He laughs. "Just joking. Now, go back to sleep. Unless you really do want me to remind you."

Staying quiet, the silence between us stretches out for so long that I think we're both holding our breath.

The air changes from light and joking, to strained and electrified. It's thick with everything unsaid, and undone, between us.

"I do," I whisper softly after a few minutes. So softly, in fact, I'm not sure if he heard me. I don't know why I said it. It's either the illusion of darkness that made me answer honestly, or all the wine I had earlier.

Probably both.

The cover of night provides me the mask I need to spill my secrets to this man, and has my mind tricking me into thinking it's okay. But in his hands, I know they're dangerous.

Ryan either doesn't hear me, or he's pretending not to have heard me, because he remains quiet, his arm around me heavy and comforting.

I breathe a sigh of relief and close my eyes, falling back asleep to the sound of his steady heartbeat.

CHAPTER 9

A hand brushes the hair from my face, and I snuggle closer to the warm body next to me.

As my eyes flutter open, the dull grey morning light allows me to see the handsome face staring back at me.

Ryan's square jaw is covered in stubble, and I reach up to run my fingertips over it – feeling the rough, yet soft, hair tickle my skin.

A small smile plays on his lips, and he closes his eyes. When they open again, the blue shines back at me – glowing like the tropical ocean in the midday sun.

"You stayed." I don't know why I keep feeling surprised at that, and needing to point it out to him.

"Where else would I go?"

Smiling, I lay my head back down on his chest. If I'm not careful, I know Ryan will send me down a spiraling hole of madness. I'm probably halfway there with the way I'm thinking right now.

"I can feel you thinking." Lifting my head, I rest my chin on his chest and he runs his finger across my forehead, and he taps my temple. "Just relax."

"Okay," I whisper, blinking slowly.

Ryan slips from the bed and curses when his feet hit the cold wooden floor. Damn, his ass looks good in sweatpants.

"Where did you get those pants?" I ask, only remembering him in his uniform last night.

"I always keep extra clothes in my truck. Consequence of the job."

"I bet," I murmur, my mind running through a sequence of events where he would need to change his clothes on the job – all of them involving women ripping his uniform clean off to have their way with him.

I'm sure the women in this town must make calls to the department over every little thing just to get Ryan to come to their rescue. Lord knows I would probably do that.

"I'm going to go make us some tea since the stove still works," he says, snapping me back to reality.

"Okay."

Rolling onto my back, my head sinks into the pillows, and I sigh, staring at the ceiling. Ryan's right, I really need to stop thinking. I'm picturing him getting naked on call-outs with random women like he's some man-whore. Which, I don't think he is.

Throwing the covers off, I slip out of bed and immediately regret it. Shivering, I hug my body and shove my feet in my fuzzy slippers.

I shuffle down the hall to use the bathroom, and catch a glimpse of my bedhead in the mirror. Sorting it out the best I can, I splash some cold water on my face, and feel a little more awake. Luckily, my skin has been agreeing with me lately, so I don't have any breakouts, but the dark circles under my eyes are another story.

I don't think I've ever *not* worn makeup around a man so comfortably before. I actually didn't even notice until now.

Smiling, I pat my face dry and brush my teeth before heading out into the kitchen. My smile widens when I see Ryan reaching for cups and saucers from the cabinet above, showing a few inches of smooth skin.

"You don't know how to make stovetop coffee by chance, do you?"

"No." He laughs, turning to smile at me. And my god, that smile. It could stop traffic – and I'm sure it has. "Tea is okay, though, right?"

"Yes, that's fine." I walk up and take the teacups from him, bringing them to the table.

When the kettle whistles, Ryan turns the stove off and carries it over to the table, placing it on a pot holder. He goes back and grabs a few boxes of tea from the cabinet and piles them in front of me so I can choose.

Reaching for the wild blueberry Bar Harbor tea, I rip open the packet and place the teabag in my cup, pouring hot water from the kettle over it. I dip the bag a few times, watching the steam rise as the water starts to darken from the leaves.

When I look up, I see Ryan watching me. "Yes?" I ask, not sure why he's looking at me like that.

"Nothing."

"Then stop staring."

"I can't. You're too beautiful."

Oh my god. My cheeks heat immediately, and I bring my cup up to my face to try and hide my smile.

"Do you have work today?" I ask, trying to avoid him watching me further. I'm afraid of what he'll see if he looks too closely.

"I do." He nods. "But I'm not leaving you here alone."

"I'll be fine, Ryan."

"No. I'm going to drive you over to stay with Jake and Ally."

"I don't need babysitters," I tell him, narrowing my eyes.

"I know you don't. But it'll make me feel better knowing you're not alone out here without power. It could be a few days before it's back on."

"A few days?" I practically shout, my eyes widening.

"Yeah." He shrugs, like it's such a normal thing to be without power for days on end.

"I can't go days without heat, hot water, or food. And my car is snowed in." Rubbing my forehead, I sip my tea and try and let the hot liquid calm my nerves.

"That's why you're not staying here."

Looking up at him, I see the matter-of-fact declaration in his eyes, and I narrow mine again. "Are you telling me what to do, sheriff?"

"Yes," he says, flashing me a satisfied grin.

"You can't," I tell him. "And I'd rather stay out here alone than with the couple who can't keep their hands off of each other. I don't need to see, or hear, that shit."

Laughing, Ryan pours himself a cup of tea, and adds a little sugar before taking a sip. Grimacing, he puts the cup back down and pushes it away.

"Not a fan of tea?" I smirk.

"No. I thought I'd try it, but I need coffee."

"Well, me too."

"Alright. Go pack your bags and I'll take you for the good stuff."

"Thank, God." Standing up, I head back down the hall. "But why do I need my bags?" I call out behind me.

"Because you're staying with me," I hear him say back, and I stop mid step before entering the bedroom.

Spinning around, I march back down the hall. "What did you just say?"

Smiling, he leans back in the chair and crosses his arms over his chest, making the sleeves of his t-shirt stretch tight against his perfectly sculpted arms.

"You heard me, sweetheart."

"Stop calling me that. I'm not your sweetheart. And I'm sure as hell not staying with you."

"You are." He smirks. "Go get your bags."

"Ryan," I say sternly, my hands on my hips.

"Ashley," he says right back, his tone lower and more threatening. "You're not staying here, and you don't want to stay at Jake's. So that leaves me. What're you afraid of?" he asks, tilting his head to the side, studying me.

"I'm not afraid," I shoot back, but I shift from foot to foot, giving away my nerves. "Whatever," I say, throwing my hands up. "Just don't expect anything to happen."

Walking back down the hall, I think I hear him mumble something after me like 'we'll see,' but I can't be sure. Yeah, we *will* see.

Letting out a frustrated sigh, I pull out leggings and an oversized sweater from my suitcase, and change quickly. Shoving the clothes I had on back inside the suitcase, I pull on a pair of thick wool socks and my winter boots.

Poking my head out into the hall, I yell down to Ryan, "If you're forcing me to stay with you, then you can carry my bags, sheriff."

"Yes, ma'am," he replies, sauntering down the hall towards me. "I'm at your service."

"As long as you know I'm not at yours." I smirk, letting him past me into the room.

Laughing, he picks up my two suitcases and follows me out into the living room. "Just these?"

"Yup." Putting on my coat, I wrap my scarf around my neck a few times, and shove my pompom hat on my head.

Grabbing my purse, I look around, and make sure I'm not forgetting anything before opening the front door. When the cold air hits my face, I turn away and shove my hands in my pockets.

"It's still snowing," I say, looking over my shoulder at Ryan. "How is that possible?"

He just shrugs. "Welcome to Maine, sweetheart."

"I said to stop calling me that." I frown, really needing him to stop. It makes it seem like there's something more between us than what there is.

Shaking his head, he smiles. "Just go wait in the truck."

"Don't tell me what to do," I huff, stepping out into the falling snow.

"You're a stubborn woman," he sighs, closing the door behind him and carrying my bags down to his truck.

"I am," I say proudly. "You should remember that."

Walking past his truck and down the driveway a little, I tilt my face up to the falling snow and smile. Spinning around with my arms outstretched, I relish in the feeling of the flakes melting against my face.

When arms snake around my waist, I blink my eyes open, the flakes that were stuck to them, fluttering away.

Smiling down at me, Ryan pulls me flush against him, and his lips capture mine in an unexpected kiss. Heat spreads down my spine, feeling it all the way to my toes.

Pulling away just as quickly as he kissed me, my heart beats fast in my chest as my breath puffs out white between us – clouding my vision for a few seconds.

"Why did you do that?" I ask, breathless.

"You looked too beautiful not to kiss you."

"Oh," I say dumbly.

"Walk with me for a minute," he says, taking my hand in his.

Tucking my head down, I run my tongue across my lips–tasting him there.

"I've always loved when it snows," I tell him, filling the quiet morning air – the only other sound being the crunching of our feet in the snow. "It's so beautiful. I like to take walks during storms when everyone else is inside their houses. It's just me and the gently falling snow."

Squeezing my hand, he places our joined hands in his jacket pocket to stay warm. "Not everyone can appreciate it that way."

"I know." I laugh. "Everyone I know hates snow. They hate

being confined inside and not being able to leave. But I love it. What better excuse to huddle under blankets, read, and drink wine do you have?"

"I was always the kid who was the first to throw his ski pants on and go play in the snow. There was sledding, building forts, and snowball fights. I always won those." He laughs.

"Of course you did." I smile, rolling my eyes. "You seem like the kind of person who hates losing."

"Who likes losing?"

"Touché." I laugh, letting my eyes wander around. The tall pine trees' branches are weighed down by the snow. So much so, they're practically touching the ground and look ready to snap.

Walking hand in hand with Ryan as the snow gently falls makes me feel like we're in our own world.

"Can I ask you something?"

"Anything," he answers, looking down at me.

"Why did you decide to go into law enforcement? And how did you become sheriff so young?"

"Well, I told you how my parents expected me to always be the good example for my brothers. They all looked at me like I was some superhero who would swoop in and save the day whenever they needed me. And I guess I took that image and made a career out of it."

"But do you like it?"

"I do. People count on me."

"Don't you ever want to *not* be the person everyone counts on? Isn't it tiring?"

"It is," he admits quietly. "I've been sheriff for five years now."

"How did you get elected so young? What were you, 30?"

"Yes, I was," he says, flashing me a smile. "And it's because I'm well-liked, sweetheart." Nudging him, I can't help but smile back, and lean into him as we walk. "But it's the truth. I was the star quarterback in high school, and then went to UMaine and played there, too."

"So, you're the town's golden boy who came back to protect and serve?"

"Something like that. Yeah."

"If you could, would you choose a different career?"

"No," he confesses after a beat. "I love being the man people count on. I used to view it as a burden when I was younger, but when I became a deputy, I saw that it was a position to take pride in. I realized I really did like being someone people could count on."

"You're a good man, Ryan," I whisper, looking up at him. Blinking away the flurries sticking to my eyelashes, his eyes meet mine.

"Thank you."

"You literally plowed your way to me to bring me food." I smile. "You went way beyond your job description to save a simple visitor of Pine Cove. So, thank you."

"I didn't do it because of the job, Ashley," he says, his eyes blazing down at me.

"You didn't?"

"No." Ryan stops walking and steps in front of me. Reaching up, he brushes away the few strands of hair stuck to my cheek. "You know why I came," he whispers, the breeze carrying his soft words to my ears.

"I do?" I ask, suddenly feeling lightheaded with the way he's looking at me.

Nodding, he lowers his head and kisses me softly, but the sting of electricity sparks something inside of me.

Ryan squeezes the hand he's holding, and I sigh into the kiss, letting him slip his tongue into my mouth. Moaning on contact, I reach up with my free hand and grip the back of his neck, holding him to me.

I can feel it – that pull in my chest that reaches out to his. I feel him everywhere.

My cold lips heat under his, and he groans into my mouth. I feel the vibrations all the way to my fingers and toes – the current flowing through my veins.

I feel vulnerable and exposed to all that's unsaid between us.

Pulling away slowly, he leans his forehead against mine, and we breathe in each other's air – eyes still closed.

We stand here for a few long seconds, my pulse pounding in my ears. Under my fingers, I can feel his thrumming strong and fast – a sure, steady beat.

Squeezing his hand, I settle back down on my feet and open my eyes. I couldn't feel the cold air before, but it hits me again, and a shiver wracks my body.

"Let's head back," he says, his voice low and smooth.

I focus on the crunching of fresh snow beneath our feet as we slowly walk back to his truck. I hadn't even realized we walked so far down the driveway.

Leaning closer to Ryan, I shove my hand deeper into my coat pocket and try not to think about how numb my fingertips are.

When we finally reach the truck, he opens the passenger door for me, and helps me inside. The moment the door closes, I huddle into myself. Getting in the driver's side, he starts the engine and blasts the heat straight away. When it starts to warm, I place my hands in front of the vents, trying to defrost them.

"They're not getting warm," I tell him, my teeth clattering.

"Come here," he says, grabbing my hands and bringing them to his lips. Blowing on them, he rubs my hands between his, the blood starting to flow again under his touch. "Better?" he whispers, his lips brushing against my fingers.

"Mhmm." I hum.

"Can't have you losing any of those fingers."

"No. They serve a lot of uses." I smile and wink at him.

Laughing, he lets go and puts the truck in drive, and we start our slow trek down the driveway.

Lowering the plow, Ryan moves the snow from our path. When we get to the end of the driveway, I look in both directions, and see nothing but blinding white.

"Are you sure we can make it?" I ask nervously. "I don't want to get stuck."

"We'll be fine. Trust me."

"Okay." I nod, but I'm still doubtful. Even with the plow shovel attached to the front, we're still only in a pickup truck.

Patting my leg, he flashes me a smile, his eyes bright like a kid on Christmas morning. "It'll be fun."

Returning his smile, I shake my head. Boys and their toys.

Revving the engine, Ryan pushes forward, the snow moving away from us like we're a boat cutting through the water. It flows to the side as we make our way down the road, a huge smile on my face.

"Holy shit, Ryan! This is awesome!"

Laughing, his smile is almost as blinding as the snow. "I know."

Turning around in my seat, I look back at the path we've cut through the road, and am in awe at how much snow has accumulated. It's definitely well over a foot by now. And it's still snowing.

We slowly make our way towards town, only having to stop and readjust the plow a few times on turns. I honestly didn't think the man could be sexier than when he's in sheriff mode – but I was wrong. Trucker mode is just as sexy in my opinion.

I still feel like we're in our own world, just making our way through the streets of another planet where we're the only residents.

There's literally no one else out here but us.

"If we get stranded, no one would know for days."

"Well, let's not get stranded then." He smiles, looking over at me.

"I'm just saying." I shrug.

"But then again, we could just keep each other warm while we waited." He winks, and I roll my eyes.

"Yeah, yeah, yeah. Just focus on the road."

"Whatever you say," he replies, the smile in his voice evident.

When we finally make it into town, I don't know why I expected the stores on Main Street to be open, but I'm surprised to see that everything is closed.

"Well, what now? Everything is closed."

"Ash, did you think they'd be open?"

"I don't know. But I need coffee and food in me soon, or things might get violent."

"I have ways of restraining you if you get too wild, sweetheart." He smirks.

A chill runs down my spine at the thought of Ryan handcuffing me – to a bed, a chair, or anything really. I think I'd like it, actually. Being at his mercy.

Seeing my reaction, Ryan tightens his grip on the steering wheel and pushes on, turning down a side street off of Main.

"You live so close to town."

"Yeah. So I'll be close in case you need me while I'm at work."

"I can take care of myself. You realize you're just taking me from one empty house to another, right?"

"Mine has power and hot water, though," he says simply, and I sigh loudly, crossing my arms over my chest.

I don't like the idea of being cooped up in his house. I want to be able to leave. I want to be able to breathe in air that I know isn't filled with the scent of the sexy sheriff. And I sure as hell don't want to feel like a damsel in distress.

With a little difficulty, Ryan plows his way into where I'm assuming a driveway normally resides.

"This is your house?"

I definitely wasn't expecting something so…normal? A two-storied, white colonial styled house with black shutters, sits in a sea of snow between red and tan houses. Bushes line the front of his house on either side of the small, roofed–in front door, and two large snow-covered pine trees sit on either side of the house.

It's beautiful.

"Yes. Did you expect something different?"

"Kind of. But I like it."

"Good. Now just wait here and I'll shovel a path to the side door."

Jumping out of the truck before I have time to protest, Ryan grabs a shovel from the back of the truck and gets to work.

I don't want him to think I'm not incapable of some manual labor. But… I really don't feel like shoveling over a foot and a half of snow right now. So, I think I'll just stay in the warm truck and watch as he does all the work.

It's not a bad view.

CHAPTER 10

Walking through the side door, I step into the laundry/mud room, and then right into a big kitchen with dark hardwood floors, white cabinets, and sand colored granite countertops. The walls are painted a light beige, and the backsplash running above the counterspace, farm sink, and stove, is white tile that's arranged in a chevron pattern.

I'm impressed with the simple, charming, style. I would never have expected this from a man like Ryan.

Following him through the kitchen, we step into the living room where there's a fireplace on one wall with a huge flat screen TV hanging above it. One either side of that, built-ins take up the rest of the wall and are filled with books and pictures of Ryan and his family.

A pang of jealously hits my chest when I see their happy smiles and arms around one another.

A complete family.

Something I haven't had in a long time.

Looking away, I take in the rest of the room. A brown leather couch sits facing the fireplace with a dark wooden table in front of it that's covered in outdoorsy magazines, and two chairs face each other across the length of the table with plaid throw pillows on them.

The windows looking out to the front yard are frosted over, but I can see the tops of the snow-covered bushes beneath the sill. It's such a warm and inviting living room that looks perfect to sit and read while curled up by the fireplace as the snow falls.

"I like it all." I smile at Ryan, knowing he's been watching me this entire time.

A small smile tugs at his lips and he nods, continuing to walk through the house. I follow him around to the foyer, where there's French doors to the right of the front door, and a large staircase straight ahead. Heading up the stairs to the second floor, we walk down the hallway, and he opens a door on the right to reveal a bedroom.

"You can have this room," he tells me, and I step inside.

The walls are painted an off-white, with pictures of the ocean and coastlines hanging on the walls. A queen bed sits in the middle of the far wall with a wrought iron frame and a tan and white striped comforter. The tables on either side of the bed match the dresser that's by the door, a blue and white swirled rug that resembles the ocean covers most of the wooden floor, and a small desk sits under the windows, looking out to the front yard.

"It's pretty, thank you."

"The bathroom is right down the hall. I'll show you."

Following him, he opens the last door on the left, and I step inside, noticing the white, tan, and blue color scheme flows into here as well. White walls and blue accents showcase the framed pictures of the ocean on the wall. They all remind me of his eyes.

"So, where's your room?" I ask, deciding to take this tour up a notch.

He lifts his chin to the last door at the end of the hall. "Right there."

Stepping past him, I grab the knob and turn it, pushing it open. And damn, I'm surprised.

Dark navy walls are highlighted by heavy, dark grey fabric curtains, and framed images of angry, storming seas. A huge–and I mean huge–bed, sits right in front of me, and takes up most of that the one wall. A navy comforter covers the bed, and white pillows rest against a dark grey leather headboard. Two dark wooden dressers sit against one wall, with a half-open closet door next to them.

"This room feels the most like you." It's very masculine, and I love it. It's dark and sexy. A lot like him.

"It does?"

"Yes. It's different from the rest of the house, but I can tell it's all you. This is your space." Turning towards him, I catch a little heated flare in his eyes before he turns away and looks out the window.

"Let's go back downstairs. I'll bring your bags in and make you coffee. Then I have to get to work."

"Sure." Walking out of his room, he closes the door behind us, and I lead the way back down the hall.

"What do you do when there's a blizzard? You don't just patrol around, do you?" I don't know why, but that thought makes my heart beat a little faster. What if he got stuck and needed help? Who would save him when he's the one always saving everyone?

"Are you worried about me, sweetheart?" he asks, and I can hear the smile in his voice.

"No," I say quickly. "I just think it's a little dangerous if that's what you intend to do."

"I don't," he assures me as we descend the stairs.

"But it also seems like a waste of taxpayer money for you to be sitting and eating donuts behind a desk, doing nothing."

His laugh behind me echoes in my ears–a deep, musical laugh that I want to hear more of. Closing the distance between us, Ryan places his hand on my lower back, and I can feel his touch through my clothes—searing me, branding me.

"Okay, I won't do that, then. I'll just have to think of another way to fill my time. Maybe I'll just make a list of all the ways I want to take you when I get home later."

My breath hitches, and a shiver runs down my spine at his words. Heat pools in my core, and my brain gets foggy with all the images of Ryan and I all over his house. The kitchen, the living room, the stairs, and finally, in that massive bed of his.

"Is that why I'm here?" I ask, breathless.

"You're here because I want you here, Ashley," he whispers in my ear.

Kissing me behind my ear, heat blooms from that spot, traveling down to my chest. The tight grip I have on my control around Ryan loosens just a fraction.

"Come on, sweetheart, let me make you coffee." He walks ahead, but I stay planted where I am, trying to regain my composure.

"I said don't call me that." Stopping, he turns to look at me, a small smile on his lips. My voice gave away that I don't really mean those words.

"Get used to it, sweetheart." He smirks, continuing on into the kitchen, leaving me to stare after him.

Taking a deep breath, I let my feet carry me the rest of the way, and I take a seat in a chair at the small wooden table in the corner. Being in Ryan's home, and in his space, makes me feel like I'm handing over a little more of my control. It's like being thrown into the lion's den, and Ryan is the big, bad lion that's hunting down his lioness.

I don't know what's going on with me. I feel like I'm going crazy.

"Here you go," he says, placing a mug of hot coffee in front of me, startling me out of my thoughts.

I reach out blindly for the mug and take a sip, letting the hot, sweet liquid slide down my throat.

Closing my eyes briefly, I feel the caffeine flowing through my body, waking me up.

"It's perfect," I whisper, taking another sip.

"I know." He winks. "I'm going to go and get your bags."

Watching him leave, I sigh a breath of relief, and sink down into the chair. I don't know why I'm so on edge around him. Maybe I'm scared he'll see too much. Or, maybe I'm scared he'll realize I'm someone not worth his time.

Why does Ryan bring out all of my insecurities?

I'm a strong, confident woman. And he's just a man.

I just need to keep reminding myself of those two facts.

When Ryan comes back in with my bags, he brings them right upstairs, and I don't even bat an eye at how good he looks carrying my heavy bags. Okay, I do, but it's when he comes back down fifteen minutes later, that I almost choke on my coffee.

Holy shit.

Raking my eyes down the entirety of his body, I take in all the glorious, sexy, powerfulness that is Sheriff Ryan Taylor.

It's the first good look I've gotten of him like this. In the café, and last night, he had his coat on. And he wasn't as put together last night as he is this morning. Plus, I was a little tipsy by the time he got there.

He's tamed his hair so that the longer part on top is slicked back, and his freshly shaven is face has my fingers itching to feel the smooth skin beneath.

And that uniform, my god. Dark brown pants with a stripe on either side do nothing to hide his powerful thighs underneath, and the khaki colored long sleeved shirt hugs his chiseled chest and arms like it was tailored for him. The badge on his chest shines like it was just polished, and the pins on his collar, and patches on his sleeves, all add to the hotness. He's so official. I would totally break the law just so he could arrest me.

If he wanted to, he could make me do just about anything while in that uniform.

I meet his eyes, and they're molten. He knows I'm appreciating him right now, and I'm not ashamed.

"Where's your... Uh"–I clear my throat and wave my hand at his belt area–"gun and cuffs and stuff?"

Smirking, Ryan walks over to the coffee pot and pours himself a travel mug. "My duty belt is in the truck. I have it locked in the safe."

"You have a safe in your truck?"

"Yeah. It's in the floor on the passenger side. I put it in there before coming to you yesterday."

"Oh." I guess he didn't want to scare me or something.

"You can call me if you need me. I'll leave my number here," he says, writing it on a notepad on the counter.

"Okay." I nod.

"Make yourself at home, sweetheart." He smiles. "I'll be back after six."

"Alright. Be safe."

He was putting a lid on his travel mug, but pauses and looks over at me with a surprised look in his eyes. "I will."

Watching him walk out of the kitchen and towards the side door we came in earlier, I feel a twinge of loss, and I hate that. I don't want to feel this attached this fast.

I really do want him to be safe, though. It's still snowing, and he's going back out there. Anything could happen. He could get stuck in the snow, or crash into a tree and freeze to death without anyone even knowing he needed help.

Oh my god. Fucking relax, Ashley. He knows what he's doing.

Bringing the mug to my lips with shaky hands, I take a sip, hoping it'll calm my nerves, but it doesn't. I'm going to need something to distract myself with until after six, or else I'm going to go crazy thinking about Ryan out there.

I'm cold again. I feel perpetually cold. No matter what, I feel it seep into my bones. It was only when Ryan was around that I actually felt warm.

I look over at the clock on the wall, and groan, leaning forward to bang my head on the table. It's only eight in the morning.

Her Maine Reaction

Letting out a frustrated sigh, I drain the rest of my coffee and pour myself another cup before wandering into the living room. Scanning his bookshelves, I find he has a lot of classics, both literature and poetry. There's Austen, Hardy, Brontë, Dickens, Eliot, Keats, Yeats, Emerson, Whitman, and Wordsworth. Wow, and that's just this shelf.

Ryan's a collector, and very well-read. I'm impressed.

Running my fingers across the spines of the beautiful old books, I pull out one with a dark green spine and gold script – a collection of Keats's poetry. When I was in college, I took an elective that was strictly his work, and I loved it. But I haven't read anything of his since.

Placing my mug down on the coffee table, I take a seat in one of the big armchairs, folding my feet under me, and pulling the blanket from behind me to drape it over my legs.

I remember having to read more than just Keats's poems. We read letters he wrote to fellow poets and his love letters to Fanny Brawne. It was in those that I fell in love with Keats's work. I think humanizing him, and seeing a peek into his real-life romance, made everything he wrote relevant and pack a better punch to the heart for me.

Sipping my coffee, I get lost in his words. And when I get to one of my favorites, I smile, thinking about how it must feel to be so in love like that. Keats writes of choosing three perfect days of love and bliss over a lifetime of mundane and common love. It makes me think. Would I rather have those three days of true love? Or have a lifetime of a lesser love?

I would like to think that I'd choose the three days, but then I'd have to spend the rest of my life feeling lonely. Or, I could have a lifetime of safe love, and never know that I was missing something better–passion and fire.

Closing the book, I stare at the bookshelves and shake my head. I don't know why it matters. It's not like I'd ever have to make that choice, or be faced with those options.

I only want burning passion for my entire life. I want a love so deep, that's it's in me forever. I want my soul branded by that kind of love.

Sighing, I stand up and stretch. I need to *not* read this. Now my mind is all over the place, thinking about love and shit.

"Aarrgg," I grumble, heading upstairs to find my phone. But when I pull it out of my purse, I forgot that it was still dead. Digging my charger out of my bag, I go back downstairs and plug it into an outlet in the kitchen.

When it turns on, a crap ton of messages from Ally pop up asking if I'm okay, and if I'm surviving the storm. But there's even more messages from our friend group chat asking me where I am and why I haven't been texting them.

Shit.

I never told Ellie and Mel that I was coming here. I only called Ally, and then packed my bags and left. We've always told each other everything. I just happened to not tell them this particular series of events.

Sighing, I type out a message, explaining myself.

Hey guys, I'm sorry I've been MIA, but I'm in Pine Cove right now. I needed to leave ASAP, and I forgot to tell you...

A minute later, I get an influx of texts from them.

WHAT?!!!? Mel texts.

YOU'RE IN FREAKING MAINE??!! Ellie adds.

Yes, calm down. I quit my job Thursday because my boss is a dick, and then I came here to clear my head. But it's anything but clear.

Why? Mel asks.

Because Ryan brought me back to his house this morning, and now he's at work and I'm alone in his house while there's a blizzard currently in progress.

WHAATTTT??!! You and Ryan?? Jake's older brother?

Yes. I have a confession to make to you... I press send and pause, wondering how to say this without causing a freak out. **We had sex at the BBQ last summer, and I haven't been able to get him out of my head. And now I'm fucking staying at his house because Dottie's lost power and his house still has it.**

My phone starts ringing a couple minutes later, and I see Ellie's name flash on my screen.

"Hey," I say when I swipe to answer the call.

"Yeah, hey, bitch. What the fuck?"

Laughing, I lean forward on the counter. "I'm in his house right now while he's at work."

"No. I mean why didn't you tell us about him?"

"I don't know. It was personal."

She's silent for a few seconds. "Do you like him?"

"Maybe," I whisper. "And I don't know what I'm doing. This is new for me."

"I know, Ash. Well, do you know how he feels?"

"I don't know."

"Okay, then. Just be you. You're fucking amazing, and he's lucky that you're even giving him the time of day."

"You're just saying that."

"I'm not. I know you, Ashley. Forgive me for saying this," she says, "but you've been messed up since your dad died. Emotionally, and mentally. The men you've chosen since were only distractions for you. You're scared because you think if you find something real, then it'll be taken away from you like your dad was. But trust me on this, Ash. You're not living if you're scared of what you can't control."

"I know, Ellie."

"Do you, though?"

"Yes."

"Good. And don't forget how much of a badass bitch you are. You're a hard shell with a soft center. Give him both."

"Yes, ma'am." I smile.

"Alright, love you, girlie."

"Love you, too."

"You better call me with updates."

"I will." I laugh. "Bye."

"Bye."

Hanging up, I send a text to Ally separately.

Hey, Al. Ryan plowed his way to the cottage last night and saved me from starvation. And then this morning he brought me back to his house because he still has power and didn't want me out there by myself. He's at work now, and I'm just trying to keep myself busy until he gets back. I'm kind of worried about him.

I'm glad he got to you before you starved LOL. I know cheese and wine only goes so far.

Yes, he brought me a big, juicy cheeseburger, a brownie, and wine. He's perfect.

Oh, is he?? Haha. And don't be worried about him. Ryan knows what he's doing.

Are you sure?

Yes. Just relax and enjoy the heat while you can. This storm isn't supposed to stop, and I don't know how much longer you'll have power. We're on a generator right now and my phone is going to die eventually.

Alight. Go have some fun with your man.

I will!

Ally and Jake are so in love, it's disgusting. They're lucky to have found one another, and it was all by chance.

I wouldn't even be here right now if it wasn't for Ally. If she hadn't come here to Pine Cove, then I never would have gone to that Taylor family barbecue, and I never would have met Ryan. I would still be living a life of dating apps and partying.

Groaning, I push away from the counter and open the fridge. I need snacks to distract myself. Pulling out sliced turkey and cheese, I make a few rollups on a plate, and take them with me to the living room. I can't believe it's only noon, so I turn the TV on, and flip around until I find a mindless reality show to get lost in.

At some point I must have fallen asleep, because I wake up a few hours later, and the room has darkened. Yawning, I get up and unplug my phone in the kitchen. Holy shit, it's already after four! I slept, for like, three hours!

Ryan is going to be home at six, so I search around his fridge and cabinets to find the ingredients I need for chicken and penne vodka, and get to work.

Cooking has always helped me to clear my head. At least for a short time.

When it's all together in a casserole dish, I put a layer of cheese on top, and cover it with foil before putting it in the oven on low.

Looking at the clock, I see it's five thirty, so I run upstairs to shower and change before Ryan gets back.

I don't know why I'm nervous, but I am. I'm staying in his house, and I made him dinner. This feels like some weird first date.

Showering, I let the hot water beat down on my tense muscles. I haven't heard from Ryan, and I hope he's okay. I could have called him, sure, but I didn't want to seem like some nagging girl checking in on him.

Sighing, I tilt my face up into the water and rinse off before stepping out and wrapping myself in a towel.

Opening the bathroom door, I run smack dab into a wall of man. "Oompf," I grunt out as arms wrap around me–steadying me.

"Sorry," Ryan's deep voice utters quickly. "I was just coming up to look for you and didn't realize you were showering."

"It's fine," I say into his chest. "But I'm getting you all wet now."

His low chuckle vibrates through me. "Funny, I thought that was my job."

"Ryan!" I laugh, smacking his chest.

Holding my towel tight, I step back out of his arms, and look up into his stupidly handsome, smiling face. But as he rakes his eyes down my wet, towel clad body, his smile vanishes, and his heated eyes meet mine again.

My wet hair drips down my back and shoulders, and I watch as Ryan's eyes follow a drop as it runs down my neck and chest, disappearing into the valley between my breasts.

"I'm going to go put some clothes on," I whisper, my pulse racing. If my skin was any hotter, the water would be steaming off of me.

His eyes dart back up to mine, holding my gaze for a long moment. Stepping aside, I walk past him and down the hall to my room in a dazed state.

I wish he would have just ripped this towel from my body and pinned me against the wall. That would have been more than fine with me.

Ripping it from my body myself, I wrap my hair up in it, and apply a generous amount of lotion all over. This cold air is already drying my skin out.

I change into leggings and an oversized sweater that falls mid-thigh and slightly off my shoulder, showing off the black lace bralette I have on underneath.

Taking the towel off my head, I comb out my hair, and put in some leave-in conditioner so my curls won't dry frizzy. Flipping it over a few times, I give it a little volume, and then move on to applying my face lotions. I don't bother with any makeup, but I do apply a little mascara to make my green eyes more enticing.

Deciding I look good enough to where it doesn't seem like I'm trying too hard, I make my way downstairs, and find Ryan in the kitchen taking the casserole dish out of the oven.

"It should be done. I was just letting the cheese melt."

"You made dinner," he says, sounding surprised.

"I did." I smile. "I take eating seriously."

He smiles back. "I do too. I'll grab the plates if you grab the forks."

"Sure." Remembering where I found them earlier, I open the drawer near the sink and take out two forks and knives and bring them over to the table. "So, how was work?"

"Good. Quiet. Mostly sitting around eating donuts." He smirks.

"I knew it." I laugh lightly. "Waste of taxpayer money."

"Hey, I did have to venture out and bring a few citizens food and water."

"You did? Who?"

"A couple of elderly ladies who live about a mile away."

"Ah, I knew it. I had a feeling the ladies of Pine Cove made calls of distress just to get you to them."

"And why is that?" He asks slyly, a smile playing on his lips and a gleam in his eyes.

"Oh, please." I roll my eyes. "You know why."

"Why don't you tell me, Ashley," he says, coming up next to me. His chest brushes against my shoulder as he leans in and places the plates on the table, my heartrate kicking up.

"Well, because, you're you."

"And what am I?"

"I am right, though, aren't I?" I ask, breathless. I can't focus on what he's asking me.

"Only sometimes," his low voice whispers in my ear, his warm breath tickling my skin.

"Seriously?"

"No, sweetheart." He chuckles. "I like that you're jealous, though."

"I'm not jealous."

"You are," he says, brushing my hair over my shoulder, exposing my neck. "But I like it."

A chill runs down my spine. "I'm not. Now sit, and I'll bring dinner over."

"I got it. You sit." With a gentle nudge to my arm, I sit in the chair I'm closest to, and watch him carry the casserole dish to the table.

He changed out of his uniform and into sweatpants and a Pine Cove High football t-shirt. And damn. Holy hot balls. Those pants hang off of his hips like they were meant for me to just tug them down, and his t-shirt is stretched tight across his broad chest, showing me every hard plane.

"So, what did you do today? Do much snooping?" he asks.

Smiling, I spoon out a decent portion of penne onto my plate, the pasta steaming up into my face, smelling heavenly. "Oh, I snooped. I love your book collection. I'm surprised, actually."

"That I read?"

"Yes." I smile. "And that you have such an extensive collection of classics. I'm surprised, and impressed."

"I'm happy to keep you on your toes." He smirks, spooning out his own portion of pasta. "This smells really good, Ash, thank you. You didn't have to cook. I was going to when I got home."

"I wanted to. And"–I look up at him–"I wanted to say thank you for letting me stay with you. Having electricity and hot water is nice. I don't think I would have lasted much longer at Dottie's if you hadn't saved me."

"You're welcome. But you would have made it. You're strong."

Smiling, I take a bite of pasta and close my eyes. Damn, it's good, if I do say so myself. Which I am.

"Ash," he groans. "This is fucking delicious."

"Thanks."

"I didn't know you could cook."

"You don't know much about me, Ryan."

"I know," he says, looking me straight in the eyes. "But I want to change that."

"Okay," I whisper, my chest constricting from the way he's looking at me.

"Tell me more about your dad."

"Oh, um, okay. Well, he was the absolute best person I knew," I tell him, not being able to hold back my smile. "We did stuff together all the time. We'd go to baseball games, football games, movies, out to eat. Anything, really. My favorite, though, was when we'd just drive around on Sunday mornings. We'd listen to Sinatra, or classic southern rock, and just run errands." I shrug. "I don't know. We'd talk and drive. It was nice."

"You really miss him, don't you?"

"Yeah," I admit, looking down, tears gathering in my eyes. But I blink them away. I really don't want to cry right now.

"I'm sorry, Ashley. I can't even imagine how you feel. But you can talk to me about it. I'm here." Looking back up at him, I meet his soft blue eyes, and the tears I was trying to hold back, fall on their own. "Please don't cry, sweetheart."

"No, I'm not sad. Thank you, Ryan. That means more to me than you can possibly know."

"It's the truth," he says, his gaze never leaving mine.

Glancing down at my plate, I try and gather myself again, but I can't. He's doing something to me that I can't help, or stop.

We finish eating in a comfortable silence, but I can feel his eyes on me the entire time.

I take our empty plates to the sink and cover the casserole when he asks behind me, "Do you want wine?" I jump. I didn't even hear him approach.

My hand flies to my heart, feeling it beat rapidly beneath my fingers. "Yes, please."

"If you grab two glasses from the cabinet above you, I'll get a bottle from my office, and meet you in the living room."

"Alright." Reaching up, I take down two glasses, and then sit in the chair where I was reading this afternoon.

"Keats?" Ryan asks, taking a seat on the couch, his eyes darting to the book on the table as he uncorks a bottle of merlot. I hadn't realized I left the book out.

"Oh, yeah. He's one of my favorites. I took a class on him in college."

"Which is your favorite by him?"

"The butterfly one." I smile, watching him pour the wine.

"'I almost wish we were butterflies and lived but three summer days – three such days with you I could fill with more delight than fifty common years could ever contain.'"

"You know it?"

"It's my favorite too," he tells me, his eyes soft, yet serious.

"Huh. What a coincidence."

"A coincidence. Sure." He smirks, handing me a glass.

"Thanks." Taking a sip, I let the wine slip down my throat and settle in my stomach–warming my insides. "Is it still snowing out?"

"Yeah. I hope it stops soon, though, or I'll have a lot more rescuing to do." Rubbing his forehead, Ryan takes a sip of wine and leans back against the couch.

"Does it snow for days often?"

"No. Maybe a couple of times in the season. But this is more than usual."

"Well, as long as we have power–" And I'm cut off by the lights going off. Great.

CHAPTER 11

"Well, I jinxed that, didn't I?"

"Definitely." He laughs. Damn, it's dark in here. I can't see him, or anything. "I'll make a fire."

"Okay."

"Don't worry, Ash. We'll be alright."

"I'm not worried."

"I hear it in your voice. You're safe with me, though. I have a fireplace, candles, food, and alcohol. We'll survive."

I breathe out a lungful of air. "Okay."

It's not surviving I'm really worried about, though. It's being alone in the dark with Ryan. With nothing to do but sit with him, I know I won't be able to resist his charming sexiness for long.

I hear him strike a match, and a flame lights up his face – his chiseled features even more sharp in the flickering light.

As he gets the fireplace going, the living room is cast in a soft, warm glow, and I feel the heat lapping at my exposed skin.

Sipping my wine, I watch Ryan as he moves around the room. He takes out a few white pillar candles from a hutch in the corner and places them on the coffee table. Lighting them, he sits back down on the couch, smirking, patting the spot next to him.

"Come here," he says in a low, seductive voice that makes my stomach clench. I'm sure he's charmed many women into doing just about any and everything with that voice. And the fact that it's working on me right now shouldn't be a seen as a sign of weakness.

Nope. I'm not weak.

But… Just maybe I am a little for this man.

It's like my body has a mind of its own, and I stand, walking the few steps towards him. Sitting next to Ryan, I feel the sliver of space separating us charged with electricity. It's like the second I come close to him, I'm immediately sucked into his atmosphere, and I feel as if I no longer have control over anything.

Sitting rigidly, I sip my wine, and take shallow breaths so my shoulder doesn't touch his.

"Relax, Ashley," Ryan murmurs close to my ear, his warm breath blowing against my exposed shoulder and neck.

"I'm relaxed," I say, even though every muscle in my body feels tense.

"Come here." Reaching out, Ryan puts his arm around me and pulls me against his body. With one touch, I sigh, relaxing into him. And despite being a solid wall of muscle, he's the most comfortable thing in the world.

The minutes pass by, and I watch the flames dance in the fireplace – listening to the crackle and pop of the wood as the sparks and embers fly.

"What're you thinking about?" he asks softly.

"Just that the fire is really pretty."

"Huh. I didn't peg you as a pyro. But then again, it's always the good girls that like to play with fire."

"Who said I'm good?"

"I read people for a living, sweetheart. You're a good person. You try and come off as rough and tough, but you're loyal and fiercely protective of your friends, and you put other people's happiness ahead of your own."

"You can read all of that from me?"

"Yes. And I can also read that you want me," he adds, stroking my arm.

Laughing, I hit his chest playfully, and he reaches up and captures my hand with his, curling his fingers around mine. Raising my head, I rest my chin on his chest – my eyes meeting his. And it's what I see there that makes the smile fade from my lips.

Ryan's eyes are serious, yet soft. They're heated, yet muted.

Taking my glass from my hand, he puts it down on the table.

Slowly, he lowers his head until he's just a breath away. My eyes flutter closed, and I can feel his lips right there, only a few millimeters separating us.

There's so much I want to say to him, and there's so much I want him to say to me. But right now, it all flies out of my head, and all I can think about is his lips. And the second they touch mine, I'm gone. I'm lost.

Gripping his hand tighter against his chest, I press into him, and kiss him back with an intensity I didn't know I had. I can actually feel my veins coursing with fire, and my skin breaking out in goosebumps.

Ryan pulls me on top of him so I'm straddling his hips, and I feel him there – right where I need him. Wrapping my arms around his neck, I roll my hips against his and we both moan into the kiss, his tongue sliding against mine. Heat licks at my skin, and I pull myself even closer against him.

Ryan grows beneath me, and I grind into him, trying to relieve the ache that's been building in me for months. One that only he can alleviate.

Groaning, he tightens his grip on my hips and slides his hands down the sides of my thighs, and then back up and under my sweater

— shuddering at the feeling of his hands on my bare skin.

Lifting my sweater up and off of me, Ryan's lips are back on mine in a millisecond. He kisses his way down my neck, raking his teeth across my flesh, his hot mouth searing my skin as he travels over my collar bone and down the valley of my breasts.

His hands grip the lace band of my bralette and he practically tears it off of me, groaning at the sight of my naked breasts. Leaning forward, he captures my right nipple with his mouth and I throw my head back, a loud breathy sigh escaping my lips as I thrust my chest into his face further.

Taking the other in his mouth, Ryan grazes his teeth over my hard, sensitive nipple, biting down. Gasping, I moan – long and low.

"Ryan," I choke out, breathing hard.

Lifting his head, he kisses me hard on the lips and picks me up, shoving the coffee table away as he lays me down on the floor.

My hands find their way to the hem of his t-shirt and slide them underneath to feel his smooth, tight abs. My fingers slide over the mounds, and Ryan's muscles clench and flex under my touch.

I love that he's as affected by me as I am by him.

Whipping his shirt over his head, I catch an eyeful of his bare chest and arms before he's back on top of me and kissing his way up my neck.

Squirming under him, his hands grip my hips as his lips sear mine with a bruising kiss. He slides his hand between us, and his fingers press against me through my leggings. Moaning, I lock my arms around his neck and buck my hips up into his touch.

Finally.

He pulls back, and I try and chase him with my mouth, but he's moving off of me. Gripping the waistband of my leggings, Ryan pulls them down and off of me in a matter of two seconds, leaving me laid out before him. Naked.

"You had nothing on under there this entire time?" he growls, staring down at me like he wants to eat me alive.

I nod, and he grips me behind the knees, pulling my legs up and open – completely exposing me to him.

With the fire next to us raging, Ryan pulls my knees towards him, my back sliding against the rug – the burn of it only heightening the heat I feel spreading out across my skin from everywhere he touches me.

"I'm going to take you every way I've thought about for months, sweetheart. But first, I'm going to have you begging for me to be inside of you," he murmurs in my ear. "And then I'm going to fill you so completely," he groans out, shoving three fingers inside of me, a strangled scream torn from my throat as I arch off the floor, "you'll never be the same."

I'm already never the same. He's already ruined me.

Pressing his thumb hard against my clit, he curls his fingers inside of me, and my eyes practically roll back into my head at the overload of sensations.

Working in and out of me, I feel myself getting closer and closer to the edge of oblivion, but then he pulls away.

"No!" I beg, my eyes flying open to find his.

"I told you you're going to have to beg, sweetheart."

Lightly, he circles my entrance with the tip of his finger, just teasing me. He slides a path up to my mound, circling me, barely touching me.

I need more. I need everything.

"Ryan," I groan, trying to move my hips up to get him to press harder. But he just shakes his head and holds my hips down with his other hand.

His eyes burn into mine as he continues to tease me ever so lightly. But I can't take it. I can't.

Squeezing my eyes shut, my hands fist at my sides, and I try and convince myself that I can beat him at his own game. But I don't think I can last much longer before I scream out for him to just fucking fuck me already.

"You just have to say the words, Ashley, and I'll give you everything, and more."

"No," I say through clenched teeth, my eyes blazing up at him.

Chuckling, Ryan just smiles his sexy little smile, and leans down so his face is only a few inches from mine. "You're going to beg me, or you get nothing." Circling my entrance over and over with the lightest of touches, my core clenches, squeezing, trying to get him closer. But he's still too far away.

Making another pass up to my tight bundle of nerves, Ryan flicks his finger over my clit, and I bite my lip trying to hold back my moan, but he just smiles like the devil over me.

He knows what it would mean if I begged him. He knows I'd have to give up everything in me to him. He knows I'd have to relinquish all control to him. It's what he wants, and he knows getting that from me, would mean he wins. He wants me to give up everything I know.

The words are on the tip of my tongue. I want to give in. I want him more than I've ever wanted anything, but it comes with the price of losing the control I've been clinging to with every fiber of my being.

I don't even know why I am, though. Something in me tells me to fight this with Ryan, but there's also another part that's telling me to give him any and everything he wants.

It's a battle of control, and I've never wanted to hand mine over to someone so badly before. But that doesn't mean I'm doing it without a fight.

"You'll give in," he taunts, circling my clit with the tip of his finger.

"I don't think so," I say back, but my voice wavers–strained.

Slamming his mouth down on mine, Ryan slowly sinks one finger inside of me, but he only goes in an inch or two before slowly removing it, and circling my entrance again.

Whimpering into his mouth, Ryan nibbles on my bottom lip, and repeats the slow plunge of his finger inside of me. I clench my inner muscles, trying to suck him in, but he just retreats and circles me.

No!

Tears prick my eyes as his hot tongue licks over my bottom lip, and he sucks it between his.

I don't know if I can do this.

I'm going to give in.

I have to.

When his finger goes inside of me for the third time–or maybe fourth, or fifth, I've lost count – I can't hold back the low whimpering moan that escapes me.

"Ryan, please. Please, I can't take it anymore. I need you, all of you. Please," I beg, my voice low, but forceful.

Pulling away, my eyes fly open, thinking he's finished, but I watch as he sheds his sweatpants.

Holy shit.

My eyes are glued to his enormously erect cock as he takes a condom out of the pocket of his pants and rips it open. Rolling it down his entire length, my body goes flush at the anticipation of having him inside of me.

Settling back down between my legs, Ryan grips my hips, his eyes locked on mine, flaring with victory and a molten desire that's all for me.

"I knew you'd beg, sweetheart," he says, pushing into me.

Screaming out, my back arches off the floor as he fills me to the hilt with one thrust. It feels like I'm being split in two.

Ryan doesn't even give me time to adjust before he pulls out and thrusts back into me.

Over and over, he pounds into me, my moans turning to screams.

Each thrust causes my back to slide against the carpet, and I feel a burn forming, but I don't care. I need him to keep going.

"You're so fucking tight," he grunts out. "So fucking good." His hands grip my hips to the point of pain, but I don't care about that either.

My breasts bounce and sway with every thrust, and Ryan

captures one, sucking my nipple deep into his mouth. I feel the zing all the way to my core, and my inner walls start to flutter.

"More, Ryan," I moan out.

Grunting against my breast, he tilts my hips up off the floor and starts to thrust into me even harder.

I can't take it.

It's too good.

It's too much.

Moving over to my other breast, he sucks it deep into his mouth, and the pull in my body is even greater.

When he bites down, my throat all but closes with the scream that's torn from deep within me.

I let go.

I let everything go.

My body breaks apart into a million pieces as I'm thrown over the edge into the abyss. Wave after wave flows through me, and over me. My eyes are pinched closed, and my mouth is open in a silent scream. Or maybe I am screaming, and I'm just deaf from them.

It's never been like this. I've never felt this.

My body feels taken.

It feels used in the best possible way.

Ryan Taylor is going to break me in every conceivable way, but I think I'm going to love every fucking second of it.

His grizzly groan hits my ears, and pierces through the haze that's taken over me as he slams into me one final time. His body stills as his grip on my hips tightens to the point where I know there'll be bruises. But I don't care. I want him to mark me, and I want to be marked by him.

We stay like this for a long while. It could be seconds, minutes, or hours for all I know, but we stay locked together.

As my heartrate settles, and my breathing becomes more even, my eyes flutter open and find Ryan's. His blue eyes are shining with something new, and they're searching mine.

There's so much said and unsaid between us in this moment,

and I have to close my eyes from the intensity.

"No," he whispers, brushing my cheek with the tips of his fingers. "Let me see you."

Opening my eyes, I find him searching mine again, and it feels like he can read every thought, and every emotion, running though me in this moment. It feels like he can see into the deepest parts of me.

This is the vulnerability I've been avoiding for most of my life.

Since my dad, I've held myself back from everyone. But with Ryan, he seems determined to figure me out, and that scares me more than I'd like to admit.

His soft blue eyes are two deep pools of mystery that I can get lost in for hours. His emotions swirl in his eyes, and I find myself falling into them – mesmerized by what I see.

"You're so beautiful," he whispers, brushing a few strands of hair away from my face, my heart thudding in my chest at his words.

Reaching up, I softly trace his face with my finger – over his brow, down his temple, across his jaw, and around his sensuous lips. His eyes close briefly at my touch, and open again, even softer.

"You're so handsome, Ryan," I confess, loving the small smile he gives me.

"It's about time you admitted that."

Smiling, I cup his cheek and lean up to kiss him. Our lips meet softly at first, but then he presses me back down to the floor and takes over.

Sliding his tongue across the seam of my lips, I open for him immediately, and he dives in – sweeping, tasting, taking.

I wrap my arms around his neck and pull him down, needing to feel his weight on top of me. We're still connected. He's still inside of me, and I can feel him growing again – a sensation unlike any I've felt before. And it brings me a new sense of power, knowing that I'm the one who turns this man on. Even so soon after just having me.

Kissing Ryan is like slow dancing under the stars on a warm summer night. That feeling of being seen, even when it's dark, and knowing that he's is right there to hold onto if I get lost.

Cupping my neck, Ryan rubs his thumb across my jaw, slowly rocking in and out of me again.

Every nerve ending in my body is still on high alert, and I feel everything. A low moan rumbles from deep within me, and Ryan swallows it, kissing me like he can't get enough.

My hands tighten around his neck, and I wrap my legs around his hips, giving myself to him.

Breaking away, Ryan leans his forehead against mine, his ragged breaths mixing with mine as he pumps in and out of me. He continues to brush his thumb back and forth against my jaw, and my eyes flutter open to see his pools of blue already locked on mine.

The slow burn builds and builds until my body explodes around him again, taking me by surprise. Falling, my neck arches up, and my lips brush Ryan's as I moan out, squeezing him with every muscle I have inside of me.

Ryan picks up the pace, pumping through my orgasm as he chases his own, and I feel another storm building in me.

"Come with me," he whispers against my lips, and I let go for a second time, my body on overdrive.

My throat closes, and my mouth remains open in a silent plea against his.

I'm never going to survive this time with Ryan if he continues to do this to me – if he continues to break me open and force me to give him all of me.

CHAPTER 12

I need air. Every breath I take seems to only make my throat close and my lungs constrict.

I can't stay here with him.

Looking away from Ryan, I watch the flames dance in the fireplace. "Will you let me up?"

"What's wrong?" he asks, tilting my face back to his.

"I just need–"

"No."

"No?"

"No. I'm not letting you run away."

I narrow my eyes. "Who said I'm running?" I fire back.

"I can see it in your eyes. Talk to me."

"I'm fine." But I know he sees through my lie.

"Stop thinking so much."

Staring into his crystal blue eyes for the longest moment, I force a swallow despite my dry throat. "I can't," I whisper.

"You can."

Closing my eyes, I take in a shaky breath, and when I open them again, I find Ryan's have never wavered from mine. I feel his penetrating gaze all the way to my core.

Kissing me long and slow, Ryan silences the questions, doubts, and fears swirling around my head.

He pulls out of me, and I whimper at the loss.

"Stay right here," he says, standing and walking out of the room.

My eyes lazily follow him until he's out of my line of sight.

Damn, his ass is fine.

Returning a minute later with a damp washcloth, Ryan kneels, and gently wipes me clean. Glancing up, he flashes me a small smile, and kisses my inner thigh when he's finished.

He leaves again, and when he comes back, he picks his sweatpants up off the floor and pulls them on, covering up my spectacular view.

"Don't worry, sweetheart," he says, and my eyes flash up to his to see him wink. "You'll see me naked again soon."

My lips twitch, fighting a smile. "I'll hold you to that, sheriff." Grabbing my sweater, I pull it over my head and tug it down so it covers everything important, but still leaves my legs on full display. "Don't worry, I'm sure you'll be seeing it all again soon, too," I tell him when I catch him staring.

"I know." He smiles, pouring us each a fresh glass of wine.

"Thanks," I say, taking the glass from him, and leaning back against the couch.

Nodding, he takes a seat next to me, his arm almost touching mine as I sip my wine and watch the flames dance, trying to recover from what just happened. But I honestly don't think I ever will. I can still feel him on me, and in me. And I know I'll never forget it, or get enough of it.

"What's your favorite movie?"

"Are you seriously asking me that?" I laugh lightly. We just had hot sex that rivals the fire in front of us, and he's asking me about my favorite movie?

I turn my head towards him, and he smiles. "Yes."

"Okay, then," I say, tapping the rim of the wine glass against my bottom lip. "Jurassic Park."

"Really?"

"Yes. Does that surprise you?"

"Sort of."

"Why? A woman can't have a thing for dinosaurs?"

"Of course she can. I just didn't peg you as a woman who did. But I love that movie, too. Now I know what we'll be watching when the power comes back on."

"Oh my God, yes! Do you have it?" I ask excitedly.

Laughing, he nods and takes a sip of wine. "I have all of them, including the new ones."

"A movie marathon it is, then. First thing when the power comes back on. Please, and thank you." I smile sweetly.

"Anything you want."

"Oh, anything? Well, then, I also want dessert," I tell him. "To start with," I add, biting my lip to keep from smiling too wide.

Reaching out, Ryan runs a finger up my bare calf. "I'll be right back."

Standing, he grabs the flashlight he left on the coffee table, and walks into the kitchen. Opening a few different cabinets, he grabs a variety of things I can't see, and places it all on a tray.

As he's walking back, I chew on my lip, watching the flames lick light and shadows across his bare chest, abs, and arms. My God, he's sculpted like a fucking warrior.

It's a sin that he looks so good.

My eyes drift down to the tray in his hands when he sits back down, and I smile. "S'mores."

Grabbing two marshmallows and a metal stick, I poke the marshmallows onto the ends, and then sit up on my knees, scooting over to the fireplace.

"I love s'mores," I tell him as I roast my marshmallows. "My friends and I used to have bonfires a lot in the fall, and they weren't complete without s'mores."

"I always had them when I'd go to summer camp. It was the best part, if you ask me."

Coming up next to me, he sits and sticks his marshmallows in the fire. My eyes take in his sculpted forearm, thinking about it next to my head as he braces himself over me – pushing in and out of me.

Losing track of time, I glance back over at my marshmallows. "Oh, shit!" They're on fire – blazing really.

I quickly pull them out and blow on them, but it's too late, they're charred beyond recognition. "Eh, I like 'em burnt." I shrug, trying to play it off that I wasn't distracted by his sexy arm next to me.

"Sure you do, sweetheart," he says sarcastically. "Just grab new ones. I have a whole bag."

Sighing, I ditch the black lumps and stab two fresh ones onto my stick to try again. I keep a watchful eye this time, pulling them out just as they catch fire, and blow the flames out quickly. Ah, cooked to perfection.

Grabbing two graham crackers and a piece of chocolate, I make my little sandwich, and bite into it right away. Moaning, I close my eyes as the chocolate melts on my tongue, and the sweet marshmallows ooze out – the perfect combination.

"Ashley," he says low and sexy, and I open my eyes to find his have gone dark and heated again. "If you keep making noises like that, I'm going to have to put something else in your mouth for you to moan about."

Coughing, I practically choke, sucking graham cracker crumbs down my throat. Swallowing a few times, I cough again, and then reach for my wine glass to down the rest of it.

"Ryan!" I scold when I can finally speak again. "You can't say shit like that while I'm eating. I could have died."

"Like I would have let you."

Eyeing him with a devilish little smirk, I make sure he's watching me as I take another bite of my s'more. Moaning again, I chew slowly, swallow, and then lick my lips to capture any crumbs stuck to them.

"You're playing a game you won't win, sweetheart."

"Me?" I ask innocently with a hand to my chest. "I'm not playing a game."

Flashing me a predatory smile, Ryan traces a circle around my exposed kneecap, and then runs his hand up my thigh – a trail of goosebumps following his path.

Reaching the bottom of my sweater, he slides under it, his blue eyes blazing into mine, just begging for me to challenge him.

But I don't. I remain still – waiting.

Inching closer to the apex of my thighs, a steady throb beats in my core – begging for his touch, begging for him.

Rounding the top of my leg, Ryan grips my inner thigh, and my breath hitches.

With a smirk, he slides a single finger through my folds and his eyes harden when he feels how wet I already am for him. Now he knows the power he has over me with just the simplest of touches.

My heart is pounding so fast in my chest, and I bite my lip to hold back the moan threatening to escape.

Ryan takes his hand away and brings his finger to his lips, sucking it clean – groaning at the taste of me. "Just as sweet as I imagined." His eyes penetrate mine, and the breath I didn't know I was holding, rushes out of me.

So that's the game he wants to play? Who can seduce who faster?

Fucking count me in.

My lips turn up at the edges and I look away shyly, playing the innocent act.

"Ryan," I purr, looking up at him through my eyelashes.

He's still licking his finger clean, and knowing that he's tasting me on his tongue, I feel a surge of power come over me.

Sitting up on me knees, I place one hand on his bare shoulder and the other on his thigh.

Dropping his hand to mine, I watch his eyes darken – flitting from my eyes to my lips.

He wants to kiss me. He wants to taste my lips just as much as I know he wants to taste more of me than what was on his finger.

Curling my hand into his shoulder, his smooth skin beckons me to feel him all over, but I resist, needing to play this little game to the end.

I slide my hand up his thigh, and Ryan takes his away, letting me explore on my own. Inching closer to the bulge in his sweatpants, I lean my forehead against his, and feel him tense up.

I know he's close to losing his composure, and I know how much he likes to be in control.

I've got him exactly where I want him.

Gripping him through his pants, Ryan lets out a low groan, and I run my hand up and down his entire length – his body jerking at my touch.

I grip his shoulder tighter, my nails biting into his skin, and I lower my lips a fraction of inch, just tempting him to give in.

Squeezing him a little harder, I rake my blood red nails down his chest, and feel his reaction in my hand, his cock twitching against my palm. I smile slyly, biting my lip.

Groaning, Ryan inhales a deep breath through his nose.

"Ryan," I whisper, my breath spreading across his lips.

"I need you, sweetheart."

Squeezing him again, I almost give in, but find the strength to hold back. "I know," I whisper, my bottom lip grazing his lightly.

Sitting back down, I pour myself another glass of wine and smile at the confused look on his face. "I win, sheriff."

"Ashley," he says sternly, a warning of some kind.

"Yes?" I ask sweetly.

"Don't play me."

"You started it, and I finished it. I was just showing you that you shouldn't underestimate me."

Taking the glass from my hand, he puts it on the table and grips me behind the knee, turning me towards him.

"I don't underestimate you," he says, pushing me back onto the rug and hovering over me, spreading my legs to make room for him. "You destroy me with your touch just as much as mine does to you."

"Don't tell me how I feel," I say, narrowing my eyes.

"You can't deny it, sweetheart. I feel it, and see it." Running his hand up my thigh, it disappears under my sweater and up my stomach. I sigh when he traces the sensitive flesh under my breast, circling his finger around my nipple. "I see the look in your eyes when I touch you. I feel your heart racing. And I feel"–he reaches between my legs with his other hand, sliding his finger through my folds–"how wet you are for me. More than you've ever been for anyone."

Stifling a moan, I bite my lip, but keep my eyes on his.

He's right, and he knows it.

"I'll always win in the end, sweetheart. Because I'm the only one who can do *this* to you." Shoving two fingers inside of me, I groan out, my hands clawing at the rug, trying to grip onto something, anything.

"Isn't that right?" he growls.

"Yes," I manage to choke out before his mouth slams down on mine in a bruising, possessive kiss.

Wrapping my arms around his neck, I pull him tighter against me, his lips molding to mine like they were made just for me.

Pumping his fingers in and out of me, a storm quickly builds, but he doesn't let me move my hips to get more. I bite his lip, trying to tell him I need more. And it works.

Groaning, he adds a third finger, and my head falls back onto the floor, knowing the end is coming quickly.

He curls his fingers inside of me, and presses down on my clit with his thumb, pushing me past my limit.

Kissing me harder, Ryan swallows every sound I make as my

body squeezes his fingers like a vice, practically sucking them up inside of me.

He kisses his way across my jaw, licking the shell of my ear, biting down. "No one else can make you come as fast, or hard. Just me."

"Yes," I choke out, trying to desperately suck air into my lungs.

His low rumble of satisfaction that comes from deep in his throat vibrates into me as he kisses, sucks, and bites his way down my neck. A shudder racks my body as heat blooms from everywhere his mouth touches me – marking me, claiming me.

Even when I know I shouldn't, I want him to claim me.

I want to keep pushing him away, and I want to keep my heart guarded, but I also want to let him in.

I want to *let* him claim me, even when he's already doing it by force.

But right now, I'm done.

I can't do, or say, anything as my eyes close and roll back into my head – darkness consuming me.

Coming to a few minutes later, my eyes flutter open to Ryan carrying me up the stairs. I curl into his chest, my face resting in the crook of his neck, and I breathe in his intoxicating scent.

Closing my eyes again, I let myself drift off in his arms.

CHAPTER 13

The dull light of predawn fills the room, and I scoot closer to Ryan, tucking my face into his chest, trying to hide from the inevitable. I don't want to wake up. I don't want him to go to work today. I just want to stay right here and keep warm in his arms.

Gentle fingers brush my hair from my eyes, and trace my face from my temple to my jaw.

"Morning, beautiful," Ryan whispers, and my heart skips. I've never been so mushy over a man's compliments, or craved them as much as I do with Ryan.

"Mmm," I hum, not ready to come out of my dream-like state yet.

But then I feel his lips press against my forehead, and I smile at the warmth that spreads across my skin from his touch.

"Let me see those eyes," he says softly, coaxing me awake.

Fluttering my lids open, I look up, and lock eyes with the most beautiful and mesmerizing blue ones.

"There they are." He lightly traces my cheekbone. "You hypnotize me with these."

I've been told countless times that my eyes are unique, and are what draws a man in. I hated that. I wanted a man to see me, but they rarely did. And while that suited me just fine for a time, this is the first time, in a very long time, that I'm grateful for them. Because I want to hypnotize Ryan, but I also want him to see more.

Tilting my chin up, Ryan plants a soft kiss on my lips, but I still feel it – the zap of electricity running through me.

Using his chest as leverage, I lean up into the kiss, wanting to feel all of him rushing through my veins. His kisses are addicting. And if I can get addicted to the feeling of my heart clenching in my chest and a thousand volts traveling through me, then I think I may have a problem.

Rolling me onto my back, Ryan presses me into the mattress, letting me feel all of him against the length of my body – his weight a welcome pressure.

Kissing me slowly, he grips my face in his hands, his thumbs stroking my cheeks.

Sliding my hands up his sides, my fingers graze the ripples of his ribcage, and his muscles contract at my touch.

I fucking love that.

I want to bring this powerful man to his knees when he's with me just as much as I want him to do the same to me. When we're together like this, I feel like a different woman – a greater woman.

Pulling away, he grabs the hem of my sweater and whips it off over my head, exposing me to the cool air. But I don't feel it the second Ryan touches me again.

Running his hands down my arms, he takes mine away from him and raises them above my head, placing them against the bedframe for me to hold. I grip the bars tightly as he slides his hands down the underside of my arms – sparks of awareness lighting up every nerve ending in my body.

Trailing hot kisses down my neck and chest, I suck in a quick breath when he rakes his teeth over my ribcage.

He's everywhere.

It's all too much.

Arching into him, I gasp and sigh, moaning out his name – long and low.

"Don't let go of the bed," he says, his authoritative tone turning me on further.

"Mhmm," I hum, not trusting my voice.

Swirling his hot tongue around my belly button, I squirm beneath him, flames bubbling just below the surface of my skin like a volcano ready to erupt.

I grip the bars tighter, fighting the urge to touch him with everything inside of me.

Ryan runs his hands up my stomach and over my breasts – caressing, feeling, and squeezing them. Moaning, I sink my head into the pillows and bite the inside of my arm to keep from being too loud.

Licking and sucking his way up my torso, I arch off the bed, needing him closer. I wish I could just grab his head and put him where I want him, but I keep my hands wrapped around the bars, restraining myself just like he wants.

Ryan teases me with his mouth, lightly grazing the skin under my breasts before rolling my nipples between his fingers. I let out a muffled groan against my arm, and squeeze the bars so tight, I think the metal will be fused to my hands by the end of this.

Sliding his tongue up my left breast, he takes my nipple into his mouth and sucks it hard, swirling his tongue around the peak.

I thrash under him, feeling completely out of control.

Moving over to the right, he pays equal attention to it, and I practically lift myself off of the bed just trying to find relief from the torture.

"Let me hear you, sweetheart. Stop holding back," he growls, and I let go of my arm, my breathy sighs and moans filling my ears as

Ryan drags his mouth back down my body, his teeth scraping against my sensitive skin.

Skimming his fingertips up the sides of my calves, he circles my knees, and then skims up my inner thighs. They fall open at his touch, and he smooths his palms against my hips.

"Ryan," I plea, not caring how desperate I sound.

"Shh," he hushes. "All in time, Ashley," he assures, blowing air against my core – a shiver racking my body. My hand instinctively falls from the headboard and onto his head, but Ryan is right there to grip my wrist and pull it away. "No," he says harshly. "Put it back, or I won't give you what you want."

Groaning, my arm feels like it weighs a thousand pounds as I lift it back above my head.

"Good girl," he praises, his fingers dancing on the skin near the apex of my thighs.

"I'm not a dog," I throw back at him, his words grating against my nerves despite the mindless state I'm in.

Chuckling, Ryan bites down on my inner thigh, and my hips buck off the bed. "I'm going to have to do something about that mouth of yours. Put it to better use." His tongue leaves behind a trail of fire as he inches closer to where I need him most. "But not yet. First, I need to taste you."

Gripping my thighs, he pushes them as far apart as he can, his hot breath on me the only warning I get before he licks his way up the entire length of my folds.

I arch off the bed, practically bending the bars beneath my hands as I try and keep them in place.

Holy fucking shit.

Pressing his tongue flat against my clit, he swirls it around, and slides it back down to my entrance – circling it, but not going any further.

I can feel Ryan smiling against me when I grunt out my protests, but he just keeps his slow exploratory pace.

Pressing my thighs open against the bed, he holds me down so I have nowhere to move. Now I can't move my hips, legs, or arms. I have no choice but to take what he gives me.

Ryan's tongue and mouth are playing tricks on me – swirling, sucking, tasting, nibbling, but not fully committing to anything long enough for me to be pushed over the edge.

My moans grow louder and louder until my throat is raw, and my mouth hangs open in a silent scream as he continues his savage assault.

Thrusting his tongue inside of me, my throat closes, and I pull so hard on the wrought iron bars, I feel them protest under my fingers.

Ryan keeps going, though. He doesn't know that I feel like my body isn't mine anymore, and he doesn't care that I feel like he's giving me something I will never recover from.

Each pass of his tongue brings on a new wave of pleasure spreading through my body, like a frayed live wire dancing on the ground in the middle of a storm.

Sucking my clit into his mouth, Ryan shoves two fingers inside of me, and I'm gone. I white knuckle grip the bars, and my body splinters off into a million little pieces, my veins flowing with pure fire.

My chest heaves as I try and suck in air, but it's not enough.

My head spins, and I close my eyes as the waves continue to crash over my head – dragging me under.

Caressing my arms, Ryan massages my sore muscles. Covering my clenched hands, he slowly unlocks my fingers one by one from the bars, allowing the blood to flow through once again.

"You taste so sweet," he whispers in my ear. "I knew that hard, spicy outer shell was only the coating to a soft and sweet filling." Kissing me behind my ear, I sigh, leaning into his touch as he brings my arms back down to my sides, kissing his way across my collar bone and shoulder.

Leaving me for a second, Ryan sheds his pants and sheaths himself, and then I feel him everywhere at once. He crawls up my body and settles between my thighs, pressing against my folds.

Tilting my hips up, Ryan slips closer to my entrance, and we both moan at the sensation. His moan vibrates in the crook of my neck, and he kisses his way up to my mouth.

With his lips on mine, I wrap my arms around his neck and arch my back, pushing my breasts against his bare chest, kissing him like my sanity depends on it – which it kind of does.

He rocks his hips forward, his tip slipping into me, and I moan into his mouth. Pushing into me slowly, I can't help the sounds coming from me, and Ryan captures all of them.

He swallows them all, and keeps them as his.

He can have everything I am if it means he'll never stop.

With one final push forward, Ryan's fully seated inside of me.

"So hot. So tight," he groans, his voice strained and gravely like he's about to lose his composure. "I need to move, sweetheart. And it won't be gentle."

"Please," I sigh, giving him permission to do whatever he wants. I just need him.

Pulling out slowly, I feel sparks shooting from every nerve ending in my body. And when he thrusts forward, a strangled moan is torn from deep within me.

Moving in and out of me, Ryan takes me with a frenzied passion.

He hits a spot no man ever has.

He fills me, and splits me open.

The dreams I've had every night since I first had him pale in comparison to the reality of having Ryan here – moving in me, with me, against me.

My imagination didn't do this justice.

I feel like I'm being pulled into a current of the swirling waters of a hurricane. I'm drowning in the perfect storm that is Ryan Taylor.

"Come with me, Ashley," he murmurs against my skin before taking my left nipple into his mouth.

With one final thrust, I let go, my body splitting in two as I come undone. My screams fill the early morning air as Ryan scrapes his teeth up my throat.

"You make me crazy, sweetheart."

"Ryan," I whisper, running my hands through his short hair.

Holding his head against me, he kisses his way up my neck and across my jaw to my lips – gently nibbling on my bottom lip before kissing me sweetly.

When he slowly pulls out of me, he rolls over, taking me with him so I'm draped over his chest. Wrapping his arm around my waist, he holds me against him, and I drift off back to sleep.

CHAPTER 14

Waking sometime later, I spread my hand out next to me, but only find cold sheets where Ryan should be. Opening my eyes, I scan the room, but he's not here, and his clothes are gone.

Eyeing the bedframe's bars behind me, I smile to myself, pulling the comforter up to my mouth. Damn, he's good.

Glancing at the pillow next to me, I find a piece of paper with large scrawling script.

Morning beautiful,

I didn't want to wake you because you looked so peaceful, but I had to go into work. I wish I could spend all day in bed with you – holding you, kissing you, and fucking you senseless. But I promise that on my next day off, we'll do just that.

I'll be home after 6.

-Ry

Smiling like a fool, I hold the piece of paper to my chest and roll onto my back. I actually feel giddy right now. I can't remember the last time I felt giddy over a man. Probably high school, if then, even. But I know I've never felt like this.

Pulling the comforter tighter around my shoulders, I curl back on my side and bring his pillow to my face, inhaling his scent that he left behind. That spicy, woodsy smell is so intoxicating.

Peeking over at the clock on the bedside table, I see that it's only nine. Oh my god, I have to kill nine hours before he gets home?

Groaning, I throw the covers off of me and shuffle down the hall to the bathroom. I hate that I can't even take a hot shower because the power is out.

Splashing cold water on my face, I brush my teeth, and try and get my curls in order, but my hair is a mess. Giving up, I throw it up in a high bun, and head back to my room to get dressed.

Today–surprise, surprise–I go with leggings and an oversized sweater. This one, though, is hunter green, and really brings out the green in my eyes.

Throwing on a pair of fuzzy socks, I head downstairs and scope out the bookshelves around the fireplace for a book to read. But as I'm scanning the shelves, I see another note for me – this one taped to the mantle.

Morning beautiful,

I hope you're dressed warm, but if not, I started a fire for you. Just add more logs when it starts to die down. And if clothes are too tiresome to put on your perfect body, feel free to wait for me naked, laid out by fire, the flames casting a warm glow across your silky skin. That'd be more than okay with me.

And if you're not naked now, you will be soon...

-Ry

Smiling, I shake my head. He thought I'd walk around his house naked? When it's freaking freezing?

He has one thing right, though. I will be naked soon…

Hmm, maybe I'll let him come home to a little surprise.

Scanning the shelves again, my eyes catch on the gold patterned spine of Jane Eyre. Pulling it out, I feel the smooth, old leather. It's slightly worn, but still beautiful.

I'm about to settle into the couch when my stomach growls in protest. Placing the book on the table, I walk into the kitchen, and find another note on the counter next to a thermos.

Morning beautiful,

I'm sorry you can't have coffee, but I made you hot chocolate, and it's in the thermos.

I wouldn't open the fridge, just to preserve what's in there, but I've left out all the good cereal options to eat without milk. And there's a bowl of fruit if you want as well. Search around for anything you'd like, though.

Make yourself at home.

-Ry

I think this man had the goal of making me like him even more when he woke up today. And it worked.

Smiling, I take a sip from the thermos, and my eyes roll back when the delicious liquid chocolate hits my tongue. Seriously, this tastes like he melted a bar of chocolate and poured it in here.

Heaven. Pure heaven.

I grab the box of Frosted Flakes, and I take it, and the thermos, with me to the couch. Popping the box open, I fist a handful of cereal and funnel it into my mouth with zero shame since no one's here to see me. I love this cereal without milk. I think it's better that way, actually.

Tucking my feet under me, I grab the blanket on the back of the couch, and cover my legs. With the hot cocoa and cereal next to me, I reach for Jane Eyre and settle in for a long day of reading and relaxing. I'm quickly realizing I need to make sure I have more of this in my life. Pure relaxation.

*****

Shivering, I look up from reading, and see that the fire has all but died out. Shit, no wonder I'm fucking freezing.

Standing, I take the fire poker and jab at the logs, making the sparks light again as I add two more logs from the basket beside the fireplace.

Sitting back down, I notice my phone on the table. I forgot that I left it down here last night. Picking it up, I smile when I see a text from Ryan.

I'm sitting here at work and all I can think about is you. You naked under me. You naked with my mouth all over you. You naked, laid out in front of the fireplace as I sink into your warm, pliant body. I should be doing paperwork, but all I can think about is you.

I think he's trying to kill me.

Letting out a frustrated sigh, I throw my head back against the couch and stare up at the ceiling.

I have to leave eventually. I have to get back and find a job. I have to try and forget this ever happened. But if I couldn't forget a night seven months ago when I was drunk, then I sure as fuck know I'll never forget these days with him.

I'm screwed.

And yet, at this moment, I'd happily take the lonely months to come if it meant I got to have these days, and nights, with him.

Chewing on my bottom lip, I look back down at my phone, and contemplate how I should respond. Hmm…

Sheriff Taylor, are you wasting taxpayer's money thinking about me instead of working? I can't say I mind, though. And I'd be lying if I said I didn't want you to. I was relaxing on your couch, drinking my delicious hot chocolate and reading, but then

I read your message... And now all I can think about is you, and you doing any and everything you want to me. It's too bad we both have to wait until six to do anything about it. Oh wait, I'm here alone. So, I guess I can...

Smiling, I pull the blanket tighter around me and sink down into the cushions. I wasn't bluffing when I said that last part.

But just when I'm about to maybe do something about the knot forming in my stomach, my phone vibrates.

Don't you fucking dare touch yourself, Ashley. I want you thinking about nothing but my hands running up your legs, my mouth on you, and my cock filling you until I'm there to do it myself.

Oh my god.

I'll know if you do. He adds. **I want your body so wound up that it's dripping for me when I walk through the door.**

Groaning, I slide down so I'm laid out on the couch, and my hand starts to drift to the waistband of my leggings. But another text interrupts me.

I said no, Ashley.

What the fuck? How did he know?

Poking my head out from the blanket, I look around, thinking he can somehow see me.

Can you see me?

No. I just know. And if you touch yourself before I get home, I'm going to have to punish you.

We'll see, sheriff. I smile to myself. Punish me? What would he do?

You've been warned, sweetheart. But I'll enjoy it either way.

How so?

Imagine my hands on you now, skimming up your calves and thighs, spreading you wide. With one pass of my tongue, I have you whimpering beneath me, the breathy moans coming

from your pouty lips making me harder than I've ever been. Sucking your clit into my mouth, you arch your back, your mouth falling open in a silent scream for more. You always want more.

Ryan...

I don't even know what else to say. I can't believe he's texting me this right now. My phone buzzes in my hand again, and I look down, my face hot. He's not done with this yet.

My thick fingers work in and out of your hot channel. And when I have you on the edge, I stop. Your eyes search mine with a disbelief that'd I'd dare stop what I was doing. But it's my cock I want you coming around, not my fingers. Spreading you even wider, I thrust into you in one swift motion. Over and over, I pound into you, hitting that spot no man but me can even reach inside of you. Your inner walls squeeze me like a vice. So tight, so hot.

Jesus, he's trying to kill me.

I take you to your breaking point, but then slow down, and drag it out. I keep doing it. I torture you, tease you, make you beg for me to stop – make you beg for me to just give you what you want. And when you do, that's when I give you everything. With one final thrust, I grind into your clit and take your nipple deep into my mouth, pinching the other one as hard as I can. You milk my cock for everything it has to give you, and I fill you so completely, it spills out.

Holy fucking shit. I think I'm going to combust just from reading this. My clit is throbbing, and when I rub my thighs together, I can feel how slick I am.

I need him. Right fucking now.

When you're with me, you're mine, Ashley.

His.

I'm his?

I like the idea of that way too much. I'm in this too deep. I have to go home in a few days, and if I start thinking of Ryan as mine, and being his, then that's going to make leaving more painful than it'll probably already be.

All Ryan did was rescue me from potential starvation and hypothermia, and then brought me to his house to stay with him until the storm passes.

But what about after? Am I supposed to pack up and leave? Go back to Dottie's? Go home?

I didn't think this through at all. I can't get my hopes up. I can't start believing that this little arrangement we have going is a real thing.

Glancing back down at my phone, though, my thoughts dissolve as I read his messages again.

I'm fucking fucked.

This man is going to break my heart. I know he is.

But if that's the case, then I might as well enjoy the ride, right? Just like Keats, I'll take the few days of bliss.

Biting my lip, I don't even think about what I want to say, I just start typing. Apparently, I'll be going down with the sinking ship that is my sanity.

What if I told you I was breaking your rule right now, sheriff? What if I told you that it's your fault? I'm flushed, flustered, and so desperately wishing you were here right now to see what your messages are doing to me.

He answers immediately. **What did they do to you, sweetheart? Are you slick between your thighs, and ready for me to just slide right in?**

A little moan escapes my lips as I rub my legs together, trying to hold off.

Yes.

Are you touching yourself yet?

No.

Do it. Take your leggings off right now.

I don't even care how he can guess what I'm wearing right now, I just hook my thumbs in the waistband of my leggings and peel them down my legs.

Okay...

Now, spread your sexy legs wide, and run a finger down your wet folds – feeling what I do to you.

Sighing, I sit up straighter, and throw one leg over the back of the couch, doing exactly as he says – a shudder rocking through my body at the first touch.

Drag it back up and circle your clit for me, rubbing it in tight little circles. Your fingers are my fingers. The little sparks running up your spine and down your legs are because of me.

Moaning, I can barely finish reading his message before I have to close my eyes and give in to his words – pretending he's here.

I peel my eyes open when another message comes.

Tease yourself, sweetheart. Insert your finger halfway, and then take it back out – spread your sweet cream up and around your clit. Press down hard, and then scrape your nail over the tight bud. Feel the shudder ripple through you – that's me.

It's working. I can hear his voice in my head, and I can feel his hands on me, even though I know it's just me.

Circle your entrance – feel the need, feel your muscles clench in anticipation.

How does he know? How can he do this to me through texts? I'm gripping my phone so tightly in my left hand, I wouldn't be surprised if I break it.

Shove two fingers all the way inside of your heat, and curl them towards you.

Sucking in a sharp breath, I bite my lip to keep from groaning too loud. I know no one's here, but it feels like I'm doing something wrong somehow.

Use the heel of your hand to rub yourself as you pump in

and out of your tight, hot, little channel. I know your shaking, but keep going. Add a third finger – mine are bigger than yours.

Oh my god. Groaning long ang low, my legs start to shake, but I do as he says. I need to.

Harder. Faster. Rub your clit. Feel me, Ashley.

Fuck.

I drop my phone on the floor, but I don't need it anymore. Closing my eyes, I snake my hand under my sweater and pull my bra down, pinching my nipple, rolling it between my thumb and forefinger.

My breathing is coming rapid. I'm so close, I can feel it.

Curling into myself, I grind against my hand. Rubbing the heel of my palm against my tight bundle of nerves, I pinch my nipple as hard as I can. Shaking, my body can't take anymore, and it hits me like a freight train.

I let go, giving into wave after wave as they wash over me, and through me.

I've never had it like that with myself before. So intense, so sensual.

Ryan just took something that is usually my own private thing, and made it his. He found a way to control me even when he's not here. This power he has over me, and my body, scares me more than I'd like to think about right now.

I rock my hips, creating little shocks that set me off again, and my core clenches around my fingers – pretending they're Ryan's.

Exhausted, I sink into the cushions and sigh, my head falling back against the armrest.

Breathing in and out, I keep my eyes closed, slowly starting to drift off in a post orgasmic haze. But a faint buzzing noise makes me turn my head, and I look down at my phone on the floor. Ryan's calling me.

Reaching for it, I suddenly feel nervous and shy about what I–or we–just did. Chewing on my bottom lip, I swipe to answer and hold it to my ear, afraid to speak.

"Ashley." His deep, gravelly voice comes through the phone and I close my eyes, loving the way it vibrates through me. "Did you do everything I said?"

Nodding, I realize he can't see me, so I open my mouth, but no words will form.

"I'll take that as a yes," he rasps, and I rub a circle around my clit again, sighing as I feel another shockwave run down my legs. "Are you still touching yourself, sweetheart?"

"Mmhmm," I hum, still not able to form words.

"Fuck," he growls, his restraint stretched thin. "I'll be home at six. Be naked, and be ready for your punishment."

Before I can even answer, or process what he said, he hangs up, leaving me staring at my phone.

My punishment?

Oh.

My foggy post-orgasm brain starts to clear, and I realize I just played right into his game. And I lost.

Damn it.

Well, at least if I'm going to lose, then I lose while in utter, and complete, bliss.

CHAPTER 15

I spend the rest of the afternoon nervous and bouncing around. Every sound I hear makes me jump, and every silent moment makes me think too much.

The hours tick by like snails trying to cross the sidewalk–slow and strenuous.

I try and read, and I try to sleep to pass the time, but neither works. When I take to pacing around his house, I all but drive myself to the point of insanity. Frustrated, I take the stairs two at a time and head into my room. I strip my clothes and grab the towel I used yesterday, and a razor from my bag, before heading down the hall to the bathroom. I don't care if the water is like ice, I need to shock my body out of this crazed state I'm in.

I turn the water on and stick my hand under the spray, a stream of curse words flying out of my mouth. It's fucking cold!

"Suck it up, Ash. Just do it," I tell myself. Rolling my shoulders back a few times, I bounce from foot to foot to get my blood flowing, trying to work up the nerve.

Tightening the bun on my head so it doesn't fall loose, I pull the curtain back and step over the tub into the shower, screaming when the water hits my skin. It feels like a thousand needles stabbing me from every angle, and over my entire body. What the fuck was I thinking?!

Sucking in breaths of air, my lungs constrict, but I force the air through anyway. My hands shake, but I shave my legs as fast as I can, and miraculously don't nick myself in the process.

With convulsions taking over my body, I reach for the rose body wash I left in here yesterday, and drop it–my hands numb.

Shit.

I bend and pick it up, forcing my fingers around the bottle, just hoping they don't snap like twigs. The icy water pelts my back and I have no idea how I'm even doing this right now. It feels like my body is slowly shutting down as the seconds pass–going numb until I won't be able to move.

Lathering my body in the soothing scent of roses, I rinse off as quickly as I can, and then shut the water off so fast I'm surprised I don't break the nob. I'm shaking so badly, it takes everything in me to lift my leg up and over the tub without falling.

I wrap my towel around me, and take slow and deliberate steps back to my room. I can barely feel my limbs. This probably wasn't the best of ideas, but it worked nonetheless. I'm not jumpy, nervous, or pacing around like a crazy person anymore. That's mostly due to the fact that I'm a human popsicle and can't think or do anything. But still, it worked.

I'm just thankful I didn't wash my hair, or I'd be even worse off. It'd probably freeze and break off like an icicle. I already learned that lesson when I was little and went outside in the winter with wet hair. It froze, and then just snapped off when I tried to put it up in a ponytail. I didn't care back then, but I sure as hell don't need that shit now.

Pulling my hair from its bun, I'm hoping it'll help warm my neck and back. Shivering, I grab my phone and rip the towel off of me, and dive under the covers. I still have an hour before Ryan gets home, and I want to make sure I'm ready for him, and my punishment. Which, I won't lie, excites me more than it makes me nervous. I know he'd never hurt me.

My phone is only on 25%, and I want to save some of my battery, but I see a bunch of missed texts from the group chat. Of course, they all want to know how it's going and if I'm having fun with my sexy sheriff.

Hey! My phone is dying, but I'm here to report that I'm still alive, it's still snowing, the power is out, and uhh... What was that last thing I wanted to say? Oh, right. I'm having mind blowing sex with the sexy sheriff...

Smiling, I send out the text and laugh at how quickly the responses come back.

So, are you leaving us for Maine now too, bitch?! Ellie asks.

What??!! No!! I'm just here having fun.

You sure?

Yes, bitch. I came here to clear my head, and I happened to find a man who has been helping me do just that. Well, he's cleared it of my job problems, but has muddled up everything else.

But it's the same man you've been hung up on for months...and didn't tell us. When was the last time a man did that?

Never. But I don't need to tell them that. They already know.

Why are you so hung up on me not telling you?

Mel takes the reigns on answering that question. **Because that means something, Ashley. You're always telling us your dating horror stories and the shit you deal with in bed. But you kept this from us...**

They don't fucking get it. I didn't want to share him with them. I didn't want him to be just another dating story. I wanted to keep him as a night just for me. I wanted to have it to pull out and think about–a secret all my own.

I'll answer for you. She continues. **He's different than the others, and that scares you.**

Stop analyzing me, Mel. I'm not one of your patients. I'm not some puzzle for you to solve. And I'm not in the mood for a lecture. My phone's dying, so I'll just talk to you guys whenever.

Turning my phone off, I toss it on the nightstand and roll over, burying my face in the pillows.

I've never talked back to my friends like that before. Sure, I can be bitch, and I speak my mind, but I'm never rude. Mel is a great nurse, and I just threw that in her face. But she's the friend in our group that is too perceptive at the worst of times. When I don't want advice, and I don't want a lecture, that's when I get one.

But I can't deal with this shit now. I don't want to.

I just want to pretend this little bubble I'm living in will last longer than it's destined to. The snow will stop, the power will return, the roads will clear, and I'll have to move on.

The bubble will burst, I know it will. But I'm not ready to deal with the aftermath of it just yet.

I want to have the best sex of my life with the sexiest man alive for as long as I can. That's not too much to ask, is it?

It is, though. Because those little fuckers called feelings come creeping into your heart when you know you can't have the happily ever after they dream of. They have a life of their own. No matter how much you tamp them down, they'll just bubble up through the cracks you tried so hard to keep covered.

I'm not letting them ruin this, though.

Feelings can just go fuck themselves, because that's all I'm trying to get out of this deal.

Squeezing my eyes shut, I try and push everything down, and lock up my heart. I don't need any more drama or complications in my life right now. I need to focus on me.

Pulling the comforter tighter around me, I start with trying to focus on relaxing my body and getting warm.

****

The rush of cold air against my skin jerks me awake and my eyes fly open.

Shit, I fell asleep. Rolling over, I'm met with Sheriff Ryan Taylor, clad head to toe in his uniform. God, this man kills me with how fucking sexy he looks. So official and powerful.

"Good, you're naked," his deep voice praises as his eyes take in every inch of my exposed body. "On your back," he commands, but I just stare at him. "Now," he snarls when I don't do it right away.

Seeing the hard set of his jaw and steely gaze, I roll onto my back, but turn my head to keep my eyes on him.

Ryan pulls the cuffs from his duty belt, the sound of the metal clinking like a siren call to my body. My breath hitches, and my heart starts to race out of my chest like it wants to run right towards the man next to me.

Placing one knee on the bed, Ryan grabs my right arm and raises it above my head. I watch his jaw tick as he focuses on me – just me. The cold metal snaps around my wrist, sending a zap of excitement and anticipation through me.

Grabbing my left arm, he brings it up to meet the other against the bedframe, and threads the cuff through one of the bars before shackling my other wrist.

The gentle skim of his fingers down my arms makes me squirm and pull at the cuffs, feeling their bite.

"The more you struggle, the tighter they'll feel," he muses, continuing to caress my skin as if I were something precious and fragile. But I'm neither of those things, especially not right now.

I want his rough touch. I want him to be in complete control. I want him to worship me to the point where he comes completely unhinged and animalistic.

I don't just want that, I need that.

Stepping back, Ryan admires his work – my body stretched out on the bed, my breasts heaving with every breath I take, and my legs rubbing together, trying to relieve the pressure.

I've never felt so exposed. It's as if he's memorizing every inch of my body and locking it away in his mind forever.

With slow, deliberate steps, he walks around to the end of the bed, and brushes his fingers over my ankle and around to the underside of my arch. Jerking away from his touch, he catches my foot, and then grabs the other one before I can pull away.

I can't move my arms, or my legs, now.

Opening my mouth, I try and say something, anything, but the words die on my tongue as Ryan climbs on the bed and pulls my legs apart – the cold air hitting my core, causing a fresh wave of need to come to the surface.

With a devilish smirk, he runs his hands up my legs, and I feel everything. His touch is filled with all the possibilities of what could be, but never will. And if I can have this, just this, then I'll take it and keep it forever. Because the look in his eyes right now has me wishing I could have all of him, but I know I never will.

This is a fantasy. It's just two people escaping into each other.

"Stay like that. Don't move." The roughness of his voice washes over me, and I close my legs, wishing that's where he was. "I said don't move." Gripping my ankles, he pulls my legs apart again, and stares down at me with a look of power, control, and lust in his eyes. Swirling together, his blue eyes mimic the stormy seas in the paintings he has hanging in his room, and I'm lost at sea.

This man has me captivated, and if he were to drag me under the waves with him, I'd welcome the black seas like I welcome my next breath – without question or hesitation.

Releasing my ankles, he stands at his full height of 6'3" – towering over me as he starts to undress.

Slowly, Ryan undoes the buttons of his shirt, letting me savor the moment as long as I can. He knows I love seeing him like this. I practically eat him alive with my eyes every time I see him in his uniform.

A grunt of disappointment escapes my lips when he pulls his shirt off and all I'm greeted with is a white t-shirt.

Smirking, he reaches behind his neck and pulls it off in one swift motion – in that way only a man can make sexy.

My eyes are glued to his body, watching his muscles flex with his movements. I wish I wasn't restrained so I could rake my nails down his chest and abs – feeling him, marking him, watching him shudder under my touch.

All I can do is watch, though. I watch him slip the braided leather of his duty belt free, and remove the whole thing from around his hips. Placing it on the floor, I watch him undo the belt and button on his pants, the sound of the zipper opening making my insides clench.

Bending, Ryan unlaces his boots and kicks them off, taking his socks with them. Shoving his pants and boxers down, he straightens, and I'm met with the most glorious piece of equipment he carries besides his gun.

Stroking himself from base to tip, a low moan escapes me as his thumb rubs a circle around his crown, spreading the beads of white that escape. My mouth waters, and my tongue darts out, sliding it across my bottom lip before biting it. I wish I could taste him.

"You got yourself off today, didn't you?" he asks, his voice husky and strained. I nod once, and his eyes seem to darken and swirl even more. "Did you pretend it was me? Did you wish it were me here to do it? Or did you like reading my words, reading everything I would do to you?"

"Yes," I whisper, answering all of his questions.

"But I did tell you you'd be punished for touching yourself before I got home. So now you can't touch me. You have to take everything I give you, and every time you pull on your restraints, you'll just be met with the harsh bite of the cuffs."

Pinching my eyes closed, I tilt my head back into the pillows and pull on my restraints, the cold metal resisting me. Damn it! This is either going to be fucking torture, or the best sex of my life. Either way, I just need him to relieve the knot I've had in my stomach since I woke up without him next to me.

"Keep your eyes on me, sweetheart." He smiles wickedly, teasing me. "I want you to see what you can't touch."

Fuck. Me.

Stroking his length, Ryan puts one knee on the bed and grabs my ankles again, bending my legs up and apart as he crawls over me. Leaning forward, he runs his hands up my thighs, hips, and ribcage before gripping my breasts. With rough, hard squeezes, he pushes them up towards my chin, and then rubs my nipples between his thumbs and forefingers.

I moan loudly and grip the bars tightly, the sound of the metal cuffs against the metal bars filling my ears. His tongue sears my skin with its heat as he circles my right nipple, taking it deep into his mouth, feeling the pull all the way to my core.

He trails hot kisses down my torso, across my hips, and lingers right in the middle. Frustrated that he stopped, I look down at him with a hardened stare.

"Sorry, sweetheart, did you want me to keep going?"

"Yes," I hiss out between clenched teeth. He can't fucking be serious.

Smirking, he lowers his head again, and licks the creases between my legs and the apex of my thighs – so close, and yet so far from where I need him.

He bites my inner thigh and I groan, trying to pull myself away from him, but he just holds my legs down harder.

Ryan runs his palms down my inner thighs and then around to grip my ass, lifting my hips off the bed as he settles between my legs. I feel him there, so close, just a little push and he'll be inside.

"All I thought about today was you, in my house, touching yourself. Coming because of me." He slips the tip past my soaking wet folds, and I moan. "I couldn't wait to leave. I couldn't wait to touch you." He pushes in a fraction of an inch. "Kiss you." A little more. "Be inside of you." He slams all the way in, and I scream out – feeling him stretch me, fill me.

He slams into me relentlessly, breaking me open to make room for him.

My nails dig into my palms as I pull against the bars so hard, it feels like I could either bend the metal bedframe, or break my wrists. Whichever gets me closer to touching him, I don't care.

His heated gaze is all over me – my swaying breasts, my flushed skin, my teeth pressing into my bottom lip, and my glazed over eyes. His jaw is set, and his eyes are focused, as he takes what he wants from me.

I've never felt so out of control, and yet still so powerful.

His rough grip on my hips tightens as he pounds into me. And knowing that he'll leave marks only makes me more eager. My inner walls start to flutter around him, and I know I won't last much longer.

"Ry–"

"Now," he growls, cutting me off. His deep, ruff voice sends me over the edge. I'm dragged under the water of the raging storm he's created, and I never want to surface.

A spark runs down my spine, electrocuting me, and numbing me, as my body is splintered into a million little pieces.

My head thrashes from side to side, as the blood rushes through me, making my ears deaf to my screams.

White dots blur my vision, and then it all goes dark.

I feel everything and nothing in this space between consciousness and the deep abyss.

Ryan's gentle hands massage my arms before unlocking the cuffs and placing them around his neck. Rolling us, I land half on top of him, and he smooths his hand down my hair, curling the ends around his finger.

Humming my approval, I rub my cheek against his chest, my

nails lightly scratching the base of his neck.

CHAPTER 16

Blinking my eyes open, the room is dark, and the solid body beneath me is no longer there. I spread my fingers out under the blanket, but all I come up with is cool sheets, letting me know he's been gone for a while.

Sitting up, I slip out of bed and pick up the oversized sweater I was wearing from the floor, and slip it on over my head. I pad down the hall to use the bathroom, and while I'm washing my hands, I finally catch a glimpse of myself in the mirror.

"Holy shit," I breathe out. My hair is a wild mess and my skin is blotchy.

Throwing it back up into a messy bun, I turn my neck from side to side, seeing that the bruises from Rick the Dick are fading away nicely. A twinge in my side has me picking up my sweater, and I smile at the little circles forming on my hips. I'll take Ryan's passion marking my skin any day.

Wait.

Fuck. Shit. Balls.

Dropping the hem of my sweater, it hits me.

We didn't use a condom.

Shit! I'm never that irresponsible.

How dare he! He never even asked me if it was okay to do that. He didn't know if I was on the pill or not. Luckily, I am, but still.

Shaking my head, I splash cold water on my face and brush my teeth. I don't know where he went, but I plan on finding out.

Taking the few steps down the hall to his door, I see it's already opened a crack, so I push it just far enough to poke my head inside. The moonlight streaming in through his open curtains shows an empty bed, but his uniform is folded neatly on the chair in the corner.

Pulling the door closed to how it was, I walk softly back down the hall and descend the stairs as quietly as I can. I don't know why I feel like I have to be so stealthy, but it feels different walking around his house knowing he's here somewhere.

I check the living room and kitchen, but both are dark and empty. That only leaves one room, and the one I refused to snoop around in while he was gone. It felt wrong to invade his office.

I see a sliver of light coming from beneath the closed French doors, and so I knock lightly.

"Yes?"

"Can I come in?" I ask tentatively, nervous.

"Sure," he says.

Opening the door, I take a step inside, and find Ryan behind a desk stacked with piles of papers and folders. He's sitting in a big leather chair, typing away at a computer, looking disheveled in an impossibly sexy way.

He looks up at me with tired eyes. "You're awake," he says simply.

"Stating the obvious." I smile, but see that he has an almost confused look on his face, so I try again. "Yes, I woke up and you weren't there."

"So, you came looking for me?" he asks, a hint of disbelief in his voice – almost accusatory.

"No, I was thirsty. I came down for water, and saw the light coming from beneath the door." A lie, but he doesn't need to know that.

"Oh, sorry." He rubs his forehead and then scrubs his hands down his face.

"It's fine."

"No, it's not. I sounded like an ass. I'm just tired."

"Are you working? It's like"–I look around until I find a clock on the wall–"three in the morning."

"I know. I couldn't sleep, so I came down to do a few things I should have done yesterday."

"Sorry." I smile, feeling my cheeks heat, knowing it was me who kept him distracted.

With a light laugh, he shakes his head. "Don't apologize. I didn't mind. Trust me."

"Okay." I nod, letting my eyes wander around his office. It's both manly and cozy. Bookshelves take up the wall behind him, filled with books on law, crime, justice, police handbooks, and everything in between. A vast change from the classics he has in the living room.

To the right are windows that look out to the front yard, and beneath are four filing cabinets, all stocked with important sheriff's business I'm sure.

To the left, a huge safe takes up a big portion of the wall, and my brows draw together in confusion. "You have a safe?"

"It's a gun safe."

My eyes flash back to his, rounded in surprise. "Oh."

"Yeah." He smiles, pushing back his chair and standing. "Want to see?"

"Uh, okay?" I've never seen a gun in person. I'm not opposed per se, I've just never come in contact with one before.

Walking over, Ryan turns the dials on the lock until it clicks.

When he pulls it open, my jaw drops. There's, like, eight guns in there.

"Um, why do you need so many?"

"I don't." He shrugs. "I just like having options."

"For what?" I ask taking a step back.

Laughing, he pulls out one of the big ones. "Here," he says, holding it out towards me.

"What?"

"It's not loaded."

"Oh, okay." Reaching out, I take it from his outstretched hand, and grip it tight. Lifting it up, I study it closely, feeling its weight in my hands.

"That's a Weatherby Vanguard Series 2."

"I was going to guess that, actually," I tell him, smiling.

"Sure, of course." He laughs lightly. "It's my favorite for hunting."

"You hunt?" I ask, my face showing my distain.

"Yes, I'm from Maine. I hunt."

"Please don't tell me you have a freezer full of venison and moose. Because I refuse to eat that."

"No, you're safe. I don't enter the moose hunting lottery, and I donate the venison."

"Donate it?"

"Yeah, when my brothers and I go hunting, we harvest the meat and then donate it to the local shelters. That's what a lot of folks do who have excess."

"Oh, that's really nice of you."

"Don't sound so shocked." He jokes.

"I'm not." I smile. "I just don't know anything about hunting, fishing, or camping. It's not really my thing."

"Well, I will say that I think you'd look sexy in camo holding a gun. And naked under the stars. And on a boat with a rod in hand while the wind blows your curls around your face."

"I think I can rock some camo. And I'm sure I'd look just as good naked under the stars as you, as well as holding your rod on a boat." I wink. "But I don't touch fish. You'd have to do that part."

His lips twitch, suppressing a smile. "No problem, sweetheart."

Facing away from him, I hold the rifle up and look through the scope. "I've always wanted to shoot a gun."

"I can take you to a range. Then you can try out a few different ones."

I smile at him over my shoulder. "Sounds fun."

We both know I won't be here long enough for that, but it's nice that he even offered.

I hand him back his gun and he puts it back in place with the others while I walk across the room to the windows. Peeking through the slats in the blinds, I gasp at what I see. "Ryan, holy shit! How much has it snowed?"

Sighing, he rubs the back of his head. "A few feet. I think three by now."

"But… How… Will it stop?"

"It's supposed to tomorrow. Don't worry, Ash, I'm keeping you safe, aren't I?" He asks, coming up behind me and wrapping his arms around my waist.

"Yes," I whisper, leaning my head back against his chest. "I am a little hungry, though. I didn't eat any dinner."

"I wonder why," he muses, kissing me behind the ear, hearing the smile in his voice. "Let's go see what I have and I'll make you something."

"Okay, but I have to talk to you about something." I'm not sure how to bring this up, but I have to. "Last night, uh, we didn't use–"

"I know, and I'm sorry. When I realized, it was too late. I've been up thinking about it for a while now."

"That's why you're down here?"

"Yeah. Ash, are you…?" He squeezes me a little tighter.

"Yeah, I'm good. I'm covered. But still."

"It won't happen again. Sorry," he murmurs, kissing my hair.

"No, now wait, I didn't say that. I just meant all you had to do was ask. I don't know where you've been."

He laughs into my neck. "What?"

"You heard me, sheriff."

"I've been inside you, sweetheart." His low voice sends chills through me. "And that's it. I've never been bare with a woman before, but I couldn't fucking help myself with you. One second in your tight, wet heat, and I was gone."

Jesus fucking Christ. My knees buckle, and Ryan catches me – tightening his hold around my waist.

Spinning me around, he captures my lips with his in a quick, bruising kiss.

"Now, let me feed you," he says against my lips, and I have no words. With a slight nod of my head, he steals another kiss and grabs my hand.

Leading us out of his office and into the kitchen, Ryan lifts me up and onto the island and searches the cabinets. "I can make you soup? Chicken noodle?"

"Sounds perfect," I tell him, my stomach growling at the thought.

Leaning back on my hands, I watch him open two cans of soup and pour them into a pot on the stove. Everything he does captivates my attention, no matter how dull the task – like stirring soup.

"Tell me something," he says all of a sudden, looking over at me.

"Like what?"

"I don't know." He shrugs. "Tell me something no one else knows about you."

"A secret?"

"Yeah." He nods.

A secret. "Okay, well… I never told anyone about us. About that night."

"You didn't?"

"No, I didn't." Looking down, I play with the hem of my sweater, rubbing the soft material between my fingers.

"Why not?"

"Did you?"

"No"–he shakes his head–"I didn't."

"Why not?"

"I asked you first."

"I, um, just didn't want it to become some funny joke to my friends. Because it wasn't that for me."

"What was it for you?" he asks, his eyes serious and penetrating.

I can't answer that question. I can't tell him that it was too much for me, and I thought about him every day since. That's not what this is. That's not what we are.

"It was more," I confess softly, hoping he doesn't press me further.

Watching me, Ryan searches my eyes. He abandons the soup and takes the few steps towards me, closing the distance. Standing between my legs, he runs a finger down and across my jaw, leaning forward and kissing me softly – sweetly.

My heart kicks up, and in the silence, I know he can hear it.

Kissing me again, he steps back and resumes stirring the soup at the stove. What am I supposed to do with that? Was it more for him too?

Clearing my throat, I play with the hem of my sweater again. "Your turn. Tell me something no one knows."

He takes a minute before answering. "I didn't want to be sheriff."

"Really?" I ask, surprised.

"Yeah." He nods. "I didn't want to give up patrol. I loved being out with the people and helping them directly."

"Don't you still do that?"

"No. I mostly do paperwork and oversee the deputies. I don't get to get out there and get my hands dirty as much as I'd like. I mean, some days I do. I can't sit behind a desk day in and out. I'm not built that way."

"Then why did you run for sheriff? Didn't you have to be

elected?"

"Yes, but I was pushed into it by my family and the people of Pine Cove. When the position opened, my dad suggested it, and then all of a sudden, the whole town was stopping me in the streets to tell me to run and that they didn't know a single person who wouldn't vote for me. I saw it as an opportunity to finally be something greater in the eyes of my family, I guess. So, I ran, and I won."

"You're a hero in their eyes. You make a difference, Ryan."

"I still wish I could do more for the people. Face-to-face. But I love being sheriff more than I ever thought I would."

"Don't sell yourself short. You take care of the people of this town. You're important. You keep them safe. You matter. And, in my eyes, your family doesn't even compare to you."

"Now I know you're just being nice." He smirks. "Chris is a doctor in the military, and Tyler is a fireman. I mean, I guess I've got Jake beat." He smiles. "He just builds boats. But then again, he was in the Navy before."

"You all have your place in this world, and you all make a difference in the lives of those around you. You're lucky you have a family, Ryan. Not everyone is that blessed."

"I know," he says softly, mulling my words over in his head. Turning off the stove, he pours the soup into two bowls. "Grab two spoons and that sleeve of crackers there, would you?"

"Sure." Hopping down form the island, I gather the items, and then follow him out into the living room.

Taking a seat on the couch, I cross my legs, and place the blanket from behind me over my lap.

Handing me a bowl, I smile my thanks, and he goes to start a fire. Sitting next to me, his knee touches mine, and I feel the connection flowing between us with just that simple touch.

"You meant that?" He asks, looking into the fire instead of at me. "What you said before?"

"Yes," I say honestly. "I think you're amazing, Ry. And being sheriff was obviously what you were meant to be, even if it didn't start out that way. That doesn't matter."

"You think I'm amazing?" He smirks, his eyes darting to mine as he eats a spoonful of soup.

"Yes. Professionally. Don't get a big head about it."

"I could give you some big—"

"Don't finish that sentence, sheriff." I laugh, knowing where he was going.

"How do you know what I was going to say?"

"Because you have a one-track mind."

"That's not true. I saw an opening, so I thought I'd take it. But since you closed it"—he smiles—"I'll just ask you some more questions."

"Alright."

"What's your biggest fear?"

"Is this a job interview?"

"Yes, Ms. Ames, it is." he says, rolling his eyes. "Just answer. Honestly."

"Fine." Clearing my throat, I think about it for a few seconds, and decide to actually answer truthfully.

"Before he died, my dad made me promise I would never settle. He made me promise I'd wait for what he and my mom had. But then he died. He was gone, and my mom was a shell of the woman she used to be. It's been eight years, and she's still broken. And even though that scares me, I've realized recently that I still want that. So, that's my fear. Never finding that person, or being too stupid to know when I do. And then I'm alone."

Looking into the fire, I take a deep breath. I don't know what possessed me to share that with him. I've never told anyone that before.

"Another thing I've never told anyone before," I whisper, focusing on my soup.

"Ashley," he finally says, and I look over at him, his eyes holding mine captive. "You're smart, beautiful, driven, passionate, fierce, caring, and about a hundred other things I could list. I'm glad your dad made you promise him that, because you deserve the fucking world, not settling for mediocre."

Yeah, I'll find it. Sure. With someone else.

With someone who's not him.

Blinking, I look away from his warm gaze. He's being so nice, and all I can think about is how I wish it were him. But I already know it can never be him. I just need to ingrain that in my head more solidly.

And yet despite telling myself that this is all just temporary, and this is all just fun, I find myself hoping for the exact opposite. Those little fuckers called feelings have now fully creeped into my veins and settled in my heart.

Why? Why? Why?

"Thanks," I say softly, acting like I'm more interested in my soup than him right now.

"Hey." Turning my head back towards him, he searches my eyes.

"I'm fine. I just never talk about this stuff with anyone."

Nodding, he releases my chin, and we both go back to eating our soup in silence.

But when I reach for a cracker, our hands clash, and I pull mine away, clearing my throat. "Tell me your biggest fear."

"I don't have one," he says, biting into a saltine.

"Come on. I told you mine, despite the fact that I never wanted to admit any of that out loud."

Sighing, he scratches his jaw and stares into the fire. "Fine. Dying on the job. I know it's a cowardly thing to say, and I do mostly desk work and shit now, but I still go out there. And anything can happen. I can walk into any situation at any time, and it could be the end."

"Ryan, it doesn't make you weak to admit that. You risk your life every day for others. It's literally your job to put your life ahead of others, and I find that incredibly heroic and selfless. And it doesn't hurt that you look like walking sex in your uniform," I tell him, making him smile, blinding me with his sexiness. "But it's more than that, obviously," I add, making sure he knows I'm serious.

"Obviously." He smirks.

"I couldn't do your job. Not many can. You're brave, even when you don't feel like you are. Remember that."

"I will." He smiles softly, biting into another cracker.

"Good." I nod, and we go back to eating, this time a comfortable silence between us.

I watch the flames dance and crackle in the fireplace as my knee rests against Ryan's. Connected in the most non sexiest of ways, and yet I feel it – the charge between us. Through our freaking knees.

The girl who always has something to say is silenced by the gentle touch of a man's knee…

I'm screwed.

Taking a deep breath, I finish my bowl of soup and place it on the coffee table. I have so many things I want to ask him, that I want to know about him, but the words won't form.

We're already in murky waters, and knowing more about him is only going to muddy the waters further.

"I think I'll go back to bed. Thanks for feeding me," I say, standing. "Sorry for interrupting your work."

"Don't be."

"Alright, goodnight."

"'Night, Ashley."

My heart thuds at the sound of my name from his lips, but I just nod, and head back upstairs. I can't read into this – us. There is no us. There's just me, and there's him. No 'we', and no 'us'.

Crawling back into bed, I curl into the comforter and stare at the wall. I'm just staying with him until the storm passes, and then I'm going back to Dottie's.

Maybe if I keep telling myself this, then it'll finally sink in. This whole 'playing house' thing needs to end before I start thinking of it as long term.

Because it's not.

CHAPTER 17

Morning beautiful,
It stopped snowing. So be ready at 6 sharp - I'm taking you out.
-Ry

I smile, reading the note Ryan left for me on the nightstand. Thank fuck, it stopped snowing!

But... If it stopped snowing, then I'll have to leave, and this is over. The huge smile I just had quickly fades.

I have a date tonight. A date that's not with some random guy I met online, or an asshole I met at a bar. It's with Ryan. The man I want, can have, but can't keep.

Groaning, I throw the covers off and dig my slippers out of my suitcase. With my feet encased in soft fur, I make my way downstairs, and find another thermos of hot chocolate waiting for me like yesterday.

Morning beautiful,
I made you hot chocolate again. Remember – 6 sharp. Stay warm.
-Ry

The thought that he can't wait to take me out makes me smile, and my heart beats a little faster.

Grabbing the thermos, I take a sip of the hot, sweet liquid, and it's like my insides are swimming in a pool of delicious tranquility. It's so fucking good. He has to just melt a bar of chocolate with milk, because this sure as hell isn't Swiss Miss.

Closing my eyes, I savor the taste. This man could seduce me with hot chocolate alone.

Grabbing an apple from the bowl on the counter, I bring it, and my thermos of heaven, into the living room. Taking the same spot on the couch as yesterday, I pick up the copy of Jane Eyre I left on the table, and open to where I left off. I was distracted by Ryan's sexy little texts yesterday, but since I turned my phone off, there will be none of that today.

It's just me and good old Jane.

I've read this book twice, and both times, it left me feeling a different way. In high school, I loved it, and I thought it was such a great love story. Rochester didn't care that Jane wasn't the most beautiful woman, he fell for her because she's smart and challenges him.

But then I had to read it again in college, and my professor ruined that rose-tinted view I had on Jane and Rochester. He pointed out that she settled for a life with him. Rochester kept Jane in the shadows of his secrets the entire time she was working for him. It was only when those secrets were literally destroyed, and dead, that she was able to return and accept his love.

She was able to take back the power in the relationship, but in doing so, she also gave up what she always wanted and worked hard for – a career.

And as I sit here reading it for the third time, my opinions are swirling together. I see the love as well as the lies and manipulation. It's almost like you can't have one without the other. Which is pretty fucked up, but necessary for this story.

Does it have to be like that in real life, though? Do there have to be lies and secrecy separating people before they can be together?

The fact that this book is still relevant 172 years later is amazing. Imagine that? A novel about a woman being admired for her wit and honesty over her looks, as well as navigating through the muddy waters of a relationship with a prominent man who thinks he can deceive a woman into loving him, still being relevant…

HA. Just kidding, that will always be relevant.

Closing the book, I stare off at nothing in particular. Maybe I shouldn't read such a thought-provoking book right now. I'm already in a state of utter confusion and am walking dangerously close to the line, where if crossed, there would be no returning.

Standing, I walk over to the bookshelf and put Jane Eyre back where she belongs. Maybe next time I decide to read her, I won't be such a fucking mess in the head.

My fingers brush along the spines of the beautiful books until I come across a little one tucked between two larger ones. Huh. Pulling it out, a slow smile forms as I read the name on the cover.

It would seem that Sheriff Taylor has a thing for love poetry. Specifically, Pablo Neruda poetry. This man just keeps surprising me. And everything I learn, I like.

Damn it!

But I love Pablo Neruda. So I take it with me over to the windows, and look out at the snow that blankets everything in over three feet of blinding white beauty. The bare trees are shadowed with snow on their branches, while the tall pine trees are bending under the weight of it. It's all so picture perfect, like the inside of a snow globe after shaking it, and the glitter settles over the scene.

There's no one walking around, and there's no cars on the road—there's nothing. Everyone is safe in their houses with fireplaces, candles, books, and maybe a loved one to pass the time with.

A snow storm like this forces us to stop and step back. To live simply. No better excuse to do nothing when you physically can't leave the house.

Walking back to the couch, I snuggle up with a blanket and open to a random page in Neruda's *Love Poems* book.

> But
> if each day,
> each hour,
> you feel that you are destined for me
> with implacable sweetness,
> if each day a flower
> climbs up to your lips to seek me,
> ah my love, ah my own,
> in me all that fire is repeated,
> in me nothing is extinguished or forgotten,
> my love feeds on your love, beloved,
> and as long as you live it will be in your arms
> without leaving mine.

Reading from the middle of "If You Forget Me," I'm struck by how it hits me. Hard.

If it were true, then what I feel for Ryan is reflected in him as well. Our fires would burn together.

I don't know how he feels, though.

He touches me like I'm his, and kisses me like he craves the taste of my lips.

Our fires might burn for one another, but maybe we're just too consumed by the now to see past the flames.

I let the pages slip through my fingers and look down at the page they landed on – the beginning of "Night on the Island".

All night I have slept with you
next to the sea, on the island.
Wild and sweet you were between pleasure and sleep,
between fire and water.

Resting my head back, I close my eyes and toss the book to the other side of the couch. I definitely shouldn't have picked up Pablo Neruda either.

All I can think of is Ryan and I laying together after he's taken me, and in that dream-like state afterwards, feeling connected to him in a way that doesn't compare to anything else – between fire and water.

Keeping my eyes closed, I hunker down into the cushions and wrap the blanket tight around my shoulders, letting myself drift off to sleep with thoughts of Ryan and me – together, burning, loving, being.

****

With a deep breath in, my eyes open to a brightly lit room. Squinting, I blink rapidly to adjust to the assaulting light. Why is it so freaking bright in here?

I scan the room, and then realize where the light is coming from. I sit up so fast my head spins, but I don't care. The electricity is back! The lamps that were on when the power went out shine like beacons of both freedom and the end.

The freedom to shower with hot water, charge my phone, watch TV, drink coffee, and eat food. But it also marks the end of this whole arrangement. I don't have a reason to stay.

Well, I have every reason to want to stay, but no reason that forces me to.

Yawning, I make my way upstairs and into my room. A few seconds after plugging my phone in and turning it on, a flood of messages blows up my screen.

Shit. Most are from the group chat, but there are some from Ally before her phone died, and then a couple from my mom.

Sighing, I throw myself on the bed and type out what feels like a blanket answer for all the inquiries in our group chat.

Sorry, guys. The power only just came back on and I plugged my phone in. Thanks for blowing that shit up. Anyway, I'm not really ready to talk about everything, but just know I'm sorry for before. I'm just feeling all mixed up and confused, but I have a date with Ryan tonight. And as excited as I am, I'm nervous.

After pressing send, I call my mom, and she picks up on the third ring. "Hi, honey," her warm voice greets.

"Hey, mom. How are you?"

"I'm concerned about you, Ashley. You haven't answered any of my messages in days. What's wrong?"

"Nothing. I'm fine. A blizzard hit, and the power went out a few days ago, and so my phone was dead."

"Oh my god, Ashley!" She gasps. "Are you alright?"

"Yeah. I've been with Ally and Jake this whole time, so we all survived together." I chuckle, trying to pass off that lie to a woman who used to always know when I was deceiving her.

"Oh, good, good," she sighs, and I can hear the relief in her voice.

"But it stopped this morning, and the power just came back on, so I'll just be a few more days probably. I want to make sure the roads are clear before trying to come home."

"Don't rush, honey. Please, just be safe. Did you call work?"

Oh, shit. I forgot I didn't tell her that I quit. "Yeah, they're fine. It's not like I can magically appear for a shift or anything."

"Just checking."

"I know, sorry. I'm just rethinking a few things, and my job there is one of them."

"You'll find what you need, honey. I know you will."

"Thanks, mom." I don't think she realizes how much I needed

her to say that to me. "I'll call you when I know more."

"Just be safe, and don't take any unnecessary risks." With the slight tremble in her voice, I know she's thinking about my dad. She doesn't want to lose me like she did him. I get it, but living with extreme caution isn't really living.

"Of course not, mom. I'll be good. Love you."

"Love you, too."

Hanging up, I heave a sigh of relief. Talking with her always leaves me feeling a little less like myself. I still feel like I'm walking on eggshells with her, even eight years later. I've seen her slowly coming back to life this past year when I moved back home, but she still has a long way to go. And I know she loves having me living with her, but I won't be there forever.

CHAPTER 18

After enjoying a steaming hot shower for what seems like the first time in weeks, I wrap myself in a soft fluffy towel and open my suitcases on the floor. I need an outfit for my date, but I don't know what to wear. It's not like I packed a bunch of dating clothes for my trip.

Pulling out all of my best options, I lay them on the bed. I don't know where we're going or what we're doing, but considering there's three feet of snow outside, I should probably dress accordingly.

So that obviously means my cute snow boots, for sure. They're white with a fur lining and trim, and pompoms on the laces. I freaking love them!

And with that decided, the rest is obvious. I go with leather leggings, a black long sleeve top, and my white faux fur vest, which I can't help but rub against my face. Oh my god, it's so freaking soft! Maybe Ryan will enjoy petting me.

HA! And I don't just mean my vest.

Smiling, I drop my towel and put on a sexy bra and panty set – a black lace bra with leather trim and a matching black lace thong. I know Ryan will love seeing me like this later.

Sitting at the desk near the window, I look out at the winter wonderland as I do my makeup, and then head into the bathroom to dry my hair. I leave it wild and curly to go with my sensual makeup – a sexy smoky eye, and a bold red lip. I want him mesmerized, and thinking about kissing me all night.

Walking around his house in lingerie makes me feel a little rebellious and naughty. Biting my lip, I grab my phone off the bed and decide to play with Ryan like he did to me.

Hey, sheriff. I'm just wondering... You don't have cameras in your house, do you?

His response is almost immediate. **Why? What're you doing, sweetheart?**

Oh, nothing.

Tell me.

Shaking my head, I smile as I type. **I'm just making sure you can't see me walking around. It would ruin your surprise for later.**

So we're playing this game, then? What if I said I did have cameras?

Then you'd know what I was wearing – or not wearing. You tell me, sheriff.

Are you walking around naked in my house, baby?

Not your baby. And no, I'm not naked – something better, I think.

There's nothing better than you naked in my house. Nothing.

Well, aren't you sweet?

No, I'm not. But I know for a fact that you are. My mouth is

watering just thinking about tasting you right now.

Jesus. I may have to change my panties before even going out tonight. *Sorry, sheriff. That'll have to wait. You said 6 sharp, and I'm expecting a date before you taste the goods.*

Fine. Just know that I'll be thinking about ripping off whatever you have on and licking every inch of your body until you're so dripping wet, I can slip right inside of you.

You could do that now.

Fuck.

Yes, sheriff, but later. You're still on the clock.

Smiling, I toss my phone on the bed and finish getting ready. It's already after five, and I have a feeling he'll be coming home early.

When I'm dressed and ready, I head downstairs to wait for Ryan, but I can't stop pacing. Eyeing Neruda on the couch where I left him earlier, I pick the small book up and place it back where I found it on the shelf – nice and hidden.

Scanning the shelves, I'm about to pull out a random book to read when I hear the door off the kitchen open, and heavy footsteps moving towards me with a hurried purpose.

Smiling, I turn around just as Ryan walks into the living room. "Well hello, sheriff," I say, a little thrill in my voice. "You're early."

Without answering, he stalks forward, his eyes boring holes into mine until he's towering over me – all six foot three inches of solid muscle and authority.

I've never wanted to break the law so badly, so long as it meant Ryan was the one arresting me.

Tilting my chin up, he lowers his mouth to mine in a gentle kiss. It's far from the fevered aggression I was expecting, but it still makes my heart stutter in my chest.

"I'm going to change, and then we'll go."

"Do you have to change?" I smirk, biting my lip.

Laughing lightly, he shakes his head and backs away. "I do."

"Fine," I huff, pretending to be upset about it. Truth is, I want to go out with *just* Ryan, not Sheriff Taylor.

I wait for him on the couch, and he's only gone for five minutes before I hear him come back into the room. Damn, this man can wear anything—or nothing—and I'm melting on the spot.

He changed into dark rinse jeans that show off his powerful thighs, and a white button-down shirt that does nothing to hide the broad chest and muscular arms beneath.

I want to fucking rip it open and see the taught ropes of muscles I was denied touching last night.

"You look so sexy, Ashley." His low, rough, voice courses through me like the waters of the Amazon River – twisting, turning, and carving its own path through my veins.

With a small smile, I reach up and brush my fingers across his cheeks, his five o'clock shadow a perfect contrast against my skin. Pushing up on my toes, I kiss his soft lips with a tentativeness that scares me. I want to go slow. I want to savor every second.

Pulling back, I see the red lipstick I left behind and smile, wiping it with my thumb. "Sorry," I say, his lips turning up beneath my touch. "I'm ready."

"For our date," he says, his eyes dancing.

"Yes." I smile. "For our date."

Grabbing my coat, Ryan holds it up for me, and I turn around, threading my arms through the holes. He shrugs his on as I button mine all the way up and tie the belt at the waist. Wrapping my scarf around my neck, I loop my arm through his, and we walk through the kitchen and out the side door, the cold air hitting me immediately.

"Are you up for walking? It's not far, and because of the snow, there's no parking." He looks down at me with nervous eyes, thinking this might be a deal breaker. But fuck it, I'd walk a mile in the snow as long as it was with him.

Oh, sweet baby Jesus, I can't believe I just thought that.

"I don't mind. I feel like I haven't been outside in a week. But I'll need this then." I pull out my white knit hat from my pocket that has a big white fur pompom on top, and my matching white knit gloves.

Laughing, he takes my arm again when I'm fully bundled up, and we start our trek. He only lives maybe a block off of the end of Main Street, so it shouldn't be too bad.

The quiet surrounds us in a calming, cleansing sort of way. Only the crunching of our boots in the snow keeps us company.

"There's someplace open on Main Street? The power only just came back on."

"Anthony's is open. They had generators to keep their freezers and refrigerators going."

"Oh, good. I'm not trying to get sick," I joke, looking up just in time to see him role his eyes.

"Like I'd take you somewhere we'd get sick. Plus, they wouldn't dare poison their sheriff. I can have them arrested."

"Ooh, look at you, just casually throwing your power around."

"A man's gotta do it sometimes." He shrugs.

"And a woman." I smirk.

"Of course. Women do it every day, though."

"What?"

"You, as a species, have an automatic power over us men. No matter how much we'd like to think we can hold on to you, or boss you around, it's you that decides everything."

"Boss us around? What is this? The 50's?"

"No." He smiles. "But you know what I meant."

"So, are you saying I have some sort of power over you because I'm a woman?"

"Yes," he says simply.

"Hmm," I hum, tapping a gloved finger to my chin. "Is there anything I can do with this power?"

"You can do just about anything, sweetheart. But I know you won't."

"What's that supposed to mean?" I ask, raising my brows.

"Nothing." Looking away, I see his lips moving, muttering

something under his breath, but I can't make it out.

Uh, okay?

"So how was work? Catch any criminals?"

"No. The snow has made people stay quiet for a few days. But it'll start up again."

"What is it you do exactly as sheriff?" I ask, then quickly add, "there's just so many branches–police, troopers, sheriffs–what's the difference?"

"Well, small towns like Pine Cove don't have separate police departments, so we are the police. I deal with courthouse transfers, warrants, arrests, and general patrol. We're everything, really."

"Sounds tiring."

He barks out a short laugh. "It is."

"But you love it." I smile, leaning into him.

"I do. I just wish there wasn't so much paperwork attached."

"Well, you should find a way to reward yourself after doing a certain amount of forms, or whatever your paperwork is. It would help keep things interesting."

"Like what?" he says low, looking down at me, his blue eyes shining. "Can I call you? Maybe do a little phone sex?"

"Ryan!" I yell, hitting his chest. "You can't be serious? Aren't there people in your office? Tape recorders?"

"I didn't hear a no in there."

"Well, no, I guess you didn't." I laugh, the white puffs of my breath a stark contrast against the night.

"So, you'd let me?" His voice is low and hungry.

I'm not a shy person, but talking about this, I feel my cheeks heat under his gaze. "Maybe."

"Alright, then." He beams, his smile blinding me, and I can't look away.

"Don't get too excited there, sheriff."

"Oh, we'll both get excited all right."

"Oh my god." The words are forced from my lips with a laugh. He's got jokes. And I fucking love it.

Turning onto Main Street, I almost slip on a patch of ice, but Ryan grips my arm tightly, holding me up until I'm steady again.

"Thanks," I say, a little breathless.

"I can't let you have a bruised ass, sweetheart. That'd ruin our night."

"Of course that's what you'd think of first. Not my safety."

"Saving your ass is keeping you safe."

"Mhmm. Whatever you say."

Taking his arm out from mine, Ryan stops walking and slips his hand under my coat to grip my ass through my leather leggings, pulling me against him. "It is what I say, sweetheart," he whispers in my ear, a little moan catching in my throat. "Got it?"

Nodding, my eyes dart up to his, and I'm met with the steely gaze I'm sure he uses to get his way at work. And I can guarantee they all do what he says, because it's a look that's causing my insides to simultaneously melt and twist in the most delicious of ways.

He's pulling me in deeper, and I'm starting to realize I've already been sinking into the quicksand, and there's no saving me now.

Another beat passes before he blinks and releases me from his grip. A rush of breath leaving my lungs.

"We're almost there," he says, taking my gloved hand in his as we continue on down the sidewalk, the lights of the shops guiding our way.

This man really throws me off my game. The sassy, quick-witted Ashley everyone–including me–knows, is reduced to a tongue-tied mess when he looks at me like that.

Only a few other people have braved the streets so soon after the storm, and all of them turn and stare at us.

"Uh, Ryan?"

"I know. It's a small town. People stare, people talk. I'm sure the news that the lonely bachelor sheriff was out holding hands with a beautiful woman will be tomorrow's fresh gossip."

"What?" Hell no, I don't want to be town gossip.

"It'll be fine, Ash."

Will it? because I really don't need, or want, the attention.

"Lonely bachelor?"

He looks down at me and winks. "It's what they all think because I'm never seen with women."

Women. He said women. As in plural. As in many.

Not that I thought I was some new revelation to him, but hearing him say it like that... I don't like it.

"So, you keep your hordes of women a secret from the town?"

Throwing his head back, Ryan's deep, throaty laugh fills the air around us. "Yes, Ashley, I do," he tells me, a wicked gleam in his eyes.

Is he joking?

"Are you serious?"

"About having hordes of women?" He smiles playfully. "Or about keeping women a secret from the town?"

"Uh, both?"

"I wouldn't say *hordes*." He laughs. "But I've learned to be careful. I have to keep my reputation clean."

"So, what I'm hearing is that you only date women who would sully your good name? And you have to keep them hidden?" I make sure it sounds like I'm joking, but even I can hear the insecurity in my voice.

"No, that's not what I meant, Ash. I just meant that I have to be a poster boy for the town, for the county, for the state. I don't need a bad breakup to effect my work, or have a woman who doesn't know what it means to be with me causing a scandal."

"And what does it mean to be with you?" I ask, my eyes darting to his face to gauge his reaction.

"I'm a public figure." He shrugs, as if that should be a blanket explanation. "Some women don't like that I'm not always around or available to them. I have duties, responsibilities. And not many understand that. And some might use that to ruin me."

"Wow, your view on women is eye opening. We're not all out to get you. And you do realize that your job attracts some women, right? It doesn't push them away."

"Does it attract you?" Such a simple question, but I feel like it's packed with about a thousand others. If I say yes, does it mean I'm admitting to him more than I'm ready to? Or want to?

"Yes." The word is barely above a whisper, but I force it out of me.

"Good." He nods, a small smile on his lips as he opens the restaurant door for me.

CHAPTER 19

Dinner was amazing. I've never enjoyed sitting and eating with anyone more in my life. Sitting across from Ryan as he told me funny stories about him and his brothers had my cheeks hurting from laughing and smiling.

The ten or so other patrons in Anthony's all came up to Ryan to say hi, and introduce themselves to me. It was friendly, but intrusive. But what else should I expect from a small town?

As we're walking back to his house, it requires a little more focus now that I've had a few glasses of wine. Good thing, though, because I can barely feel the bitter cold against my face now.

A gust of wind blows my hair across my face as snow falls gently from the trees–swirling, twirling, and drifting down like glitter–and I tilt my face up to meet each flake like a gift.

Blinking away the snow from my eyelashes, I focus on the man in front of me. His stare is intense and penetrating, and heats my cheeks despite the cold air.

"What are you looking at?"

"You love the snow, don't you?"

"Yeah." I smile, walking a few steps away from him. Closing my eyes, I lift my arms and spin. "The cold air makes me feel alive, and the snow feels like a gift just for me. When the trees are covered, and everything is blanketed in white, it makes even the ugly look beautiful, and the beautiful even more so."

Two strong arms loop around my waist from behind, and pick me up, pulling me against a rock-solid torso.

"Hey!" I laugh, squealing at the sudden rush of being swept up in the air.

"Hey, what? I couldn't take another second of not holding you. And I agree, you look more beautiful when you're in the snow," he rasps.

"Oh, okay." I smile up at him, stretching my neck back to kiss his chin before he lowers me to the ground. Holding my hand out for Ryan to take, we continue on walking.

I don't know if it's the wine I had, or the magic of the snow, but it feels like nothing but the here and now matters.

All of my fears and doubts can wait until the morning.

Whatever this is between us, I just want to let myself have it. I want to give in to the fact that I'm falling so hard for this man, and not worry about what that means for my heart tomorrow.

I just want tonight.

I feel lighter, somehow.

It's new, but I know what it is. Happiness. I'm happy just to be around him, and even though it's only been a few days, they've been the best days of my life.

I've been free to just be me. Something I haven't been able to do in a very long time.

As we walk up his driveway, I'm only half paying attention to where I'm going, because I miss the huge patch of ice and my feet are suddenly sliding out from under me.

"Whooooa! Ahh!!" I scream, knowing I'm about to fall flat on my ass.

Ryan reaches out to try and steady me, but he just ends up slipping on the same patch. Spinning, we start to fall, and the air rushes out of my lungs as we land in the snow mound next to his truck.

Ryan protects me in the steel cage of his arms, and my face is plastered to his chest.

The cold snow enveloping us starts to seep through my clothes, and I burst out laughing, my whole body shaking against his.

"Something funny, Ashley?"

"N-n-o-o," I manage to stutter through my laughter.

"Really?" he asks, a smile in his voice.

"Mhmm," I hum. "Ah! Ryan!" I scream as he rolls us over, the cold, wet snow slowly numbing my legs.

I open my mouth to say something, but I'm silenced by his wolfish smile before he slams his mouth down on mine. Moaning on impact, I wrap my arms around his neck and pull him as close as I can.

His kisses warm me from the inside out, the heat quickly spreading through my veins – the cold no longer on my mind.

A shudder rocks my body, and Ryan rolls us back over, taking my place in the snow. Licking the seam of my lips, I open for him, and our tongues come together in a slow dance I never want to end.

My god, he's addicting. I don't think I could ever get tired of kissing him.

As the fire in me builds, I rock my hips against his, needing to relieve the pressure building inside of me.

"Ryan," I whisper, moaning against his lips as I feel him harden beneath me.

"Stand up. I need you. Now."

Scrambling to our feet, Ryan all but drags me the rest of the way inside of his house, when my body finally catches up to me. The snow seeped into my clothes, and my body is starting to shake where

I stand.

Sweeping me up into his arms, Ryan carries me upstairs and into his room, placing me down on the edge of his bed.

He rips the hat and gloves from my body and tosses them to the floor. I try and untie the belt on my coat, but my shaking hands make it nearly impossible, so Ryan shoves them out of the way and takes over, a determined look on his face.

I don't do anything but stare at him, watching his eyes laser in on the task – his tongue peeking out from his mouth, and his perfect teeth pressing into the cushion of his bottom lip.

I can't wait to feel his mouth on me, his teeth raking down my neck, and his tongue licking paths of fire on my skin.

When he frees the final button of my coat, Ryan pushes it off of my shoulders and tosses it on top of my hat and gloves.

He makes quick work on my vest, top, and boots, but pauses when he sees me in my bra, his hands gripping the waist of my leather leggings.

With a heated look, he starts to peel them down, and I lean back, lifting myself up so he can get them over my hips. Slowly, he pulls them down, his eyes taking in every inch of my legs that he exposes.

"Fuck," he growls when he frees me of them, looking up at me from his knees.

I give him a sly smile and hold my hand out for him to pull me up. Standing, he drinks me in from head to toe, his eyes molten and his nostrils flared.

"Turn," he commands, and I don't hesitate. "Fuck," he growls again, and a sting flashes across my right ass cheek.

Collapsing forward, my hands reach out to brace myself on the bed, bent over the edge, my ass on full display for him.

"This is what you were walking around in earlier? You just love teasing me, don't you?"

"Yes," I breathe out, my skin hot.

Another flash of sting comes, this time on my left cheek, and I suck in a sharp breath, loving this side of him.

Gripping the thin material of my lace thong in his fist, Ryan rips it from my body, plunging his fingers into me straight away.

"You're fucking drenched," he growls behind me, running his free hand up the length of my back.

Groaning, I arch into his touch, asking for more.

He kisses his way up my spine, and I push back into him, his thick fingers working in and out of me as my breathy moans and sighs fill my ears – my arms threatening to give out on me.

He's inside of me, touching me, kissing me.

I feel him everywhere at once, my body in overdrive.

He knows exactly how to make me forget everything but him. He knows exactly how to make me lose my mind and every semblance of a coherent thought.

All I can think about is feeling.

All I can think about is him.

Pulling his fingers out of me, Ryan grips my waist and flips me over, pushing me onto the bed.

Tearing his clothes off, he keeps his eyes on me, letting me see the hunger and need in them.

It's what I need.

I need him to want me with everything in him. I need him to want me with such an intensity–that if he doesn't have me now–then he'll fucking lose it.

Gripping my thighs, Ryan opens me wide, spreading me so he can enter me in one swift motion – filling me to the point of pain. But a pain that flames into a wild burn for him to take me with every ounce of hunger I see in his eyes.

"Ryan," I moan out. "Don't hold back. Take me. All of me."

His eyes harden, and he tightens his grip on my hips. Pulling out of me slowly, the slow burning drag makes every muscle I have contract, trying to hold him inside.

When he's almost fully out, he thrusts forward, slamming into me. I scream, arching off the bed as I scratch at his comforter trying to grip it, but my nails come up with nothing.

His eyes stay on me, watching my face as he pumps in and out of me – splitting me, filling me, taking me higher and higher until I'm no longer here.

I'm flying, soaring. And when I can't take it anymore, my body shatters, transforming into a thousand birds all taking flight amongst the stars.

Ryan soon joins me, and we both take the night like we own it.

He owns it. He owns me.

CHAPTER 20

I wake up to the slight movement of the bed next to me and warm lips on my forehead.

"Mmm," I hum, my eyes fluttering open to a dimly lit room and Ryan over me, his warm blue eyes shining. "Are you leaving?" I ask groggily.

"Yeah, I have work."

"Do you ever have a day off?"

"Yes." He smiles regretfully. "I was supposed to have today off, but I have to go in. With the storm, we have a lot to do and we're stretched thin."

"Okay," I whisper, bringing the blanket up to my chin. "I'll see you later, though?"

"Of course, sweetheart." He chuckles. "This is my house, remember?"

"Oh, yeah." I smile sleepily. "Sorry."

"It's okay, go back to sleep."

"Mhmm," I hum, closing my eyes again, snuggling deeper into his bed.

The next time my eyes open, the room is brighter, but empty. He hasn't had a day off since I've been here, and I wish he didn't have to work so much, but I know it comes with the territory. And normally I wouldn't mind because I love my alone time, but I'm just here, by myself, in his house. At least if he was here, then we could just stay in bed all day and only leave when we got hungry.

Mmm, his bed feels like a warm hug. I love it way more than the guest bedroom's bed I've been staying in. Come to think of it, this is the first time I've even been in here besides when he gave me a tour that first day.

It seems the bars of the headboard in there are more suitable for his needs since the one in here is leather, and there's nowhere for him to cuff me.

Smiling at that thought, I bite my lip and roll over onto my other side, feeling a throbbing in my core.

He's fucking amazing.

Last night. I have no words. We started out rough and frenzied, not being able to get to the end fast enough. But sometime in the middle of the night, after losing count of how many times he took me, Ryan rolled me onto my back and slipped inside of me.

Slowly, he made me burn for him as he took his time.

His eyes were on mine the entire time, and I felt it – that shift inside of me. My heart squeezed in my chest, and then kicked up double time, racing like a horse in the derby running straight for the finish line.

Ryan is my finish line.

The slow burning fire turned into a 5-alarm blaze as my body ignited, burned, singed, and turned to ash under him.

He's had me since that night last summer. And these days with him have only solidified that fact.

I refuse to believe he didn't feel it too. He had to have.

Flashes of us pop into my head and I groan, covering my head with the blanket.

I'm utterly and completely fucked, in all aspects and meanings of the phrase. I've completely fallen in love with Ryan Taylor.

I can't deal with it, though. And before I can overthink it, I slide out of bed and go and take a shower. The hot water hits my skin, and I try and let it wash away all of my doubts.

I'd like to think Ryan feels the same, but I don't know. I know he likes me, but love? I think I might be the only one crazy enough to fall for someone so fast.

Finishing up, I turn the water off and wrap myself in a fluffy towel. Heading back into my room, I sit on the bed and grab my phone, seeing it blinking with a new message.

Hey, Ash! Want to meet for lunch? You've been holed up with the hot sheriff and I want some time with my bestie.

Yes! I need to leave this house, lol. I've already spent too many days alone here while Ryan's working.

Yay! I'll pick you up at twelve.

Okay. I'm getting dressed now.

Tossing my phone aside, I dig through my suitcase and pull out a pair of leggings–shocker–and a quarter zip sweatshirt.

I throw on thick boot socks and dry my hair before braiding it into one long plait down my back. I apply a light layer of makeup to cover up the fact that I was kept up most of the night by a relentless Ryan – not that I'd ever complain about that.

Padding back into his room in search of my snow boots and jacket, I find all of my clothes draped neatly over his chair to dry, and my coat is hanging from the top of the closet door.

Slipping my feet into my boots, I drape my coat over my arm and grab my phone and purse from my room before heading downstairs, just in time for my phone to buzz with Ally telling me she's outside.

Closing the door behind me, I climb into her car and hug her straight away. "I feel like I haven't seen you in forever! Even though it's been less than a week."

"I know! It feels like the past five days have been stretched into weeks. Not that Jake and I have had any problem filling our time."

"Yeah, me too." I smile, and Ally swerves, barking out a laugh. "Oh my god, focus on the road!" I yell, laughing.

"How's that going by the way?" she asks, pulling herself together.

"Good. Really good, actually. Last night, it was…" I sigh, biting my lip as I think about how different last night was.

"You're falling for him," she states matter-of-factly, glancing over at me. "It's written all over your face."

"You don't know my face."

"We've been best friends since high school, bitch. I know your face."

"Okay, and?"

"And… That's my point. Also, I had to endure all three of you telling me last summer about how I was different, and I was in love – blah, blah, blah. Now I'm doing it to you because Ellie and Mel aren't here."

"Blah, blah, blah? That's how you describe falling in love with Jake?"

"No." She smiles. "But you know what I mean. It's all in the things that you can't explain. All the things unspoken between you. Every look, touch, and kiss. It's all there."

"I know," I whisper, looking out the window as she parks in a spot outside of the café. The plows must have been out early today, because there was nothing here last night.

Ally climbs out of the car, and I follow her. The bells jingle above us as we walk through the café's doors, and I inhale the heavenly scent of fresh coffee.

"Oh my god, I haven't had coffee in daaayyss," I groan, my body practically pulsing with need.

"Ashley!" Courtney screams, coming out from behind the

counter to hug me. "You survived! How have you been? What did you do in the storm? Or should I say who?" She winks.

"What?" I cough out, choking on air.

"I told her." Ally shrugs.

"Who else knows?"

"Practically everyone. People saw you two out last night and rumors started flying because you were seen walking from his house."

"Who saw us? The streets were empty until we got to Main Street and the restaurant."

"Oh, there are eyes everywhere, Ashley. It's a small town."

"Okay, well, I need a coffee. ASAP." Sighing, I walk down the cases of treats and survey my options. Courtney has the absolute BEST pastries. "And a bear claw. And a blueberry glazed donut."

"Oh, so it's a double pastry afternoon I see."

"It is." Courtney hands me my coffee, and I add a little cream and sugar and then take a seat at the empty table in the corner where my back is to the door and no one will see me.

I don't need to draw any attention to myself while I enjoy shoving sugary goodness into my mouth.

Ally takes the seat in front of me with her blueberry crumb cake, and Courtney places my two treats down on the table and takes the seat next to me.

"Thank you."

"No problem. Now, spill. I told you at that barbecue to go after the good sheriff because he needed a little fun in his life. Have you provided that?" Courtney asks, smiling.

"Um, maybe?"

"Come on." She gives me a pointed look.

"Okay," I sigh, rolling my eyes. "I'll tell you that he's freaking amazing, in *every* way. But that's it. That's all I'm saying. I'm still sorting things out in my head."

"Okay, okay," she says, holding her hands up defensively. "Just know that I'm here when you're ready. I like to think that I helped make this happen in some small way." Smiling, she stands and goes back behind the counter.

"Ashley, talk to me," Ally pleas.

"Let me enjoy this bear claw first, then we can talk."

"Fine," she sighs, sipping her coffee.

Biting into the delicious, sugary sweet pastry, I moan softly, savoring the divine perfection.

"You sound like me." Ally laughs, biting into a forkful of her crumb cake, a small moan escaping her lips too. "Jake always makes fun of me for how much I love food. But why shouldn't I? We should always enjoy what we put in our mouths." She smirks. "And not just food."

"Jesus, Jake has you thinking about sex 24/7."

"And Ryan doesn't for you?"

She's not wrong. "Maybe," I admit.

"Those Taylor brothers," she sighs. "They'll turn your life upside down in the most terrific of ways."

"So, you've been with all of them then?"

"What? No. I just meant—"

"I know what you meant." I laugh. "And yeah, he has done that for me – turn my life upside down."

"How?"

"What do you mean how? He just has."

"Oh my god, Ashley!"

"How are you exasperated with me right now?"

"Because I'm just trying to ask you what he does to make you feel like he's different, that he's the one."

"The one? Aren't you getting a little ahead of yourself?"

"I knew with Jake pretty quickly. I may not have been thinking 'the one' right away, but I knew I was falling too fast and too hard for it to be anything other than something serious."

"Well, that's you, not me. And you were living here, I don't. I have to leave eventually, Ally. Most likely in a few days."

"What? Why?"

"I have to find a new job. I have to start all over again."

"Why can't you do that here?"

"Are you serious?"

"Yes, completely. I did it."

"Even if the idea has crossed my mind, which I'm not saying it has, I can't."

"Why not?"

"Ally," I say seriously, making sure she's looking at me. "I like Ryan. A lot. More than a lot. But I can't just decide to stay. He has to ask me. I'm not putting myself on the line like that for him to just crush me."

"How do you know he'd crush you?"

"Because I'm falling for him. Hard. I'm trying to resist, but last night… Last night I gave in. To myself, to how I was feeling, to how much I want him to want me with the same insane, crazy need.

"It's all fucking crazy, Ally. He's just a man. We had sex once, and then I couldn't get him out of my head. I still felt him. Everywhere. All we had was an insane, impulsive, and amazing one-night stand. Actually, it wasn't even a night. It was in the woods… At his parent's house… During a fireworks show. There was no date, no bed, no sleeping, and barely any talking.

"But it stayed with me. The passion, and the way he made me feel utterly insatiable and irresistible. No man has ever done that."

Rubbing my forehead, I stare at my coffee. For all the mornings I've craved it while the power was out, I find myself wishing it were a hot chocolate instead.

I let my wine and snow infused state of mind–that was running high on an amazing date with Ryan–convince me it was okay to let myself give in to a night of believing what we have could be more. I shouldn't have been so weak.

"Ashley. Look at me." Ally's low, soothing voice, forces my eyes to hers. "I get that you're thinking, 'maybe this is all just an intense physical connection and I'm blinded by his hotness'. But ask yourself this. What are the moments like between you two when you're not physical? How does he make you feel then? Does he only make your heart race when he's touching you? Or do you feel it all the time? Do you like just being with him? Around him? Not naked? It's *those* moments that make it all real. Amazing, off the charts, mind blowing sex, is just the cherry on top of an already delicious sundae if you have those other moments. You two, as people, is what makes it all real."

I don't know what to say, so I take a sip of my coffee. "I keep thinking about how this all started because I was drunk and wanted him. And for the past seven months, I've been calling myself crazy for being so attached. But since I've been here… The second I saw him, Ally, it felt like I could breathe again. After months of building him up in my head—to the point of insanity—there he was. And I felt it all over again – that connection. And the more time we've spent together, the more we've talked, and the more we've just been around each other, I've fallen head over ass for that man."

"Well, that's a new way to put it." She smiles. "I like it."

"It fits." I shrug, taking another sip of coffee. "But I don't know what to do. I've never been in love before, Ally, you know that. I don't know what I'm doing."

"No one does, Ash."

"Well, that's helpful," I say sarcastically.

"I didn't know what I was doing at first." She scoffs. "And neither did Jake. Trust me. But we've figured it out together. And I sure as hell don't know how to be a wife. But I'll figure that out too. *With* Jake. Just like you'll figure all of this out *with* Ryan. Relationships are a two-person machine."

"Okay, Dr. Phil."

"Ashley," she says sternly, letting me know she's trying to be serious here.

"Sorry, it's just that I feel like I'm stranded in the middle of the ocean, treading water. I can see land ahead, but I'm not sure if I'll make it. Maybe I'll just be stuck swimming towards something that's not even there – a mirage I created in my delusional brain."

"Wow, okay, that was a powerful metaphor. Now who's Dr. Phil?"

"Ally, come on," I groan, shoving the rest of my bear claw in my mouth. I need the sugar to distract me from the seriousness of this conversation. I'm not used to it. I'm not used to laying it all out there.

I'm the girl who keeps shit bottled up and plasters a smile on my face for the world so no one sees how I'm really feeling. I laugh and joke my way through life because I'm afraid to be real. My mom and dad were real, and it was ripped from them.

But this is real. My life right now is real, and I don't know how to handle it.

"Has he said anything to you? About what happens next? I mean, you're living at his house for Christ's sake."

"Yeah, and I have no idea for how long. I mean, I have to go home at some point. How do I bring that up?"

"You should use that to see what he'll say. With the thought of losing you, he'll realize that you should stay."

"Maybe." Or maybe he'll be relieved.

"No maybes. Men need a push in the right direction or they'll never figure their shit out. They're all the same in that way."

"True. Men are quite dumb."

"Yes, they are," she agrees, and we both finish our pastries.

"But, enough about me, please. Tell me about the wedding. How is the planning going?"

"Oh." She smiles, her whole face lighting up at just the mention of her upcoming nuptials. "I'm having so much fun with it! It's hard, of course, but Jake and I just want a simple, fun wedding to celebrate with our friends and family. Which brings me to my next question. Will you do me the honor of being one of my bridesmaids?"

"Oh my god, yes! Of course!" I squeal, quickly getting up and hugging her. "Now I get to help plan the bachelorette weekend!"

"Uh, nothing too crazy?"

"Uh, yes, bitch! Of course it will be crazy! Do you know your friends at all?"

Laughing, she just shakes her head. "Oh, I do."

"Have you asked Mel and Ellie yet?"

"No, I was waiting to ask all of you in a cute way by mailing you boxes, but since you're here, I couldn't wait. My sisters are my co-maids of honor, and then you three are my bridesmaids."

"So, what color dress am I wearing?"

"Burgundy. A deep merlot."

"Ooo, okay, I can rock that."

"I figured." She laughs, rolling her eyes. "Since it's in the fall, I thought that'd be the perfect color. The details are still being worked out on the tablescapes and flower arrangements, but think dark, woodsy, and romantic, all rolled together. An enchanted forest."

"Oh my god, I can't freaking wait! That sounds amazing, Ally! I'm so happy for you and Jake."

"Thanks," she says, smiling shyly. "He's amazing."

"I'm glad you came here and found him. It was—"

"Fate," she finishes for me.

"Yes. As cheesy as that sounds, it definitely was."

"And my coming here has also brought you something, too."

"I guess. But right now, all it's giving me is a headache."

"Alright, enough boy talk and pouring our hearts out. I need to go buy some new paints, want to come with me?"

"Yes, please give me a distraction. I can't go back to his house yet."

Laughing, we stand and bring Courtney our plates. "Thanks, Courtney. I'll see you soon."

"Yes, you will. Because I need the juicy details!" she yells after us as we're leaving the café.

"Yeah, that's not happening," I tell Ally when we're outside. "She'd have to get me drunk to share that shit." I laugh, wrapping my scarf a little tighter around my neck. The wind biting at me.

"I wouldn't put it past her. Trust me. That's how she got me to tell her my secrets when I first got here. She's crafty, that one."

Dodging snow mounds and patches of ice, Ally and I somehow make it across the street without falling on our asses.

The hardware store is only a few storefronts down, and the second we walk in, an older man behind the counter beams at Ally, his whole face lighting up. His kind blue eyes are framed by the laugh lines of a man who's lived a good life.

"Ally, my dear, how are you?"

"I'm good, Jim, how are you?"

"Oh, good, good. You know, just trying to bounce back after the storm."

"Yeah, it was a rough one. My friend Ashley here actually got stranded out at Dottie's when it hit."

"Oh my, well hello, Ashley. I'm Jim," he greets warmly, sticking his hand out for me to shake. "I hope you stayed safe during the storm."

"Good to meet you Jim. And yes, I did. I wasn't sure I'd make it at first, though." I laugh, hoping I don't have to confess I was rescued by–and taken home with–the town's beloved sheriff.

"A true Mainer can weather any storm. We're built for it."

"Well, then, I guess maybe I can be an honorary Mainer since I made it out the other side unscathed." On the outside at least.

"Of course, young lady. We welcome newcomers here in Pine Cove."

"Thank you. I'll keep that in mind."

"Good." He nods. "Now, Ally, go on and pick out some new colors." He smiles, knowing her all too well.

"I plan to." She smiles. "Oh, and if Jake comes by for his order, don't tell him I'm in here. I'm getting supplies to make him something special and I don't want him to know."

"My lips are sealed."

"Thanks, Jim."

Walking to the back of the store, there's a whole section dedicated to art supplies. "Wow, this is more than I expected," I tell Ally.

"I know," she says. "Jim's wife was an artist, so she had him stock the good stuff for her and her students. She passed away a few years ago."

"That's so sad. He seems like such a nice man."

"He is." She nods, crouching down to look at the tubes of paint on the bottom shelf.

"So why all the secrecy with Jake?" I ask, curious.

"Oh, nothing," she says, waving her hand in the air to dismiss my query.

"Uh, okay." Yeah, I definitely don't want to know then. It's probably some weird sex thing, and I don't need those images in my head.

Leaning against the shelf of wood stains and primers, I let Ally be Ally, and give her a few minutes of peace while she decides what paints she needs.

Standing here, my mind wanders to Ryan. Of course it does. Give me two seconds to think, and it'll go there on its own. I can't help it.

I hear the door to the shop open, and it brings in a voice that's all too familiar. "Hey, Jim," I hear Jake say, making Ally jump, and then fall on her ass.

My hand flies to my mouth, and I bite back my laughter, shaking silently.

When a cramp hits, I bend forward, one hand gripping my side, and the other on my mouth as Ally rolls on the floor, silently laughing her ass off too.

"Jake, Ryan, how are you two? It's always good to see you boys together," Jim greets.

Oh my god, no. Ryan is here too?

"I'm good, Jim," Jake replies.

"Me too," Ryan's deep voice follows, and my stomach takes flight. "How did you manage through the storm?"

"Oh, I was fine. Just missed a couple days of work, but I was due."

"You deserve some time off. When was the last time you went fishing?"

"It's been a while," Jim says, a longing in his voice.

"Next time Jake and I go, you're coming with us."

"Deal." And just like that, Ryan stole another little piece of my heart. That damn man.

I hear their boots against the concrete floor, and I duck even farther down with Ally. I don't know why we have to hide, but Ally shuffles herself over to sit next to me, linking her arm with mine.

"So man, Ash is staying with you?" Jake asks Ryan, and I immediately go stock still, holding my breath so I don't miss what he says.

"Yeah, and?"

"What do you mean 'and'? *And* what's going on with you two? You're not exactly known for taking women in."

That makes me breathe a little sigh of relief, but my heart still pounds in my chest.

"Well, she was stranded. What was I supposed to do, leave her out there alone?"

"No, but you could have just brought her to my house. She's one of Ally's best friends, and could've have had company. I'm assuming you just left her alone all day while you were at work."

"She was fine," he says defensively. "And I didn't want to plow down your mile-long driveway."

"Bullshit. You just wanted her with you."

"And so what if I did?"

Smiling, I tuck my knees to my chest, hope blooming in my chest.

"What do you plan to do next, Ry? Is she going home? Staying with you? What?"

"I don't know. But it's not like we're dating. We're friends. We're just having fun. Her life isn't here."

My heart sinks to the floor so fast I think I might pass out. Just having fun? That's how he sees this? Us? I thought... Well... I thought we were more than that. Especially after last night.

"Are you sure that's it? You took her on a date last night."

"Of course you already know that," Ryan sighs, and I can picture him rubbing the back of his neck as he stretches his head from side to side. "That *is* it, though. Trust me. I don't see her that way. She's just a distraction. A really good distraction, don't get me wrong, but…" he trails off, not finishing his thought.

"If you say so, man."

The sound of their boots starts moving away from us, and their voices sound muffled as they talk to Jim at the counter. My ears are going deaf to the world around me, and all I can hear is the blood rushing to my head.

My body is numb, and my eyes just stare straight ahead at the wall of paint tubes. What was a wall of colors before, is now just shades of grey to me.

He doesn't love me. He doesn't even like me.

He doesn't see me as anything but a friend.

A friend he can kiss and fuck, but not one that's good enough to warrant anything more.

We're nothing.

The fact that I'm in love with him means absolutely nothing now. I'm just an idiot who fell for a man I knew I couldn't have from the start.

I told myself repeatedly to not get attached. But did I listen? No, of course not.

Those mother fucking feelings crept into my heart and nestled themselves in deep.

CHAPTER 21

"Ash," I hear Ally whisper next to me. "Ashley," she repeats, grabbing my arm. "Ashley!" she says a little louder, shaking me out of my stupor.

"What?" I respond flatly, all emotion drained from me.

"Are you okay? You look like you're about to either pass out or throw up. I can't tell."

"Both."

"Come on, let's get up."

"I can't move."

"I'm going to kill Ryan. I'm going to go to prison because the sheriff is a little fuck boy. I'm going to have some words with Jake about what a dipshit his brother is. He can't do this to my best friend."

"Ally. Please." I just need her to stop talking. She's not helping in the least.

"Sorry. Right. Okay, well you need to stand up so we can get the hell out of here."

Hooking her arm with mine, I manage to muster enough energy to pull myself up, using the shelf behind me as leverage.

"Ally." My voice cracks on her name.

"It'll be okay, Ash."

"No. Because I'm in love with a man who thinks I'm just a friend he can have sex with but who's not good enough to be with."

Ally mutters something under her breath I don't catch, but I can assume it's not good.

Shuffling down the aisle, we make our way past Jim, and he must see the look on my face, because his eyes widen. "Are you okay? Is she okay, Ally?"

"Oh, she'll be fine, Jim. A migraine just hit her like a ton of bricks. I'll be back tomorrow for my paints. Thanks."

"Sure." He nods, looking concerned.

Ally pushes us out the door, and I walk like a robot to her car. It's like I'm aware of what's around me, but it's all just white noise and a blurry picture.

I fold into the passenger's seat and methodically buckle up, staring straight ahead, the ice on the windshield my new fascination.

"Ashley, talk to me."

"About what?"

"What we just heard. What Ryan said."

"There's nothing to say. He said his peace, and that's that. Now, I think it's time I went home."

"No, Ash, come on. Don't leave yet. You can come and stay with Jake and me for a few days."

"No, Al. I need to go. I can't be here anymore. I just want to be alone."

"But–"

"No. Just take me to his house so I can get my stuff while he's at work."

Silently, Ally starts the car and backs out of the spot. I know she wants to say something, but it's not going to help or change my mind in leaving. Ryan was crystal clear in what he said, and I refuse to be here anymore.

Pulling up to his house, my chest tightens. I really grew to love this place. It felt like home.

No.

Shaking my head, I tell Ally, "Just wait for me. I'll be back in five minutes."

Climbing out of her car, I walk up to the side door and turn the knob.

Shit.

I don't have a key.

I'm so stupid. I locked the door behind me earlier without even thinking about a key to get back in.

Groaning, I pound on the door with my fist, collapsing against it. I did this to myself.

I begrudgingly walk back to the car. "I forgot I don't have a key," I tell her when I'm enveloped in heat once again. Not that it's helping. I'm cold from the inside out.

"Oh."

"Take me to the cottage, please. I'm just going to leave my stuff. Maybe you could stop and pick it all up for me tomorrow and just keep it with you until you come back to Jersey? Whenever that is. I don't care."

"Ashley, come on. Let's just stop and get the key from Ryan at the station. You can stay in the car and I'll run in."

"No." The word leaves my mouth so fast my head spins. "He'll think something's up and want to come out and see me. Just please take me to my car."

"Isn't it snowed in?"

"Jesus, Ally, please!" I yell, almost at my breaking point. "Please. I need to get out of here."

"Fine. But we'll have to stop and get Jake's truck. He has a plow on the front."

"Whatever." Leaning my head against the window, I let the cold glass sooth my pounding head.

When we pull up to her house, she releases a breath. "Good, he just came right home before. He should be in his garage now, so I'm just going to run in and steal his spare key."

Nodding, I watch as she goes inside her house. Her house. Which is Jake's house, but they've made it theirs now. A stabbing pain hits my chest, and I lose my breath for a second.

I'll never have that.

Ally comes running out and opens my door to help me out. I honestly don't think I could walk on my own right now.

She shoves me up into the cab of the truck, and rounds the front to hop in herself.

"Okay, so Jake let me drive, uh, once. But don't worry, he showed me how to work the plow in case I ever needed to and he wasn't around."

"Great," I say flatly, not really caring about what she's saying.

With a sigh, Ally starts the monstrous pickup truck, and we make our way through the pine tree lined streets of Pine Cove. The roads are mostly cleared of the three feet of snow, but there's still a thin layer of snow packed neatly on top for traction. It crunches beneath the tires as we drive the winding roads for what will probably be my last time.

I'm going to miss seeing these beautiful trees covered in snow. I'm going to miss a lot of things about this town.

I don't want to think about the fact that I'll have to come back in the fall for Ally and Jake's wedding and see Ryan again. He'll be standing at the alter with his brother, looking sexy in a tux, and I'll be standing with Ally trying not to cry.

"Shit."

"What?" I ask absentmindedly, just watching the landscape go by in a blur of white. How mistaken I was to think snow was magic.

"Nothing. I just forgot how long Dottie's driveway is. But at least half of it was already plowed by you know who when he–"

"Yeah, I got it."

Ally masterfully pushes the snow away as we make our way down Dottie's driveway, and I'm impressed with how she managed to get the hang of it so quickly.

When the little blue cottage comes into view, I breathe a sigh of relief.

I can leave.

I can try and start forgetting everything that's happened.

But when we make it all the way to the end, my moral is dimmed when I see the state of my car. It's literally buried.

"Oh my god."

"It's okay. We'll dig it out," she assures.

Reaching out, I curl my hand around her arm. "Thanks, Ally. For everything."

"Anything, Ash," she says simply, but it means so much.

Hopping down out of the truck, Ally takes two shovels from the back and we start at digging out my car.

When it's finally cleared, my back is killing me, my arms are sore, and my neck has a creak. But now I can leave.

"I'm just going to see if I left anything inside, and then I'll give you the keys back."

Walking through the cottage, tears prick the backs of my eyes, but I refuse to let them fall. It's just a little place. I didn't even spend that much time here. But there's something about it. Something that draws you in like a home cooked meal on a Sunday, and embraces you like a warm hug when you walk through the door.

I take one last look around after checking all of the rooms, and I say a silent goodbye before locking the door behind me.

"Ash, I'm sorry," Ally says, her voice full of emotion. "When I invited you up here, I had no idea this would be the outcome."

"It's okay, Ally. I'll be fine. I always am."

"It's okay to not be fine, too, though. You know that, right? You don't have to pretend all the time."

"But I do," I confess, an emotionless smile forming on my lips as I pull her in for a hug.

"Love you, Trash-ley," she whispers in my ear, my favorite joke nickname my friends call me not even making me smile like it usually does. "I'll get your stuff tomorrow and bring it to you in the next couple of weeks. I'm due for a visit, anyway."

"Okay, thanks."

"It's going to be dark really soon. Please be careful. You can stay with me tonight and then leave in the morning if you want. I'll make sure Jake doesn't let Ryan anywhere near you."

"No. I'm just going to go now."

Nodding in defeat, Ally steps aside and lets me get in my car. I'm hoping it hasn't frozen over while buried, so I take a deep breath, and pray that it'll turn on as push the start button.

"Thank you, God," I whisper when the engine turns over. I'm going to have to let her warm up for a few minutes before taking off. But having time alone to think isn't a good thing for me right now, and Ally is still next to me, sitting in Jake's truck.

Pulling out my phone to text her that she can leave, I see a new message from Ryan waiting for me. The pain in my chest spreads down my arms, and my hands shake as I open it. I shouldn't, but I read the first two words in the preview, and I prepare myself for the torture.

Hey, sweetheart. I'm sitting here with a pile of paperwork as tall as me, and I got to thinking about how you said you could help me with a reward system...

He wants to have phone sex right now? Is he fucking serious? Of course he is. Because all I am is a warm body for him to play with.

I'm so embarrassed. I just handed myself over to him on a silver platter, so I only have myself to blame. I knew this would happen, but I wasn't prepared for how it would leave me feeling like some floozy whose past finally caught up with her.

When my phone starts to vibrate in my hand, and I see his name flash on my screen, my heart jumps. I want to answer it, I want to hear his voice one last time.

But I can't.

I can't listen to any more lies without completely breaking.

It eventually stops buzzing, and the breath I didn't know I was holding rushes out of me.

You can leave. I'm just warming my car up. I text Ally, my frozen fingers shaking as I type.

I want to make sure you're okay.

Ally, please. I just need a few minutes.

Ugh, fine. You're impossible. You better text me, though, when you're leaving, and when you make your first stop. I want to make sure you're safe.

I will.

Love you, Ash. I'm sorry.

Text you soon.

I can't type the words 'I love you' back. It's tainted for me now – a bitter taste on my tongue.

Ally waves to me as she drives away, and then disappears behind the trees.

Resting my head back, I close my eyes.

I need to bottle this up and keep it sealed somewhere deep within me where I won't be able to find it. This is what I do, this is what I'm good at – keeping it all to myself.

Every touch, kiss, and moment comes flooding to the surface in waves, crashing down on me, and a few tears leak from the corners of my eyes.

I can do this.

I'm strong.

A man doesn't define me and my happiness, only I do.

I know who I am, and if he doesn't want me, then fine. I'm leaving. By the time I see him again, I'll be back to the old Ashley, just living for the fun of it.

But even as I think those words, my stomach churns.

I don't want to go out and meet guys and party.

I want to curl up on the couch with the man I love and watch Jurassic Park while drinking hot chocolate and roasting marshmallows.

Fuck this. No.

Opening my eyes, I wipe my face dry and throw my car in drive.

I must have had my eyes shut for longer than I thought, because the sky has quickly darkened to a dull navy.

Leaving Dottie's blue cottage in my rearview mirror, I focus on the road ahead. I have to keep looking ahead. I don't know what's in store for me, but I have to know that it's better than this.

At some point in my life, something has to work out for me. Doesn't it?

Turning on the radio, I blast the pop station and make a left out of the driveway. I need to flood my brain with something other than thoughts of Ryan.

"No!" I yell when a slow love song comes on and I quickly change to the rock station – letting the electric guitar and pounding drums drown out my senses.

Glancing at the clock, I realize I've been driving for fifteen minutes now, and nothing looks familiar. Did I make a wrong turn? Or miss a turn? Everything looks the same when it's covered in three feet of snow. And the street names are hidden behind the snow that's blown over and stuck to the signs.

Damn it!

Why didn't I turn on my GPS before leaving?

Stopping, I put my flashers on, and turn on my phone's GPS. Luckily, there's no one out on the road, so I have time to sit here for a minute.

Oh my god. I have to backtrack like two miles! Damn it! I just want to get to the highway and drive as fast as I can away from this place.

Slamming my hand on the steering wheel, I make a k-turn in the middle of the road, and head back in the direction I came from. But then bright headlights shine directly in my eyes, and I can't see a damned thing. Shit!

I turn the radio off to focus, and I look off to the side, blinking rapidly to try and clear my eyes of the white dots, but it does nothing.

I can't see anything but the blinding lights.

All I can do is grip the wheel as hard as I can and hope I'm driving in a straight line, and not directly at them.

Time slows, and I hear the loud, heavy engine of a truck rumbling towards me, and the whoosh of air as it whizzes past my little car.

My heart thumps wildly in my chest as I scream at the top of my lungs, squeezing my eyes shut for a brief second, praying I'm not about to be crushed to death.

But then it's quiet again, and my screams die in my throat.

I blink, trying to focus on the road, but my eyes are blurry from tears I don't remember shedding. Rubbing them only makes it worse, and my throat feels like I swallowed knives.

Panicking, my heart beats even faster, and my breathing becomes rapid.

I focus on where I think the road is, but the bright headlights left my eyes seeing spots.

I feel the tires sway beneath me, losing traction, and I turn the wheel in what I think is the opposite direction to try and regain control. But it doesn't work.

The car starts to fishtail and slide to the left and right as I desperately turn the steering wheel, not even knowing in what direction.

I start to spin out, and when I think I'm hitting the breaks, I hit the accelerator, sending me flying off the road and into a snow embankment.

CHAPTER 22

My heavy eyes open to nothing.

My head beats a steady rhythm, throbbing painfully. I reach up and touch it, sucking in a sharp intake of air.

What happened?

I look at my hand and see that it's covered in blood.

Why am I bleeding?

Where am I?

My eyes are too heavy to stay open, and I don't know where I am.

****

I'm so cold.

Why is it so cold?

I can't move my body, it's too numb. I can't feel anything but the bitter cold seeping into my bones.

Where am I?

My head is pounding, and everything is fuzzy, until the darkness drags me back under.

****

Flashing blue lights penetrate the black behind my eyelids, and I try and lift them. But they're too heavy. I have no strength.

I hear faint voices yelling as streaks of white light dance in front of me.

It's so pretty. I wish I could see them better.

The voices start to get louder and closer. It almost sounds like they're calling out my name, but I don't know why they would.

I start to slip back under the black fog holding me down, but then a bright light shines in my face.

No, no, I'm not ready. I don't want to die. Please, I'm not ready.

Ryan.

I want to see Ryan again.

I need him.

Please don't make me leave him.

"Ashley!" The voice of an angel says my name, and I know this has to be the end. I know he's not here.

I open my mouth to protest, but all that comes out is a whispered, "Ryan."

Then it's black again.

****

Bright. So bright.

I try and blink away the light, but it remains.

Groaning, I turn away, my throat protesting at the vibrations.

"Ashley, baby, sweetheart." It almost sounds like Ryan. But I know that it can't be.

"Please, Ash, look at me," the voice begs desperately.

"Ryan." I mouth his name, only a slight whispered breath leaving my lips. I wish I could see him just one last time before I have to go.

CHAPTER 23

A steady beeping sound breaks through the dense fog that's been covering my brain, and my eyes flutter open to harsh fluorescent lighting.

What happened? Where am I?

My eyes lazily take in my surroundings. I see pale blue walls cut in half by wainscoting, a TV is mounted in the upper right corner playing the local news, stiff, stark white sheets cover my legs, and next to my head are machines that won't stop beeping.

I'm in a hospital.

Closing my eyes, flashes of what happened play behind my lids, and a chill runs through me.

I was in a car accident, I think. I was trying to leave, and I was blinded by headlights, and then I spun out.

The rest is all a blur. I only remember snippets of what happened after.

It was dark, I was cold, and my head hurt. It still does.

A warm hand brushes a curl from my forehead, and I open my eyes to a familiar pair of worried blue ones.

Then it all rushes back to me. Why I was leaving last night, and where I was going. Home.

"Go," I tell him, my voice dry and rough as I pull away from him. Too fast, though, because the sudden movement causes my head to spin.

"What's wrong?"

"Leave. Go. I don't want you here."

"Ashley, sweetheart, it's me. Ryan."

"Don't call me that. Don't call me anything." I look over at him with emotionless eyes. "Just go."

The hurt look in his eyes stabs me in the gut, and my heart clenches in my chest.

He has no reason to be hurt. I'm hurt.

"Why? Tell me why, or I'm not going. Don't push me away."

"Push you away?" I scoff. "You already did that."

Closing my eyes, I try and hold back the tears threatening to fall, but a few leak out the corners of my eyes and slip down my temples, splashing into my hair.

"I heard you, Ryan," I whisper, his name burning my lips to even say.

"Heard what?" he asks, confused.

But before I can answer, the door to the room opens and in floods Ally, Courtney, Jake, and Jack, all gathering around the bed.

"Ashley," Ally gushes, tears spilling down her cheeks like rivers. "You're okay."

"I am," I assure her, even though I'm anything but okay.

"I'm glad you're okay." Courtney sniffs, turning to wipe her eyes so I can't see. Her husband, Jack, puts his arm around her, looking down at her with such love and devotion.

Jake is the same. He hugs Ally from behind and kisses her neck, just letting her know he's there for her.

That's all I've ever wanted. My dad used to do that, and be that, for my mom. He was her rock, and he was there. Always.

Tears pool in my eyes and I look up at the ceiling. I start counting the tiles to try and distract myself from the throbbing in my head and the sinking of my heart.

But my eyes eventually find their way back to Ryan's tired ones, the confusion and hurt still swirling in his pools of blue. He's still waiting for me to answer his question.

His hair is messy like he's been running his fingers through it, and he looks disheveled in his uniform. His shirt is wrinkled and the top two buttons are undone.

I look at Ally, knowing she can see what I'm feeling and what I'm trying to tell her. Please make him leave. Please.

I beg her with my eyes.

Nodding once, she clears her throat, and gives Ryan a hard stare. "Ryan, I think you should go. Ashley needs to stay calm and rest."

"What's that supposed to mean, Ally?" he asks harshly. "What's going on?" His eyes dart around the room and then land back on me. "Ash, I thought–"

"You thought what?" I interrupt, my voice hard, and filled with unshed tears. And he just stares. "Exactly. We're nothing. Now leave."

I could swear the flash of pain in his eyes is genuine, but he covers it up so quickly I can't be sure.

"Hey, Ry, let's take a walk," Jake suggests, motioning to the door with a nod.

Growling low under his breath, Ryan shoves his chair back and stands, my head spinning at the sound as he stalks out. Jake looks at me apologetically, and then follows his older brother out of the room.

"Ashley..." Ally starts, but then pauses. "Hey, guys," she says to Courtney and Jack, "give us a minute?"

"Sure." Courtney gives me a small smile and walks out hand in hand with her husband.

When Ally looks back at me, her face says it all. I know a lecture is coming.

"I need water," I rasp, my throat bone dry.

"Oh, of course." Grabbing the Styrofoam cup from the food tray to my left, she holds the straw up to my mouth.

When the first splash of cold water hits my tongue, I close my eyes as it runs down my throat, soothing the pain.

"Thank you," I tell her, sounding a little more like myself.

"Ash, he's been here the entire time. He hasn't left your side."

"How long have I been here?"

"A few hours."

"That's nothing, Ally. I can sit in a chair for a few hours, too, without leaving."

"He's was so scared, Ash. I've never seen a grown man so scared. He really cares about you."

"Stop. Please. You and I both heard him. He just didn't want to lose a good lay. Now, I need you to leave, too."

"Ashley," she pleads, taking a step towards me. But my glare tells her to not take another step. Sighing, she throws her hands up. "You need to deal with your shit, Ash. You could have died, and all you're doing is pushing everyone who cares about you away."

"My head is pounding. I need to rest." Closing my eyes, I turn my head away.

"You love to tell Mel, Ellie, and me what's on your mind, so I'm going to give you a little taste of how annoying it can be."

"I'd rather you didn't." My head is killing me. Do they not supply pain meds in here?

"Too bad. Now listen. You're strong and independent, and you've spent years running since your dad died, searching for something in every man you've met. Now you've found it, and you can't handle it. One little bump in the road and you run. You don't even want to talk to him about it, tell him how you feel, and see if he feels the same. Maybe he was just talking out of his ass with Jake. He's a guy, they're dumb. And now you're being dumb."

"I'm lying in a hospital bed, Ally. Thanks for calling me dumb. I'm really not in the mood for this." I press the red button on my bed for the nurse, needing something to help me sleep.

She runs her hands through her hair and lets out a frustrated sigh before storming out of the room. Luckily, when it opens again, a woman in her forties in navy scrubs walks in.

"Hi, Miss Ashley, I'm Emily, your nurse. What can I do for you?"

"Hi, my head is killing me. Can I have something for it?"

"Yes, I just need to ask you a few questions first now that you're awake."

"Sure."

"What do you remember about last night?"

Squeezing my eyes shut, I focus on remembering through the pain and slight fog that's still veiling my complete memory. "I was blinded by the headlights of an oncoming truck. It was so bright. I thought I was going to crash head-on with it. And when I didn't, I thought I was okay, but then I still couldn't see. I hit a patch of ice or something, and I couldn't control my car, and then I spun out. The rest I don't know. I went in and out of consciousness, I think. I only recall flashes of light and sounds. And I was so cold." A shiver racks my body just remembering being out there.

"Okay, that's good that you remember. Now, how is your head? On a scale of one to ten, ten being severe, how would you rate your pain level?"

"Eight, nine maybe? I don't know."

"Okay." She writes something down on her clipboard and then looks back at me. "Do you hurt anywhere else?"

"I don't know, I don't think so. I just can't get past my pounding head."

"Of course, and I'll give you something for it before we discharge you."

"I'm okay to leave?"

"Yes, we did x-rays and a CT scan, and you don't have any

fractures or brain swelling. Just a head abrasion and severe concussion."

"Okay, thank you."

"Of course, let me just go and get you some Tylenol."

"Is that all I can have? I don't know if that's going to cut it."

She smiles warmly at me. "Yes, sorry."

"Fine," I sigh, resting my head back in the pillows as she walks back out the door, closing it firmly behind her.

No one better come in here unless it's her bringing me drugs. I can't hold any semblance of a rational conversation right now.

I hear the click of the door opening again, and I lazily turn my head in that direction, cracking one eye open.

Oh, good, it's just Emily again with a little paper cup in her hand. "Here you go, Ashley," she says, handing me the cup with three little pills, along with my Styrofoam cup of water.

"Thanks." I toss back the pain killers and wash them down with the fresh, cold water.

"Just rest, and I'll be back in a little while with your discharge papers for you to sign. You won't be able to drive, so do you have a ride? Will one of your friends out there be taking you? I'll have to leave them with instructions for watching you."

"Oh, um, I don't know. Maybe. I'm not sure who is, or where I'll be going actually." Even I can hear how pathetic I sound.

"Would you like me to ask them? They're all sitting out there, and I don't think they're leaving." She smiles, thinking that'll cheer me up or something.

"Sure. I just want to be alone right now, though."

"Of course." She nods. "I'll make sure you're not disturbed."

"Thank you," I whisper, closing my eyes.

The moment I hear the door click closed, the tears I've held in for the past twenty-four hours pour from eyes, and my body starts shaking violently.

I'm still so cold. Why can't I get warm?

I pull the thin blanket over my shoulders, but the shivers still rack my body as I cry harder than I have in the past eight years.

The sounds coming from me are foreign to my ears, but I can't help it. Everything has been building in me for such a long time, and I can't take it anymore.

Loud voices and scuffling from out in the hall remind me where I am, but I can't help it.

"What do you mean I can't go in there?" I hear Ryan's muffled, angry tone, through the door. "I can hear her crying! She needs me."

"I'm sorry, sir, but she asked to not be disturbed. She's resting."

"She's not resting," he growls. "Do you not hear her?"

"I'm sorry, sir. The patient has the right to deny visitors."

"Fine. I'm not a visitor, then. I'm Sheriff Taylor, and I have questions for her about the accident."

There's a beat of silence before I hear nurse Emily reluctantly say, "Alright."

The moment I hear the door open, I turn away from him. I don't want him to see me like this.

I hear his boots heavy on the floor, taking slow steps towards the bed – my back to him. I curl into myself, staying huddled on the edge with the blanket wrapped tightly around me.

I'm still shaking. I'm still cold.

The bed dips behind me and I feel him there, radiating heat like the summer sun. Ryan lifts the blanket and climbs on the small bed, wrapping his arms around me – pulling me into his warmth.

I don't resist him.

He doesn't say anything, and I don't say anything. I just let him hold me as I let out everything I've held inside of me for what seems like a lifetime.

His presence is all I need. His comfort and strength envelope me, and give me the closure I need.

My head throbs even harder from crying, but I don't care. I did this to myself. I always mess everything up.

When a fresh wave of tears pours out of me, Ryan slips his other arm under me and flips me so I'm facing him. But I don't want him seeing me. I grip his shirt in my fists and burry my face against his chest.

I can feel his heart beating, and his even breathing. His chest rises and falls beneath my forehead, and I take solace in that simple motion.

"Ashley," he whispers softly, stroking his hand up and down my back. "I'm sorry, sweetheart. I'm sorry."

"Please," I beg, my voice cracking. I don't want his pity.

"I thought I was going to lose you. I saw your car half buried in that snow embankment…" he trails off, taking a deep breath. "I've never felt so helpless in my life. Then I got to you, and saw your head. Blood was dripping, and dried, all down your face. And I swear, Ashley. My heart stopped beating.

"I thought I'd never hear your voice again, or look into your mesmerizing eyes, or feel your heart beat against mine, or hold you." His arms tighten around me, and his heart beats a little quicker.

"The second I laid eyes on you again in the café, it felt like my world was righting itself. Something in me told me to not let you go again. I should have never let you go last summer."

"I heard you, Ryan," I croak, my throat raw. "In the hardware store. I heard you."

"I know. Jake just told me." Tilting my chin up, his eyes search mine, swirling shades of blue swimming with regret, sorrow, and apology. "You have to believe me when I say it was all meaningless. I was just talking, trying to get Jake to stop asking me questions I didn't want to answer. Not to him, at least. When I got home and you weren't there, but all of your stuff was, I called you. And when you didn't answer for a while, I called Ally, but she wouldn't tell me what happened, just that you left. I was driving around, and then it came in on the scanner that a car was spotted…"

"Ashley," he whispers, cupping my cheek, smoothing his thumb back and forth. Ryan closes his eyes, and when they open again, I see the look. The look I've been waiting for my entire life. The look that holds more meaning and weight than any words ever could. "Why did you run? You and I... I thought... This, us, is real. You know it is."

More tears fall from my eyes as what he says sinks in.

"You see me as more?"

"So much more."

Wiping the tears from my cheeks, Ryan presses his lips to mine, and I feel everything. He pours all of the unsaid words and emotions into this kiss, and my heart swells.

This man is everything I've always needed, but didn't think I could have.

The pounding in my head slows, and is replaced with the pounding of my heart. Ryan's kiss soothes me, and mends me from the inside out.

"I'm so glad you're okay," he whispers against my lips. "Next time you want to run, just promise me you'll talk to me first."

"Next time?"

"It's probably inevitable if you're with me," he says, and I can hear the twinge of sadness in his voice.

"No, it's not." Reaching up, I brush my fingers across his forehead and down his jaw. "When I heard you say it, confirm what I feared most, I just... I didn't want to hear it again if I came to you. So I ran." I swallow the lump in my throat. "But I didn't want to go, Ryan."

Kissing me, he smiles softly. "Will you stay with me, sweetheart?" He strokes my cheek. "Stay with me."

A few tears fall from my eyes and I nod, my pulse racing, as his mouth captures mine in a searing kiss that I feel all the way down to my toes. Heat spreads through me, finally warming my chilled body.

I tuck my head into the crook of his neck, and I close my eyes, breathing in his intoxicating scent, letting it calm me.

CHAPTER 24

"It's time to go, Ash," Ryan whispers, waking me from a deep sleep.

"Hmm?"

"It's time to go."

"Where?" I mumble.

"Home. I'm going to take you home."

"I already am," I mumble, snuggling closer into him.

"To my house," he whispers, rubbing circles on my back. "And you have to sign some papers."

"Okay," I say around a yawn, stretching out my stiff limbs.

Ryan slips out of the bed and I press the button to raise it to a sitting position, leaning back against the pillows.

"What time is it?"

"Almost dawn."

"I feel like the last twelve hours have been the longest of my life."

"How does your head feel?"

"It hurts, but it's better. You helped."

"It's my fault you're in here," he says, rubbing the back of his neck. "I wish I could take all of your pain away."

"What do you mean it's your fault? Ry, it's *my* fault. I'm the idiot who thought it was a good idea to drive at night right after a blizzard."

"Because of me."

"Ryan, no."

"Ash, there's nothing you can say to make me think otherwise." He tucks a loose curl behind my ear. "But I'm going to spend a very long time trying to make it up to you. Starting with taking you home and making you hot chocolate and s'mores."

"And Jurassic Park?"

"Anything you want, sweetheart." He smiles, leaning down to kiss me sweetly.

But I need more than just a sweet kiss. Grabbing his shirt, I pull him closer and press my lips harder against his, headache be damned.

God, I've missed kissing him. I know it's only been a day, but that was before I thought I was never going to be able to do it again. I want to believe him when he says I'm more to him. I want to believe that this will work out between us. I want to trust him.

I just want him.

"Oh, excuse me. Sorry. I have your discharge papers." I was too wrapped up in Ryan to hear the door opening. "How are you feeling?"

Tucking my face in Ryan's neck, I smile against him, feeling his pulse beneath my lips. I peek over his shoulder and see nurse Emily smiling apologetically and holding a clipboard of papers.

"I feel better, thanks." Pushing on Ryan's chest, he steps back, a huge grin on his face.

Emily hands me the clipboard and shows me where to sign.

"Now, I already briefed the sheriff here on what to watch for in the next few days. And if you start feeling dizzy, or are vomiting, or your headaches get worse, then you need to come back immediately."

"Okay." I nod. "Thank you." I sign all of the highlighted lines and hand her back the clipboard.

"Make sure to get a lot of rest in the next few days, and don't do anything too strenuous."

My eyes dart to Ryan and he winks. "Sure, of course. No activities, and rest." Doing no activities with Ryan is going to be torture.

She walks out, leaving Ryan and I alone again, and I slide my legs over the edge of the bed.

"Let me help you," he offers, coming around to support my weight as I stand.

"Thanks."

"Aren't they supposed to roll you out in a wheelchair?"

"I think that's just in the movies."

"But what if you get dizzy and fall? Are they sure you're okay to leave?"

"Ryan, relax. I'm good, I promise. Maybe you could just hold my hand, and then I won't fall."

"I can do that," he says. "I won't let you fall on my watch." Ryan grabs my coat from the closet door and holds it up to help me put it on.

"Where is all of my other stuff?" I ask. "My car? My purse? Anything else I had inside?"

"I have your purse. And your car was towed to the impound. We can go and get it when you're feeling better. Don't worry, I took care of everything."

"Thank you. Is my car a goner? Can she be saved?"

"I'm not sure. I came straight here to be with you."

"Oh," I whisper, the breath leaving my lungs. He came straight here to be with me. He was worried. He cares.

Taking my hand, we walk down the halls of the hospital, and I feel every step pulse through my head. I have to focus on putting one foot in front of the other.

Squeezing his hand, I move to loop my arm with his, and he looks down at me, his eyes filled with concern.

"You okay?"

"Yeah, I just need to lean on you a little."

"Are you sure? Do you need me to get a nurse?" He looks around for one, but I shake my head.

"No, I just need you. I'll be fine. I'm just a little off balance."

"Are you sure?" he asks again, my heart swelling at his concern.

"Yes, I'm fine. Don't worry."

Continuing on, we make turn after turn until we finally make it to the sliding doors, the cold air hitting me hard.

"I'm just over there." He nods toward his SUV cruiser parked in the 'official vehicles only' spot.

"I see you're abusing your power for me. Do I have to ride in the back?" I smile, my mind going straight to handcuffs.

"Do you have some sort of criminal/being arrested fantasy? Because we can play that out, sweetheart," he muses, a gleam in his eyes.

"Oh my god, Ryan." I laugh, rolling my eyes. "I don't know if I do, but maybe when I'm feeling better, you can pull those cuffs out again."

"That's a given." He smirks, opening the passenger door and helping me up. Spreading his hand out on my thigh, he slides it up. "I loved having you at my mercy, laid out and ready for me. I've never seen anything sexier in my life."

"Are you trying to make me dizzier? Because it's working." My head is spinning, and I wish it wasn't so banged and bruised, or I would be jumping him the second we got back to his house.

Leaning into the car he kisses me, his tongue sliding along the seam of my lips.

"Not helping," I rasp, my breathing rapid.

"Not sorry." He smiles, kissing me again before closing the door.

"There's a lot of buttons and gadgets up here," I say when he gets in the driver's side. "What do they all do?"

He points to a series of switches. "These are for the siren, lights, and speaker. And then there's my laptop, radio, and scanner."

"Oohh, can I turn the lights and siren on?"

"Sure. I'll take a backroad so you can go crazy." Smiling, Ryan pulls out of the hospital parking lot, the sky lightening with the rising of the sun.

I can't believe the accident was only last night. It feels like I've been out of it for days, but on the other hand, my body is exhausted like I haven't slept for days.

The morning winter sky is streaked with orange, pink and yellow. A beautiful, bright, contrast to the stark white of the snow.

Winding our way through backroads as we make our way back to Pine Cove, Ryan looks over at me when we turn onto a desolate road with no houses.

"Alright, Ash, light it up."

Bouncing in my seat, I ignore the protest in my head, and I rub my hands together – warming them up for the task.

I flip the switch for the lights, and smile when blue lights start flashing all around. Next, I flip the switch for the siren, and a girlish giggle bubbles out of me.

When I press the button next to the switches, the siren makes that whooping sound, and I laugh again.

Switching it off, I look at him hopefully. "Can we find someone to pull over?"

"What? No, Ash, we can't." He laughs. "I'm taking you home to rest. I'm not on duty, either. I took a few days off, actually."

"You did?" I ask, all joking aside.

"Yeah, I did." He nods, looking over at me, unsure. "Is that okay?"

"What? I mean yes, it is. I'm just surprised. I know you're busy."

"Not too busy for you. I want to make sure you're okay, and I was given strict instructions to watch over you."

"Isn't the town going to fall apart? Won't criminals be running around on the loose?"

"Yes, Ash, the town is going to go up in flames and be brought down by criminals running rampant while I'm sitting at home watching movies with you."

I place my hand on his forearm. "Ryan," I say softly, "thank you. The fact that you took off of work for me. I…" I swallow the lump in my throat, tears pricking the back of my eyes. My pounding head is making my thoughts all jumbled, and I'm feeling too emotional.

Taking my hand, he brings it to his lips. "You don't have to do everything by yourself, Ash. I'm here for you. You can depend on me."

I really want to. I want him to be that guy for me.

"Okay."

Nodding, he intertwines his fingers with mine and places our joined hands on his leg.

The ride back to his house is quiet and comfortable, the streets empty at this early hour. I close my eyes and lean my head back, trying to block out the pounding in my head.

"We're here," Ryan says gently, waking me from a light sleep.

"Mhmm." Blinking awake, I unbuckle by seatbelt and climb out, gripping the door for support.

"Hey, let me." Ryan rushes to my side and wraps his arm around my waist.

Walking into his house, Ryan brings me over to the couch.

"Just relax, I'll be right back."

"Okay." Closing my eyes again, I lay on my side and drift off, waking again to the scent of chocolate. "Mmm."

"I knew that'd wake you."

"How do you make this? I need to know. It's like liquid gold."

"I'm not telling you."

"Why not?"

"Because then you won't need me to make it for you."

"Fine," I huff, taking the mug from his hands. "Keep your big secret to yourself."

"It's not the only thing that's big." He winks. "And I don't want to keep it to myself."

"Oh, I know." I smile, holding the mug up to my lips and inhaling the delicious aroma.

Putting a DVD in, Ryan comes back and sits next to me, and I lift the blanket up so he can join me. I lean my head on his shoulder and he places his palm on my leg, running it up and down.

Sipping my hot chocolate, I let myself relax into this moment.

****

Ryan's been taking care of me for the past four days, and they've been bliss. We've watched movies, drank hot cocoa, slept in each other's arms, and talked about any and everything.

But he has to go back to work today, and I'll be left alone again, missing him.

"I'll be home at six," he tells me, bending over the bed to kiss me on the cheek.

"Okay." I nod, my voice low.

He sees the look in my eyes, and scratches his jaw. "I mean, I could—"

"No, it's okay." I smile weakly, pulling the blanket over my bare shoulder. "You have to save the world. I'll be fine, I promise."

"Call me if you need anything. I'll come right back."

"I'll be fine. But, thank you."

"I'm still going to call and check on you."

"Okay." I smile, biting my lip. "Will you be needing a stress reliever?"

"Don't tease, Ash," he says, his voice strained. "Because I've been needing you."

"Me, too." Grabbing his uniform shirt, I pull him down to my lips and kiss him hard.

My head isn't pounding as much as it was a few days ago, and

I've been needing him too. I know he hasn't touched me since the accident because of my concussion, and he doesn't want to hurt me, but I can't take another day, or night, of being with him and not ripping his clothes off.

"You better not be late tonight," I murmur against his lips.

"Six sharp," he rasps, kissing me back into the pillows. Groaning, he pulls away and stands up straight, staring down at me with molten eyes. "Be by your phone," he tells me before walking out without a second glance, and I can hear his boots fading the further he storms down the hall.

Smiling, I bite the comforter and roll over, hunkering down deep into the bed.

****

My phone ringing wakes me with a start.

"Hello?" I answer groggily.

"Hey, Ash."

"Ally, hi."

"Can I come over today? I'll bring lunch."

"Yeah, sure. Ryan went back to work today, so we can hang here. I wanted to talk to you."

"Me too."

"Noon?"

"Sounds good. See you then."

"See you."

Hanging up, I breathe out a sigh of relief and stare at the ceiling. I've been meaning to call her, but nothing I thought to say sounded good enough. I was an asshole in the hospital, and I haven't talked to her since.

Seeing it's already after ten, I get up and take a hot shower, letting the water soothe my muscles. I haven't been able to do much in the past few days, and I'm feeling cooped up. Add being tense from not getting any from my man, and I really need this hot water to relax me.

Well, I need a lot more than hot water to relax me, but I have to wait until six until I get that relaxation treatment.

This is going to be the longest day ever.

Getting dressed, I throw on a pair of leggings and an oversized sweater for another day of lounging around. I was down to my last pair of clean panties and leggings, so I'm glad I was able to do laundry yesterday – something that felt very domestic for me to do in Ryan's house.

Heading downstairs, I straighten up a little and put on a pot of coffee, smiling when I see a note left for me on the counter.

My sexy Ashley,
I'm writing this after you so rudely teased me upstairs. I wish I could crawl back in bed with you and be the one to tease you for hours...
I'll be calling you soon.
-Ry

Smiling, I fan myself with the note and then re-read it. If he thinks he's going to tease me, he's got another thing coming.

Oh, I'll answer his call today, and he'll see what it really means to tease someone.

Pouring myself a cup of coffee, I go and sit in the living room, and scroll through my phone while I wait for Ally.

Oh, shit! I can't believe I never called my mom!

Dialing her number, it rings twice, and then she answers.

"Hi, honey, how are you?"

"Hi, mom, I'm good. How are you?"

"Good."

"Um, I sort of need to tell you something. I should have called days ago, but I, uh, was distracted."

"I already know, honey. Your nice young man called me when it happened. And he's called me every day since to update me."

"What?" I ask, the words barely making it past my tight throat. He did?

"He's a good man, Ashley. I'm happy you found him."

"Mom," I croak, tears gathering in my eyes.

"I don't know why you didn't call me, honey."

"I… I didn't want to worry you. Because of…"

"I know. But I'm your mother. I don't want you to be afraid to tell me things just because you think I can't handle it."

"Mom, that's not it."

"It is. And that's on me. I lost myself when your father died. He was my everything, Ashley. I wasn't ready to lose him, and I didn't know what to do when I did." I can hear the sadness and unshed tears in her voice. "I wasn't able to be there for you, and I'm sorry. I'm so sorry, honey. You may as well have lost both parents that day."

"Mom, no." Tears spill down my cheeks, and I pull the phone away from my face to try and gather myself. "I lost my dad. I didn't lose you. You had to heal in your own way, and I had to in mine."

"But I should have been there for you more. We should have healed together."

"It's okay, mom. I was twenty. I found a way."

"That's still a baby, honey. You needed me."

She's right, I did need her, but I understood.

"I love you, mom," I whisper, my heart squeezing. She's finally saying the things I've always wanted to hear.

"I love you, too, honey. And I promise I'm going to be better. I started seeing a therapist last month. I'm learning to cope."

"Mom, that's amazing. I'm so proud of you."

"It's a start."

"I want you to be happy again."

"I'm learning to focus on the future again, and moving forward."

"I know you loved dad, mom. And he loved you. I won't ever think any less than that if you start moving on and living again."

"Ashley," she chokes, and I can hear her crying through the phone. "Thank you. Thank you, baby."

"Mom, please don't cry," I beg, tears streaming down my face.

"I'm sorry, I can't help it. I'm just glad I didn't lose you, too. But you have to promise me you'll stop hiding things from me. I'm your mother, I should know if you're hurt."

"Sorry," I whisper, feeling like a shitty daughter. "Then I should probably tell you that I had to quit my job at the bar because my boss cornered me and I punched him in the face."

"Ashley, why would you hide that?"

"Because of what happened at the law firm. This is the second time a man has thought I'd been leading him on, and the second time a man's thought it was okay to put his hands on me. I don't know what I do that makes them think—"

"Ashley," she interrupts, "it's not you. It's them. Those little pricks think because they have a higher position of power, then they can do whatever they want."

"But—"

"Let me finish," she interrupts again. "You're a smart, beautiful woman. And most men think that just smiling at them is flirting. Trust me, honey, it's not you. It's them. Men are famously dense when it comes to women."

"Thank you," I say softly. I should have just talked to her from the beginning. I don't know why I thought she'd think differently of me, or blame me.

"Now, let's talk about your new man."

Smiling, I pull my knees to my chest. "Well, his name is Ryan. Ryan Taylor. He's the sheriff of Pine Cove, and, uh, Ally's fiancé's older brother."

"Oh, scandalous."

"Mom." I laugh.

"He sounded handsome on the phone when he called me."

"He is." I bite my lip. "Very handsome. And pretty freaking amazing."

"I can tell. He's been taking care of my daughter, and that's no easy task. I would know, I raised you."

"Mom, oh my god. That's rude."

"It's not, honey." She laughs. "And it means a lot that you even let him take care of you. It means he's important to you."

"He is," I admit, pausing before I tell her, "I love him."

"I know. I can hear it in your voice."

"I haven't told him yet. And I don't know if he feels the same, but he told me he wanted more. So, I'll wait."

"Oh, Ashley. That boy loves you. He's called every day for the past four days. I hear it in his voice like I do yours."

"How did he call you when I was with him? How did he get your number?"

"Don't worry about it, honey." I can hear the smile in her voice. "I'm glad you found a man who cares so deeply for you. I know he'll take care of you."

"I'm fully capable of taking care of myself, mom."

"That's not what I'm saying. I just know that you'll be taken care of, and loved, by a man worthy of you. Your father would approve, too."

Tears prick my eyes at the mention of my dad. I know he would like Ryan. He would love talking to him about small town life and being a sheriff.

"I know he would," I croak, my throat tight again.

"I didn't mean to upset you."

"You didn't. I'm glad we can talk again, mom."

"Me too, honey. I love you."

"Love you, too."

"Will you be calling me more, then, I hope?"

"Yes, I promise."

"Alright. Well, I'll let you go. Make sure you rest."

"I will. Bye, mom."

"Bye, honey."

Hanging up, I lay my head back against the couch and sigh. I've missed my mom so much these past eight years, and I feel like I'm finally getting her back now. I wanted her to get help, but I didn't want to be the one to suggest it. I wanted her to *want* help.

My phone ringing brings me back, and I swipe to answer.

"Hey, Ally."

"I'm here."

"Okay, go to the side door. I'll be right there." Standing, I wipe my face and walk through the kitchen to open the door for her.

"What's wrong?" she asks right away.

"Nothing, why?"

"It looks like you've been crying. What did Ryan do?"

"Whoa, okay, relax. Please come in." I motion for her to enter, and wait for her to close the door before telling her about my mom. "I was just on the phone with my mom. And we talked. Really talked."

"Oh, sorry," she says, her face regretful as she places a bag on the counter. "I brought us subs from a deli a town over. I discovered them last fall, and now I crave them."

"Sounds perfect." I smile. "Do you want a cup of coffee?"

"Yes, of course. You don't even have to ask."

Reaching up, I grab a clean mug from the cabinet and pour her a cup. "Cream is in the fridge."

"Thanks." She adds a splash of cream to her coffee, and turns to me, leaning against the counter. "Now, let's talk."

"Yes, let's. I'm sorry I was an asshole to you."

"I was, too. And I know you were just trying to deal in your own way."

"Yeah, I was." Looking away, I stare at a random spot on the counter.

"You and Ryan talked?"

"We did. In the hospital."

"Good. Did you work it all out?"

"Sort of? We've just been enjoying each other's company. He said enough that day. For now."

"Okay…"

"I'm happy, Ally," I tell her, looking her in the eyes so she can see. "And it's because of him. I knew he was different from the moment I laid eyes on him. Do you remember?"

"Oh my god, how could I forget?" She laughs. "Ash, you two ate each other alive with your eyes. I had to drag you away from that grill before you jumped him right then and there."

"Well, come on. He's so sexy. Of course I wanted to." I smile.

"You told him you wanted a juicy wiener!"

"He was grilling! I was just taking advantage of the situation."

"Oh my god," she groans, slapping her forehead. "You're too much."

"Which is why you love me. Admit it."

"True." She smiles, taking a sip of her coffee. "Now, let's eat, I'm starving."

"Yes! I need food."

****

Ally and I have been sitting and catching up for a couple of hours when my phone rings. "Oh, Ally, uh, I have to take this call." I smile, biting my lip. "Upstairs, though."

"Okay?"

"It's Ryan."

"Okay?"

"Uh, the short version is that I'm going to go have phone sex with him, and then hang up before he can finish."

"I'm sorry, what?!" she exclaims, her eyes bugging out.

"You heard me." I smirk. "It's this whole thing," I say, waving my hand dismissively in the air. "But he challenged me this morning, and I'm trying to prove a point."

"That's the Ashley I know and love. Alright, go get 'em! Give him hell."

Laughing, I walk out of the room and yell over my shoulder, "I always do!"

Swiping open his call, I make sure to use my most seductive voice. "Hey, sheriff. I've been waiting for your call."

"Have you, now?" His gruff voice does something to my insides, but I tamp it down.

"Yes," I purr, walking upstairs and down the hall. "I'm in your room. In your bed."

A low groan comes through the phone and I smile, loving that he's ready to fall into my rap.

"Are you alone?"

"I'm in my office. No one can see or hear me."

Sitting on the edge of his bed, I get comfortable. "Have you been doing paperwork all day, sheriff? Do you need a reward?"

"Yes. I need you."

"I know," I whisper. "Now, picture my hands running up your chest, my lips on your neck, kissing and licking my way up, swirling my tongue around the shell of your ear, whispering everything I want to do to you."

"And what's that?" he asks, his breathing heavy.

"Everything," I tell him, and he groans. "Unbuttoning your shirt, I rake my red nails down your chest, marking you as mine. My fingers dance across your hips, and I unbuckle your belt, popping the button open and pulling your zipper down." I hear him through the phone, doing just that. "I slide my warm hand into your pants and find you already hard as I grip you in my palm."

Another groan from Ryan.

"Squeezing you, I'd slip down to my knees under your desk, and spring free your massive cock."

"Ash," he breathes.

"Yes, sheriff? Would you like me to stop?"

"No," he says sternly, and I bite my lip.

"Are you hard right now for me, sheriff? Ready for me? Wishing you could feel my hands on you?"

"Yes," he says through clenched teeth, and I go back to

torturing him.

"Leaning forward, I lick you from base to tip, searing you with the heat of my tongue. Gripping you with one hand, I take the thick head of your cock into my mouth, sucking, swirling my tongue, feeling you grow even harder in my hand."

"Ashley," he groans out, low and long.

"Can you feel me, sheriff?" I whisper, knowing he's already gripping himself. I only get a grunt in response.

"I'm taking you deep, my hot mouth sucking you in until you hit the back of my throat. You taste so good, Ryan." Moaning, I lay back on the bed, wishing I wasn't so turned on listening to his grunts as he touches himself. But I have to focus.

"Your musky, heady, taste fills my mouth, and I moan around you, the vibrations traveling the length of you, and down your legs."

Ryan's heavy breathing has me holding back a moan of my own. I love that I can do this to him. I almost feel bad for what I'm about to do. Almost.

"Are you almost there?" I ask huskily, letting him hear the roughness in my voice.

"Yes," he hisses.

"Good." I pause, listening to the small grunts he's making. Fuck, it's sexy. "Now, sheriff, this is what I call teasing," I purr, "not what I did this morning. I'll see you later."

"What?" he sputters, his voice ruff and confused.

"Bye, sheriff."

Hanging up, I cover my mouth with my hand, a giggle bursting out of me. I can't believe I just did that.

My phone starts ringing in my hand almost immediately, and it's Ryan. Laughing, I press ignore, and head back downstairs, an extra spring in my step.

"So, how did it go?" Ally asks when I walk back into the living room.

"Very well." I laugh. "I left him right on the edge. And then I hung up."

"Oh my god, Ashley," she groans, covering her eyes.

"What? It's fun teasing him. And it'll be worth it later." I wink, smiling wickedly.

"I'm glad you're feeling better." She laughs, sipping her coffee. "Happiness looks good on you."

"I could say the same for you."

"It's weird, right?"

"What?"

"Feeling happy."

"Yeah." I smile. "It is. But I think I'll adjust just fine."

CHAPTER 25

After my little phone call with Ryan, Ally and I had the best afternoon. We talked and laughed, sharing stories about Ryan and Jake. Apparently being sexy alphas who are kings in the bedroom is a family trait.

"I've missed this," I tell her.

"Me, too. Do you think that you'll be staying?"

"Staying?"

"Yeah, here in Pine Cove."

"Uh, I don't know. He asked me to stay when I was in the hospital, but I don't know if he meant permanently."

"But you want to."

"Yeah. I just don't want to be the one to bring it up."

"How about I invite Jake over, and we all have dinner together? Maybe I can find a way to bring it up organically."

"I don't want an audience for that, Ally."

"Okay, fine," she sighs. "But I still think we should have dinner together. How fun would it be? Brothers dating best friends?"

"I guess…"

"Okay, good. I'll tell Jake to come over. When will Ryan be home?"

"Six. But, uh, he's going to expect us to be alone."

"Well, too bad. You can have sex after we leave."

"Oh my god, fine. I know you'll just get your way anyway."

"I will. Now, what should we make?"

"Ryan went shopping the other day after having to throw everything out from the fridge. So, it's stocked. Let's go look." Walking into the kitchen, I open the fridge. "How about chicken parm?"

"Yes, perfect!" she exclaims, clapping her hands. "Let's start. It's already five."

Ally shoots off a text to Jake, and we wash our hands, getting to work. I haven't made chicken parmesan in a really long time, but I still remember. My dad taught me when I was a teenager, and I spent years afterward perfecting it.

At six sharp, I hear the side door off of the kitchen open, and the telltale sound of Ryan's boots on the floor. I may not have told him that we were having company tonight, so I hope he's not too mad.

Walking around the corner, he stops short when he sees Ally at the stove, stirring the angel hair pasta as it cooks.

"Oh. Hi, Ally."

"Hey, Ryan."

He looks back and forth between Ally and me. "I didn't know we were having company."

"Well, you are. I invited Jake, too," Ally tells him.

"What?"

"Sorry," I apologize. "Ally insisted. But it'll be fun." Walking up to him, I stretch up on my toes and kiss his cheek, whispering in his ear, "Don't worry sheriff, we have all night for me to finish what I started earlier."

Wrapping his arm around my waist, Ryan pulls me against him. "Oh, you can be sure of that, sweetheart," he growls in my ear.

Catching my moan before it spills from my mouth, I bite my lip. I've been wanting to taste him for the longest time.

Releasing me quickly, I sway on my feet, sighing. I have no problem finishing what I started earlier. I can't wait to bring this man to his knees. He'll be at *my* mercy this time.

"I'm still here," Ally says flatly, draining the pasta in the sink.

Oops, I forgot. "Sorry."

"I'm going to go change," Ryan says, his heated eyes on me before walking out of the kitchen.

"Oh my god, Ash." Ally smiles. "You two are hot," she says after he's out of earshot.

"Uh, thanks?" I laugh, taking the chicken out of the oven. I add a generous layer of cheese to the top of the dish and I put it back in to melt. "I'm so glad you think so."

"Oh, shut up." She laughs. "It's a good thing. You have to have passion to survive and thrive."

"Thanks for the relationship advice."

Rolling her eyes, she brings the bowl of pasta over to the table and places it in the middle. "I'm just saying."

"Well, don't worry about us keeping the passion alive. The good sheriff knows how to use his cuffs."

"Ahhh! Oh my god!"

"Shhh, he'll hear you."

"Well, I'll be looking at him differently now. In a very good way."

"You're engaged to his brother. Reign it in."

"Oh, please. Jake keeps me *very* satisfied."

"I don't need to hear about my brother and my soon to be little sister," Ryan says, walking back into the kitchen in jeans and a long-sleeved t-shirt.

"Sorry," Ally says, her face turning a light shade of pink.

"It's okay." Ryan laughs, bringing her in for a hug. "I'm glad Jake has you, but I don't need to hear about the details of your sex life."

"No problem," Ally murmurs, blushing harder.

"Ry, stop embarrassing her. Can you take the dish out of the oven? It should be done."

"Sure. What did you make?"

"Chicken parm."

"Oh, baby, yes. That's one of my favorites."

"Not your baby, sheriff." I hate being called that. Men who've called me that always grated on my nerves, and meant it in a derogatory or condescending way.

"Sorry, sweetheart. I forgot." He smiles, throwing me a wink.

"Well, aren't you two cute?" Ally croons, looking back and forth between us.

I open my mouth to say something back, but the side door opening stops me.

"Hey, Ry," Jake greets, slapping his brother on the back before walking over to Ally and kissing her deep.

Jake is a huge, Viking, Thor type of a man, and when he turns to me, he envelopes me a big bear hug. "Hey, Ash. I'm glad you're okay."

"Thanks. Me too."

"Unhand my woman," Ryan says, placing the chicken parm on the table.

"Relax, Ryan," I sigh, rolling my eyes. Grabbing four wine glasses, and a bottle from his cabinet, I place it on the table and uncork the bottle.

"Can you drink?" Ally asks.

"Yes, would you like to see my ID?"

"Don't be a smartass, Ash," she says, pinning with me a stare. "I meant because of your concussion."

"Oh, I think I can?" I look over at Ryan. "Am I? Did the nurse at the hospital say I couldn't drink?"

"She said not while you're still healing."

"Fine," I sigh, sitting down. "Let's eat, then."

Ally laughs. "Don't pout, Ash. It's not a good look."

"Whatever bitch. I'm the one with a concussion, so I'll pout if I want."

"At least hitting your head hasn't changed you." She smiles.

It sort of has, though. Hitting my head, although painful and scary, made Ryan and I face what we were too scared to talk about.

****

Dinner went smoothly. Ally and Jake are fun to watch. He's normally stoic, but around Ally, she makes him smile and laugh.

"Jake is actually kind of funny," I say to Ryan after they leave, and we've finished cleaning up.

"That's all Ally. He was a grumpy ass for years until she came along. She brought me back my brother, and I'm forever grateful. She's good for him."

"And he's good for her. He makes her so happy. I've never seen her like that."

"Speaking of happy," he says, circling my waist with his arms, pulling me close. "You make me happy."

Smiling, I smooth my hands up his chest and around his neck. "You make me happy, too."

Kissing me long and hard, I moan into him, raking my nails against the nape of his neck, pouring all of my emotions into this kiss.

Groaning, he pushes me back against counter, his hot tongue tangling with mine – sweeping, tasting, claiming, owning.

He owns me, body and soul.

Pulling back, he rests his forehead against mine. "Ashley, I want you to stay. Here. With me."

"What?" I ask, breathless.

"I want you stay here, with me."

"In your house?"

"Yes."

"How would that work?"

"What do you mean?"

"I mean, are you asking me to move in with you? Stay here, in Pine Cove, with you?"

"Yes."

"But—"

"I asked Bill Jenkins, the lawyer in town, about a job today. And he said that Mrs. Grady, his current paralegal, is retiring at the end of the month and he's looking for a replacement."

"What?"

"But if you don't want to work there, you can do whatever you want. I just happened to run into him. Whatever makes you happy, you can do."

I'm stunned. "You're asking me to move in with you, and saying I have a job at the law office if I want it?"

"Yes." He nods.

"Yes?"

"Ashley." He smiles. "How are you not getting this?"

"Not getting what?"

"I love you."

What? How was I supposed to get 'I love you' from that? Speechless, I just stare at him.

"I love you, Ashley. I haven't stopped thinking about you since that night in the woods. The way you felt, the scent of pine and flowers on your skin, how you responded to my touch. So open, ready, and willing. So beautiful. You were fire in my hands." He brushes his fingers across my cheek. "But it was the look in your eyes that captivated me. It felt like you could see into my soul. Past the surface.

"I've closed my eyes thousands of times since, and saw your eyes there – staring, willing me to come to you. But then you came back, and the second those gorgeous hazel eyes met mine again, I was fucking gone. Done. It was like a punch in the gut. And then you brushed me off"–he smiles–"and I knew, right then, that you were perfect."

"What?"

"I may not have said the words, Ash, but I've showed you how I feel."

"You did?" I whisper.

Sorting through my muddled brain, I try and think.

But all I come up with is that I love him.

Everything he's done has made me fall in love with him. Every look, touch, and note he left, made me fall head over ass in love with him.

Oh, I guess he has shown me.

Looking into his eyes, I see it there.

Pulling him down to my lips, I sear mine to his, willing them to never be separated.

Heat blooms in my chest, and a fire ignites. My veins are overflowing with the love I have for this man.

I can't get enough of him.

He's unlike anyone I've ever known.

I now know why no man has ever captured my attention. It was because none of them were Ryan.

Ryan is who my dad told me to wait for. I never settled for mediocre because I always knew he was out there, waiting for me, like I've been waiting for him.

CHAPTER 26

1 month later...

"Ashley, come on, sweetheart!" Ryan yells up the stairs to me.

"Relax, Ry!" I yell back. "I'll be down in a second!"

"Don't make me come up there to get you!"

"I think I'd like that very much, sheriff!" Smiling, I do a little spin in the mirror. If he came up here, I know he'd never let me leave. Not that I would mind. It's kind of my plan right now. We won't be going to dinner if I have any say in the matter.

It's been a month since my accident, and a month since I moved in with Ryan. I still can't believe that. I never thought I'd move in with a man after just a week. But I've always kind of done whatever I wanted.

My concussion stopped being an issue almost two weeks ago, but Ryan just won't listen. And so I'm ready for a night of seducing him until he gives me exactly what I want.

Him.

Unhinged and blinded by passion.

He's been too afraid to take me like he did before the accident, and I'm going crazy. Don't get me wrong, I'll take him any way I can–gentle, loving, caring. But I need that dark storm that brews inside of him.

It's what drew me to him in the first place.

I love seeing that dark side of the good sheriff.

So, I've decided on bringing out the big guns. My leather trimmed lingerie awaits him under my carefully chosen outfit. I've gone with a short leather skirt over my sheer black polka dot tights, thigh high stiletto black suede boots, and a tight black, off the shoulder sweater.

I straightened my hair, and then curled it in big, loose waves that fall down my back, and my makeup is sultry, with a smoky eye and bold red lip. I know he won't be able to stop staring at my lips, which is exactly what I want.

With one last look in the mirror, I smile, ready to face my man.

"Ashley!" he yells again, but stops when he sees me walking down the stairs. His heated eyes start at my feet, and travel up the length of my body, his stare like a caress.

"Eyes up here, sheriff." I smile, his eyes watching the curve of my red lips as I take the last step. My hand reaches out to rest on his chest. "You look good," I whisper, taking in his freshly shaven face. I love that I can smooth my hand over his jaw and feel every sharp plain and masculine line.

"You're beautiful." His smooth voice covers me in a blanket of warmth, and I lift up on my toes to kiss the corner of his mouth, careful not to give him a full kiss yet.

"Let's go, I'm hungry," I tell him, watching his eyes darken. "Starving, actually."

"Me, too," he rasps, wrapping his arm around my waist, pulling me against him. "But not for dinner."

His mouth captures mine in a kiss that holds so many promises, so much weight.

Pushing him away, I suck in ragged breaths. "Ryan, I had a whole plan. Don't ruin it."

He flashes me a wicked smile. "Oh, I know you did, sweetheart. That's why I'm going to give you exactly what you want. What I want."

Picking me up, Ryan takes the stairs two at a time, and stalks down the hall, kicking open the door of the room he'd first given me when I was brought here.

Tossing me on the bed, I bounce once, and crawl back until I hit the pillows. But Ryan shakes his head and grabs my ankle, dragging me back down the bed.

Pulling my boots off, he drops them onto the floor and traces a single finger up my left leg, his touch practically burning my tights, clearing a path.

Unzipping the side of my skirt slowly, he tugs it down, tossing it aside. I sit up, and he grips the hem of my sweater, pulling it up and off of me, leaving me in only my leather and lace black bra and tights, my hair spilling out all around me.

The look in his eyes is pure need. Pure desire. And my body melts at just that single look.

Walking around to the bedside table, Ryan pulls out a pair of cuffs.

Biting my lip, I lift my hands above my head and grip the bars, my eyes pleading with him, needing him. But he shakes his head, turning his finger in the air.

"Turn over," he commands.

When I don't comply right away, he grabs my ankles and flips me onto my stomach. Gripping my hips, he lifts them in the air, and runs the cold metal up the length of my back.

Taking my left hand, he clamps the cuff around my wrist and then feeds it through the bars of the bedframe and clamps it closed around my other wrist.

"So beautiful," he murmurs in my ear, trailing hot kisses down my spine.

Slowly, Ryan peels my tights down my legs, his mouth planting open-mouthed kisses as he goes. I squirm beneath him, but he keeps going until he's removed the thin layer separating him from all of me.

Sliding his hands up the back of my thighs, he grips my ass, each hand getting their fill.

He groans, his finger running under the lace waistband of my thong. "I love seeing you like this. Mine for the taking."

"Yes," I moan out, turning my head to the side to see him.

He runs his finger over my right cheek, and up the lace covered slit between my thighs.

"Already so wet for me."

"Always," I moan again, trying to close my legs on his hand, but he just chuckles behind me. Gripping my inner thighs, he pulls them as far apart as they go.

I hear the buckle of his belt releasing, and the sound of his zipper sliding down sends a chill through me. Ryan sees it. He knows what he does to me.

His clothes hit the floor, and the mattress dips as he places a knee on the bed. Gripping the lace between my thighs, he pulls, tearing it from my body, exposing what's his. But he doesn't touch me yet.

He runs his hands over my ass and up my back, coming around to grip my breasts through my bra. Pulling the cups down, he rolls my hard nipples between his fingers, and my back arches, my head falling to the side, moaning.

His knee pushes my legs apart again, and I feel him there, the blunt head of his thick cock at my entrance.

"I can't be gentle anymore, sweetheart."

"Don't be," I groan out, and he shoves into me in one push, splitting me open.

I pull at the bars, and the cuffs tighten, the metal biting into my wrists.

His grip on my hips is hard and bruising, but I need it.

Pulling out, he thrusts forward, and I slide up the bed, sparks igniting across my skin.

I've been needing him like this, desperate for him to take me like this again.

Finally.

I grip the bars so tightly, that with every stroke, my arms go numb and my shoulders ache. But I use that. The pain mixed with pleasure is unlike anything I've ever felt. Everything is heightened.

My moans grow louder, until my screams fill my ears, and I'm so far gone, that I'm pushed off the cliff – free falling into oblivion.

Ryan's roar breaks through my senses as he stills behind me, filling me, joining me.

His soft kisses pepper my back and he pulls out of me.

I collapse onto my stomach, no longer able to hold myself up. I can't feel anything but his mouth on my sensitive flesh.

He unlocks the cuffs and brings my arms down to my sides, massaging them as he goes.

Lying down, Ryan rolls me over so I'm draped over his chest, my leg intertwining with his, and my arm flung across his torso.

He plays with the ends of my hair, and I tighten my arm around him, my heavy eyes drifting closed.

Sleep starts to claim me, but I smile to myself, loving that I was able to get him to play right into what I wanted.

"I love you," Ryan whispers against my temple.

"Mmm," I moan, curling into him, my nails digging into his hip. "Love you too, sheriff."

ACKOWLEDGMENTS

Thank you to my friends who inspired this badass group of girls in the series. Ashley, Melanie, and Elizabeth, you three are forever my girl gang.

Thank you to my friends and family for your continued support, and loving me even more when you saw a peek into my brain with my first book.

Dara, thank you for telling any and every one we meet that I write romance, and they should all buy my book. You have no idea how much I love it!

And lastly, thank you to everyone who had kind words to say about my first book, you all pushed me to continue on this journey of following my dream.

ABOUT THE AUTHOR

Rebecca is a dreamer through and through with permanent wanderlust. She has an endless list of places to go and see, hoping to one day experience the world and all it has to offer.

She's a Jersey girl who dreams of living in a place with freezing cold winters and lots of snow! When she's not writing, you can find her planning her next road trip and drinking copious amounts of coffee (preferably iced!).

Website, blog, shop, and links to all social media:
www.rebeccagannon.com

Follow me on Instagram to stay up-to-date on new releases, sales, teasers, giveaways, and so much more!
@rebeccagannon_author

CPSIA information can be obtained
at www.ICGtesting.com
Printed in the USA
LVHW030539041220
673318LV00010B/1852

9 781712 274033